# *Laura*
## *the*
# *Explorer*

# SARAH BEGG

Published by Sarah Begg, 2019
Sydney, NSW, Australia

This book is a work of fiction. Any similarity between the characters and situations within its pages to actual persons, living or dead, or situations is unintentional and co-incidental. Any real location has been used in an entirely fictional way.

A catalogue record for this book is available from the National Library of Australia

ISBN: 978 0 9876415 0 2 (paperback)

Cover Design by Hazel Lam
Cover image courtesy Getty Images

www.sarahbegg.com

To Mum, who inspired my love of reading.

And to Dad, the best storyteller I know.

# 1

"Don't forget you always have a room at home, darling," Mum said, her concerned face peering around the side of the passenger seat at me.

"She's fine, Cath," Dad scolded, but I saw his eyes crinkle with worry as he studied me in the rear-view mirror.

I sat up straighter and rolled my eyes at them. "Thanks, Mum, I know. And don't worry, I'll be fine. I *have* lived out of home before, remember?"

Mum shot Dad a look before turning back to face me. I was actually surprised she was able to swivel so far around in her seat with the seatbelt clutched to her chest like a life vest.

"Yes, darling, but you know—you were married then," she said in that soft and caring voice that made tears spring to my eyes all over again. I didn't need to be reminded that I was twenty-seven and already getting a divorce. Nor did I need to be reminded of the past six months living back at my parents' house, the first few of which were spent holed up in my old bedroom, with its pink wallpaper and unicorn feature wall, hugging Starlight, my old My Little Pony toy, while watching *The Notebook* on repeat and going through mountains of tissues and green tea.

On the plus side, I did lose about five kilos. But anyway, I was determined to put that in the past and move on. It was time to get my life back together and stop dwelling on my failed relationship.

"The apartment is really nice!" I said brightly. "And it'll be good for me to have roommates."

"What are they like?" Dad asked.

"Well, Ben is really nice, he's the one I met the other day when I went to see the place."

"Ben?" Mum sounded intrigued. "You didn't mention you were living with boys!"

"Only one boy," I said hurriedly. Knowing Mum, she'd probably romanticise this whole situation and convince herself Ben and I would become an item. "Plus, Ben is way younger than I am—I think he's only twenty-three. So it'll be like living with a little brother."

"And the other roommate—she's a girl, isn't she?" Mum asked hopefully.

"What's she like?" Dad piped in.

"Erm, I haven't actually met her yet," I said.

That was probably a mistake, because Mum swivelled around and eyed me again. "You haven't met someone you're going to live with?" she demanded. "What if she's a fruitcake! She might go into your room when you're not home and put on all of your underwear!"

"Muuum." I shook my head. "I'm sure she'll be great. She's British, apparently."

Mum and Dad glanced at each other in alarm.

"This is the street, isn't it?" Dad asked as we turned down a narrow road lined with low-rise apartment buildings.

"Yes—this is it!" I leaned forward, eagerly trying to see out the front window. "That's the building over there!"

"Are you sure?" Mum asked, peering out the window with a new look of concern on her face. "It looks a bit … old."

"Well, yes. But you know what they say—go for the worst house on the nicest street and all that."

"I think that's buying a place, love, not renting," Dad said.

"We're here now," I said positively. "Come on, wait until you see the actual apartment, it's really nice on the inside."

Dad pulled in to the visitors' parking space and we all clambered out of the car. I hurried over to the front door and pressed the intercom button for unit three.

"Hello?" said a male voice.

"Ben? It's Laura."

"Come on up!"

There was a loud buzzing sound and I pulled open the front door.

"Don't worry about that yet!" I shouted at my parents, who already had the boot open and were starting to pull out my quilt and table lamp. "Come up first and have a look."

We filed up the stairs, Dad carrying the table lamp, anyway. As we reached the landing, the door swung open and a young friendly guy with shaggy blond hair grinned at us.

"Hey, Laura!" He stood back and let us file through. "You must be the parents, nice to meet you!"

Dad seemed pleasantly surprised as Ben shook his hand enthusiastically, and Mum even giggled and blushed as Ben gave her a big hug and a kiss on the cheek.

The apartment was warm and cosy—not too big, but not small, either. There were surf boards decorating one wall, a funky driftwood coffee table surrounded by two lived-in couches and two beanbags, plus a big TV on one side.

"He's a bit young, isn't he?" Mum whispered to me, as Ben headed over to the other side of the room.

"Young for what?" I looked at her quizzically. She was eyeing Ben with a distinct look of disappointment on her face.

Mum sighed. "Oh, I don't know. I guess I hoped he might be more …

your type."

"Mum!" I managed to make my whisper convey a decent amount of outrage. "He's my new flatmate, not my boyfriend!"

She huffed quietly again. "Well, at least this building is in a nice spot. There are lots of good-looking boys that live on the northern beaches, you know."

Ben started walking back towards us and I felt my face flush. Oh God, trust my mother to make things awkward straightaway.

"Come and look at the view!" I said loudly, drawing my parents over to the best part of the apartment. I shuffled them out onto the small balcony and indicated the spot, in between the two apartment buildings shadowing ours, where you could see a glimpse of the ocean beyond.

"It's the beach, Mum!" I clarified, in case she didn't spot it.

Mum wasn't admiring the view, though—she was looking towards one of the other apartment buildings instead. "There's a naked man walking around in there!"

"What? Where?" I peered eagerly and—okay, wow. There was definitely a naked man in there. He was quite fit for an old guy.

"We call him Fabio!" Ben said happily, joining us on the balcony. "He likes to do naked yoga in front of the living-room window in the mornings."

Mum's eyes had turned into saucers.

"Come see my room!" I herded my parents back inside and away from the view of Fabio, who was now doing lunges across his apartment. Honestly, I know you need to try to get your knee on the ground when lunging, but he was likely to end up with carpet burn on a different appendage doing that.

We made it inside and crammed into my new small room. My parents looked around and made some polite murmuring noises, and did the same thing when I gave them a quick tour of the bathroom.

"Okay, let's bring my stuff up," I said.

Dad sprang into action, taking charge of the move, and Ben chipped in eagerly, chattering away to my dad about cars and suspension. Mum flittered around, trying to help but mostly getting in the way.

I'd just dumped a bag of clothes on the floor when I found myself alone in the apartment, everyone else down at the car. It seemed eerily quiet in there, and I walked into the living room, surveying my new home.

*Well, here I am.* A new, fresh start. In a weird deja-vu moment, I remembered a similar time, barely more than a year ago when Jack and I stood on the verandah of our brand-new cottage. Well, the cottage wasn't new—it was an old, practically falling-down shack. But to us it was new.

Newlyweds. High-school sweethearts. *How sweet it is, Laura, how romantic, that you married your first and only boyfriend*, everyone had said. *Such a fairytale, how rare.*

Eleven years we'd been together. Eleven years! That made me sound so ancient. But when you start "going out" when you are fifteen, the time quickly adds up. When we got engaged at twenty-four, everyone said it was "about time". We'd been together for almost a decade by that point, after all.

And then the wedding. Oh God, the *wedding*. I squeezed my eyes shut, forcing the tears away. It was such a beautiful day. I remembered Mum and Dad's proud, shining faces, and the faces of all our family and friends. They all saw it. They were all witness to us pledging our lives to each other, vowing to love, honour and respect each other for the rest of our lives.

What a joke that was.

I walked over to the balcony and took a few deep breaths of fresh air, wrapping my arms around my chest as if I could squeeze the memory into non-existence. Because that was the most embarrassing part of all this. The fact that we were married. It was such a public statement, a huge announcement that you know each other best in the world and want to spend the rest of your lives together.

Only as it turned out, I didn't know Jack best. I was his partner for eleven years and I didn't know. And now, when people looked at me—people who knew why we were no longer together—I felt the shame and humiliation burning in me every time.

# 2

I cracked the top off my beer with a wooden penis bottle opener.

"It's Kalina's, honestly!" Ben said when I raised my eyebrows at him. "All the other ones keep disappearing."

My parents had finally gone home. It had been a mission trying to get them out the door. Dad and Ben wouldn't stop chatting, and Mum kept trying to steal glances out the windows at Fabio and asking for more cups of tea.

"So, where's Kalina?" I asked, slumping down onto one of the couches. My other new flatmate had been conspicuously absent all afternoon.

"She's at work," Ben replied, flopping onto the other couch. "At least I think she's at work."

"On a Saturday?"

"Yeah—she works down at The Pony."

"What's that?"

"The Blonde Pony? Haven't you ever been there? It's one of the bars down in Manly."

"Oh, right. No, I haven't been there. I haven't really had a social life for the last … well, for a while. And there weren't many bars around where I used to live."

"You lived somewhere out west, didn't you?" Ben asked, crinkling his forehead thoughtfully.

"Yeah—sort of near Windsor." I smiled, knowing he'd have no idea where the tiny suburb was. "But I've been at my parents' place for the last six months."

"Right. So not many bars around there, then?" he asked.

"There are a few. Just not any people around that I wanted to go out with."

"Don't you have a sister?"

"Yeah. But she's been overseas ever since I moved back home—trekking around South America with some friends." I smiled wistfully, imagining letting Elle take me out with all her 21-year-old mates. While she'd skyped me from overseas as much as she could, the age gap between us was pretty big and I didn't think Elle really understood how devastating the whole Jack-thing was for me.

"That sucks," Ben said, taking a swig of his beer. "Well, The Pony's a pretty weird place. You get some interesting people down there, which is why I think Kal likes it—she loves talking to weirdos."

I raised an eyebrow. "And how would you define a weirdo?"

"Oh, there're all sorts. Anyone you'd normally steer clear of in a bar, she'll walk right up to them and start a conversation."

"And that's not your idea of fun?"

"It's certainly entertaining to watch."

I squished myself further down into the couch as Ben turned on the TV. The Food Network came on and we watched for a few minutes as an American chef tried to cut up vegetables with his arms tied to a giant wooden pole across his back, his competitor attempting to cook chicken in a jaffle maker.

For a while, I was totally engrossed in just how nice the moment was. Sitting on a couch, drinking a beer on a Saturday afternoon without having my parents flapping around telling me to get up and do something. I'd really missed living out of home. Though in the previous scenario, I would have been snuggled up on the couch with my husband. Me blissfully happy, Jack obviously hiding how unhappy he was.

My stomach gave a little violent twist. It had been doing that a bit lately. It was like every time I thought I was doing well, and really getting over Jack, a new memory would surface and then the pain would jump out at me again and shout, "Surprise! You're not over him yet!"

I once read that it took half as long as you were together with someone to get over them. If that was true, then I still had five years left to get over Jack.

Ha. Ha. Ha.

"What do you normally do for dinner around here?" I asked, trying to distract myself. "Is it communal cooking or an every-man-for-himself type thing?"

"Lately, it's been just me cooking," Ben said with a laugh. "Kalina refuses. Or maybe I banned her." He looked thoughtful for a moment. "Anyway, whatever you do, don't let Kalina cook for you. She's terrible at it."

"Noted."

"One time she cooked for us—we had Dave living in your room then— and it was this thing that she called a 'fish pie'. But it turned out to be frozen fish fingers and cheese wrapped up in puff pastry with tomato sauce and scrambled eggs on top. I think it was the first and only time I ever saw Dave not finish a meal."

"Wow. But with all that egg-and-fish goodness?"

"I know. How could those flavours *not* go together?"

"Okay. So no cooking by Kalina. I'm guessing there are lots of takeaway nights, then?"

Ben shrugged. "I've always done a lot of cooking. I have a pretty big family and my mum's always been a bit laidback in the kitchen. She thinks most things come from jars and packets. I started cooking a few years ago when I lived at home, and I cook most nights here now. Kalina normally just chips in for groceries, and I get to pick what we eat."

"Well, I'm also happy to buy groceries." I smiled hopefully. Not that I couldn't cook. Of course I could. But I was more of a "Ben's Mum" type of cook. I mean, weren't Patak's and Old El Paso mixes dietary staples?

"Sure, if you want." Ben shrugged, not seeming bothered. "Though I'll be honest—Saturday nights are takeaway nights."

"Excellent—I'm starving!"

～♋◯

The next morning, I woke early and saw sunlight peeking in around unfamiliar blinds. *Oh God, where was I?* But then—oh, right! I was in my new bedroom, in my new apartment, on the other side of Sydney from where I used to live.

I took a moment to peer around at the room while holding the quilt up under my chin. I'd unpacked and set up all my things the night before, so aside from the fact that I was somewhere completely new, the place had a nice, homey feel.

I was half tempted to scrunch down in the bed again and go back to sleep for a few hours, but I mentally shook myself and pushed away that idea. The last few months had been filled with long sleep-ins and depressive afternoon naps. So much sleeping, in fact, that my parents had started to entertain the idea that I'd somehow developed chronic fatigue. I could have been a polar bear in hibernation, except that instead of trying to survive I appeared to have given up the will to live.

But anyway. This, now, was supposed to be my fresh start. I'd already promised myself that it was time to get my life back together, time to start "seizing each day" so to speak.

After determinedly throwing off the blankets, I went across to the window and the beautiful, welcoming view made me smile. Sure, I was mostly looking directly into another apartment building (in fact, I was looking right into Fabio's place), but just like from the balcony, I could also see a tiny glimpse of the sea.

I gazed at the view for a few minutes but then felt at a loss regarding what to do next. The whole day was stretching in front of me, long and empty, with nothing planned. It was weird no longer having that partner there that I could do everything with. My parents had helped fill that gap over the last six months with an almost manic need to get me doing things. Most Sundays they'd be up early knocking on my bedroom door, offering eggs or pancakes or French toast or whatever they thought would make me feel better that morning, and then dragging me off to some flower nursery, or boat expo (they've never been able to afford a boat, but they liked to pretend they would one day).

But I wasn't at their house anymore. No one was going to come barging into my room with a bright idea of what we should be doing for the day. I was now independent. Alone. Well, sort of. I'd chickened out a bit on the whole "living on my own" thing by moving into a share house. Plus, I'd made sure my two potential flatmates were both single before handing over the bond. I actually had a look at a different share house with two other girls, but they both had boyfriends and the thought of sitting on a couch next to some happily cosy, cuddling couples made me want to retch.

Taking a deep breath, I turned back and surveyed my tidy room again and then realised that I did have a lot to do that day. First up, I needed to go and buy myself some food. Because that's what people did when they shared flats with others. They contributed to the household.

I started rummaging through my drawers and wardrobe until I located my workout clothes and runners. They weren't what I'd usually go to the supermarket in, but hey, this was Manly! Maybe I'd go for a quick run along the beach while I was at it. Pulling the garments on and sweeping my hair back into a ponytail, I made a quick trip to the bathroom.

My reflection looked back at me from the mirror. A bit too pale, eyes a bit too sunken. At least I no longer had that exhausted, slightly ill look that had become very familiar after my marriage meltdown. For a good month there, I'd barely even washed my hair. I think I went three whole weeks before my mum had a fit and insisted on literally washing me herself, scrubbing brush and all. That humiliation had snapped me back into a regular bathing routine. And now, I had started thinking about that phase in my life as the Black Period; a sinkhole in time that just sucked everything away and morphed it into a lump of memories that was best forgotten.

As I brushed my teeth, I surveyed the seemingly hundreds of products lining the sink, windowsill and just about every available surface. There were hair products, skin products and makeup everywhere. Ben had his own en suite bathroom, so everything in here (aside from the small section of space I had commandeered last night for my things) was Kalina's. My eyes shifted to the shower and I paused, mid-tooth brush.

A Tupperware container sat in the shower caddy with … butter chicken? I sniffed at it dubiously, and yes, that was definitely butter chicken with rice sitting there in the shower. Interesting. Come to think of it, I had woken up at some point in the night and heard a lot of banging around in the kitchen—obviously Kalina arriving home.

I rinsed my mouth and vacated the Indian-dinner crime scene, quietly exiting the apartment amidst snores coming from one of the other two bedrooms.

The air was fresh and crisp when I stepped outside, and as I took a few deep breaths of the pine-scented breeze, I felt my mood start to lift. I took a few wrong turns in the back streets of Manly, but eventually I found my way down to a gorgeous sunny walkway that ran all along the beach.

And wow—there were so many people already down there! I thought I was doing really well getting up so early, but there were people everywhere—

women power-walking together, others running along with their prams, couples walking dogs, and some just strolling along with coffee in hand. Down on the sand, people were already sunbaking in the early-morning sun, their bags full of supplies for the whole day sitting next to them. Out in the water, surfers bobbed along, waiting for a decent wave.

And everyone was wearing super-trendy clothes. There were girls in patterned leggings with matching crop tops, fluoro visors and delicate silver jewellery. Guys jogged along in brightly coloured sneakers and black shorts, most of them sans shirts, which I didn't mind.

I didn't mind that at all.

*Gawd—look at that one!* Dark, Mediterranean skin, small chest tattoo. Broody eyes and dark hair. Oh shit, he started looking at me.

Awkward.

But anyway, there was something strange going on down there. Something ... unusual. I couldn't quite put my finger on it until ... yes! I knew what it was: everywhere I looked, no matter what people were doing, they all seemed to have one thing in common—they were all really fit. It was different to where Jack and I used to live. I mean, in the western suburbs' defence, it was a totally growing, cosmopolitan area. Sure, there may not be a nice beach-front walkway to jog along and show off your new workout wear, but there were loads of restaurants, cafes, shopping centres and superstores. Plus, far more paddocks and wildlife. In fact, you could probably go do some horse wrangling if you really wanted to give your activewear a go.

I glanced down at my own clothes—semi-worn-out leggings and an orange top that I only just realised had totally faded in the washing machine. Hmm. Note to self: get down to Lorna Jane and update fitness clothes.

Second note to self: get fit. And buy some fake-tan spray.

I picked up my pace and got into a power-walking swing. I even smiled wanly at a few people that I passed, but they gave me weird looks, so I stopped smiling and tried to swing my arms marginally less.

Up ahead, I could see a big cluster of volleyball nets along part of the beach with heaps of people playing. As I passed, I slowed to take a better look, and they were pretty good!

It didn't seem possible, but the girls playing volleyball were even more fit-looking than the ones I had already seen. They had ripped stomachs, toned arms and powerful-looking legs, all of which were being shown off in tiny sports bikinis.

And the guys. Oh wow.

My eyes were drawn to one guy in particular—a tall, tanned, well-muscled guy who looked to be about thirty. He was wearing nothing but board shorts and he'd certainly be described as fit. Super fit. Seriously, I didn't know abs could actually look like that. He also had that longish, shaggy hair that seemed to be popular with surfers, which he kept flicking back off his face as he waited for the ball to be served.

My eyes slid down over his lean chest and stomach and my steps started to falter of their own accord. The sunlight caught on his eyes, which were a brilliantly vibrant blue.

He looked up at me.

Our eyes locked and I felt my breath catch. *God, his eyes are amazing.* It was like staring up at the sky on a cloudless day and admiring the beautiful, crystal blue that was stretched out above you. I was becoming lost in them, drawn in like Narcissus.

And then he frowned.

Oh shit, what was I doing? Heat rushed into my face as I realised that I'd just completely stopped walking and was staring at him, no doubt with a weird kind of drugged-out grin on my face. *Stop being creepy, Laura. You can't just stand around staring at people!* And then he was looking at me quizzically, as if trying to work out if he knew me.

I broke contact and turned away, my face burning. Argh! How super awkward.

Luckily, a running group suddenly engulfed me, with people jogging past and blocking his view of me. I made a split-second decision and started running with them, caught up in their midst. I was like David Copperfield, doing a great disappearing act.

The group was moving really fast and some of them gave me annoyed looks, so I dropped out again, breathing heavily. Looking back, I was a good fifty metres away from the volleyball nets. I could still see the hot guy, but he'd returned to the game, his back to me.

*Ahh ... what a back!* It was all lean and muscled, with sweat running down the middle ...

I forced myself to turn away and keep walking, though I couldn't help a smile cracking over my face. Spotting a supermarket along the next street, I remembered the reason I'd come out walking in the first place.

Picking up a basket at the entry, I started strolling around the aisles and grabbing random items. But I was having trouble concentrating on what I needed, my thoughts absorbed by the shirtless, golden-skinned volleyball guy with the shaggy hair and sky-blue eyes that seemed to have imprinted themselves on my mind.

The thought sent a warm glow through me and I shivered, surprising myself. Obviously, dating and sleeping with new people was going to be part and parcel of being single, and of course it had crossed my mind. But this was the first time since Jack and I had split that I'd actually looked at another person (i.e. a real person, not Ryan Gosling or Chris Hemsworth's on-screen characters) and *felt* something. As in, felt that I wouldn't mind getting all naked and pressing up against another person again.

Huh. Maybe I really was ready for this new beginning—in every way.

# 3

It was mid-morning when I got back to the apartment. Ben was sitting on the couch, bleary-eyed and messy-looking, eating a bowl of cereal and watching TV.

"Morning!" I said cheerily as I walked in with my armful of groceries.

"Mor-fing," he replied zombie-like. He was even chewing his cereal as if in a trance.

I left him be and started unpacking my things. Just as I was finishing up, I heard Kalina's bedroom door open, and a moment later a girl wearing an oversized *Sesame Street* t-shirt appeared in the kitchen yawning loudly and stretching her arms dramatically.

"You must be the new flatmate!" Kalina said brightly in a London accent.

"Yes." I smiled. "Laura."

"I'm so glad you're a girl!" she said, walking past me to the fridge and pulling out a bottle of orange juice. "It's been a total man-cave around here for too long."

"It wasn't a man-cave!" Ben called out from the couch.

Kalina rolled her eyes at me before opening the juice and drinking it straight from the bottle. "Ben's not so bad," she whispered conspiratorially. "That Dave, though—hopefully, he hasn't left any residual man-smell in your room."

"I haven't noticed anything," I said, scrunching my nose up. "But I'll double-check later."

"Good idea. So, Laura, you're single, aren't you?"

My stomach clenched involuntarily.

Single. I hated that word.

But yes. Yes of course I was. At least "single" sounded better than "separated". And soon it would be "divorced".

"Yeah, I am," I said, trying to make it sound like a positive thing. "You are too, right?"

"Yep." Kalina grinned, putting away the orange juice. "Ben and I both are. It makes things a lot more fun around here."

A sudden image of bizarre naked orgies appeared in my mind, and for a second I wondered if I'd made a terrible decision. What did she mean by that comment? Do Ben and Kalina sleep together? And would *I* be expected to participate?

"I'm working at The Pony again tonight," Kalina continued, not noticing my startled expression. "You should come down for some drinks. You too, Ben," she added. "It's a great place to hang out in—loads of awesome people there. What do you say, Laura?"

I hesitated, frowning briefly. "I have work tomorrow."

"So what?" Kalina replied. "Sunday sessions are the best! You don't have to stay out long. And it really is just around the corner from here."

Okay, I wasn't really expecting that. I mean, of course I was sort of hoping that my new flatmates might want to go out drinking together (God knew I certainly needed to go out with people my age, having had my parents act as my "best friends" for six months). But I'd only just met Kalina and was still feeling drained after the move.

"Go on—I'll come down too if you want," Ben called from the couch. "It can be a 'welcome to the flat' sort of thing."

"Yes, perfect!" Kalina said, looking at me as if I was a new and exciting pet. "What do you say? I'll even make drinks on the house. Well, so long as my boss is out," she added with a wink.

"Well ... okay, yes!" I said, smiling.

Work tomorrow? Fuck it. This was operation "fresh start" after all, and sitting on the couch watching TV all night wasn't conducive to that plan.

"Wicked! We'll have a great time." Kalina grinned again as she walked past me and headed into the bathroom. "Oh!" I heard her exclaim loudly from inside. "There's my curry!"

∽ℑ◯

God, was I ready to be going out to a bar? I mean honestly, I'd only just moved in yesterday and that was a huge step in itself. My body imprint was probably still sitting there on my parents' couch. Was I ready to start acting like a single person?

But obviously, yes, this was one of the objectives of moving into a shared flat in a trendy area—to go out and make new friends, far away from my old disaster of a life. To help me to move forward. Plus, it was a "Sunday session" as Kalina called it. Just a small group of new friends, sitting in a bar drinking casually together. Nothing to worry about.

The "interesting patronage" description that Ben used for the clientele at the Blonde Pony was pretty spot on. The place was half-full with a mix of uni students, musicians or couples out on their second date.

The decor was fabulous—all vintage-style posters and shelves of trinkets reminiscent of an old British pub. There was a long bar with stools for individuals or couples to chat or watch the bartenders, and Ben and I commandeered two of said stools so Kalina could entertain us.

"That guy over there," she said, indicating with her eyes a middle-aged man wearing chinos and a Bintang t-shirt. "He keeps offering to take me out on his boat one weekend. He's loaded, he reckons, just got rid of an ex-wife, too."

"What's stopping you, then?" Ben asked, eyes twinkling.

"Hey, I'm not that bad!" Kalina said. "Besides, if I wanted a sugar daddy I wouldn't just take up the first offer that came along."

"So she says." Ben winked at me.

An ice cube sailed across from behind the bar and whacked Ben on the shoulder.

"You're too young to even know about such things, little Benny," Kalina cooed patronisingly.

"Hey, just don't get any cougar ideas on my friends," Ben shot back.

I happily watched the banter between Kalina and Ben, already feeling the effects of—what was it, my third beer? They'd shared the flat for over a year and had obviously become really good friends in that time. I'd also dismissed my earlier fear that they hooked up every now and then; they acted more like brother and sister than anything else.

"How about you, Laura?" Kalina asked, and I realised I'd tuned out of the conversation.

"Hmm?"

"Worst first date you've ever been on," Ben repeated.

"Oh."

Well, this was embarrassing. I should have expected it. I mean, isn't that what single people do—sit around and compare dating stories? But Jack and I were high-school sweethearts; we didn't even really have a first date as such, we just started hooking up behind the music hall. And since then—well, apart from my mother's attempts to set me up with Eric, the guy who works at the RSL bistro we'd been frequenting every Friday night for the past six months—there'd been no movement on the dating front. In fact, up until very recently, the very thought of dating had me bursting into tears.

"Actually, I haven't been out with anyone since I split up with my ex. I mean, we're still technically married." I gave a phony kind of laugh, which I was sure neither of them bought.

"That's right, Ben mentioned you were recently separated," Kalina said, frowning. "But what about your first date with him? Or before him?"

I could barely meet their eyes as I mumbled my response. "Well, Jack and I never really had a first date, we just sort of started seeing each other. And there wasn't anyone before. I mean, we were fifteen when we first got together."

I looked up, giving a weak smile as if this was all just a funny story. But their reactions were far from delighted. Instead, it was like I'd just dropped a grenade right there, in the middle of the table. There was a moment of confusion when I could see their minds working—doing the maths. And then that tiny recoil, that look of shock as they figured it out.

"Noo!" Ben said, right as Kalina gasped, "What?!"

"Yeah." I gave that weak, forced smile again, dropping my eyes to my beer glass. "Funny, isn't it?"

"Hang on, hang on, hang on!" Kalina shook her head. "How long were the two of you together for?"

"Eleven years." I stared morosely into my beer.

Ben pressed his hands onto his head as if his mind was going to explode out of it. "Eleven years ago I was only twelve!"

"Wow, you *are* a baby," I said, trying to make a joke.

"So, let me get this straight." Kalina looked at me intently. "You've only ever dated the one guy?"

"Yes," I mumbled.

"Does that mean that you've only ever *slept* with one person?" Kalina asked, leaning in conspiratorially with a look of fascination on her face.

I glared at her. "Well yes, obviously!"

"That must be *so* strange! I mean, how do you even know if he was any good in bed? You'd have nothing to gauge it by. I mean, you might have been putting up with really awful sex all these years and you'd never even know!"

If only she knew the real story, it would be funny how accurate she probably was.

I shrugged. "Plenty of people marry their high-school sweethearts or first boyfriends. It's not that unusual."

Ben and Kalina shared a wide-eyed look.

"So, if you were together for that long, then you must have done loads of experimenting in the bedroom, right? Like, kinky stuff with toys and costumes and—"

"Okay, way too much info!" Ben stood up abruptly and walked off towards the bathroom.

Kalina turned back to me with delighted anticipation. "Come on, the longer you're together the kinkier things get, right?"

Oh God. I could feel it. This was the moment it was all going to come out. Kinky? The absurdity of that suggestion made me unsure whether I was about to start laughing hysterically or crying.

"Things didn't get ... I mean ..." I shook my head. "Kinky is not really how I'd describe the situation." My voice sounded hollow, dead.

"What happened?" Kalina asked softly, leaning even closer. The atmosphere had suddenly shifted, and I knew Kalina realised it, too.

What happened? That one question was enough to make the memory of that day come flooding back to me, like a blinding light suddenly flashing across my eyes, completely unavoidable and just as painful ...

It was a normal Saturday morning, just like every other Saturday morning since we'd moved into our cottage. The mortgage payments were a killer—neither of us had really anticipated just how much we'd miss those extra few hundred dollars each week. But that didn't matter. We were working through things. I was sure I'd be able to get a pay rise, maybe even a promotion at work soon. And Jack was on the up at his law firm. Soon he'd be earning a great income. Which was good, because I was already doing the research into maternity leave. I mean, imagine! Nine, maybe twelve months off work! It was what dreams were made of, wasn't it? No longer going into the office, no longer doing the nine-to-five (Or the eight-to-six as it more often was). I'd almost entirely convinced myself I was ready for kids (was anyone ever *really* sure?) and one of my best friends, Louise, was also talking about starting a family with Simon. Plus, Mum had already offered to come round all the time to babysit once we needed it, which would be good, because then Louise and I could go shopping or go get our nails done or whatever it was that new mums did.

I pulled on my oversized fleecy dressing gown and padded my way out into the kitchen. Jack was already sitting on the couch in the living room eating cereal, watching *Weekend Sunrise*. As I put the bread in the toaster and put the kettle on to boil, I wasn't really thinking about anything important. Probably imagining what we could have for dinner that night. Picturing the drive to Woollies, where I'd park so I could pop into Priceline at the same time.

I didn't even notice Jack appear in the kitchen. Didn't realise the TV had been turned off and that Jack was standing there quietly at the end of the kitchen bench.

"Morning," I said with a yawn, barely even looking at him as I started spreading peanut butter on my toast. I mean, why should I look at him closely? Why should I expect that this was not a normal morning? Maybe if I had paid more attention, I might have noticed the way he was standing, a certain stiffness to him.

"Laura, there's something we need to talk about," he said.

"Okay," I replied easily. Closed the peanut butter jar. Finished making my tea. Walked past Jack, nodding at him to follow, as I walked to the lounge. That's when I noticed the TV wasn't on anymore. Funnily enough, that's probably the first moment I realised something was wrong.

"Everything okay?" I asked, taking a seat and biting a huge chunk of toast into my mouth. And then I looked at him properly.

There was something strange about his posture. He seemed nervous, restless. Skittish, even. For a moment he couldn't meet my eyes. He just stared down at his hands. What I remembered best of that moment was my eyebrows creasing in concern. Funny, that of all things, I really strongly remembered my own eyebrows.

"There's …" Jack paused, took a deep breath. Looked up at me finally. "There's something I need to tell you."

Still, at this point, I wasn't overly worried by this conversation. "Yes?" I said magnanimously, patiently. I took another bite of toast.

"We can't have kids together," he said quietly.

I frowned, trying to comprehend. What did he mean? Of course we could have kids. Or, did he have something medically wrong with him? Was he not able to have kids?

Jack took a deep breath. "We can't have kids together because I'm gay," he said in a rush, his voice louder this time.

Gay? That's not a reason to not be able to have kids. Gay people could have kids. But what did Jack mean? He wasn't gay. He was married to me, a woman, so of course he couldn't be gay.

"I'm sorry, Laura." His voice became anguished, his posture introverted and defensive. "I'm so, so sorry. I've … I've been trying to ignore this for so long. Trying to pretend I'm not, trying to *make* myself not be. But I can't, I just can't bring children into this."

The other thing I remembered about that morning was that I had a chunk of toast in my mouth still. It suddenly felt like dry cardboard, as if my mouth was the first part of my body to comprehend just what Jack was saying, turning itself dry, retreating from regular function in horror. And I also remembered suddenly feeling really self-conscious that I was wearing my big, ugly, oversized fleecy dressing gown. The one that I knew looked awful but was just so warm and cuddly. Because you shouldn't be wearing ugly clothes when your husband tells you he's gay and that he doesn't want to have children with you, should you? That just wasn't fair.

"What … what?" It was the only thing I could say.

"I can't do this anymore. I can't keep doing this to you. You deserve a better life. You deserve someone who … someone better than me."

"What … are you saying?" I remembered the weight of the little bread plate in my hand. The half-eaten toast sitting on it. I was gripping that plate really hard. And my eyes felt watery. I blinked a few times.

"We need to break up. Get a divorce," Jack said, his voice sounding rough but firm.

And then, because I couldn't even process it, didn't want to face it, I did the one thing that could turn my morning back to normal.

I picked up the TV remote and turned *Weekend Sunrise* back on.

Jack quietly left the room as the tears started running down my face. And the rest of that toast just sat there on my lap until it was cold. I stared down at it and thought, *What a waste.*

Kalina was still looking at me expectantly, a concerned look on her face. But of course, that memory had flashed through my mind in no more than a nanosecond. It was the kind of thing that could now be delivered in one great walloping packet—bam! And I was left feeling completely gutted and mortified all over again.

As if surfacing from a swimming pool, the buzz of the bar—the music, the laughter—all washed over me again, and I forced myself to take a deep breath. Normally, I'd make up something to answer Kalina's question, or I'd mumble a dismissive and generic response. But maybe because I'd had a few drinks and I was feeling brave, or reckless, or maybe it was because Kalina seemed so open and generous and somehow, weirdly, caring, I decided to tell her the truth; to lay out the ugly reality right there on the bar.

"It turned out Jack was gay," I said quietly, managing a weak smile, as if somehow that would show I was okay with the situation.

"Fuck no!" Kalina said, her eyes going wide. "Are you serious?"

I laughed, just once. "I'm serious."

"Holy shit! And you … I mean …" Kalina trailed off, watching me as my face heated up. I knew all the questions she wanted to ask; wondered which one she would pick first. How did I not know? Weren't there any indications? How did he pretend to be straight for eleven years and how did I not notice?

"Shit," she repeated in a kind of awed voice. Then she reached over for a bottle from the back shelf of the bar. "Whisky?"

A genuine laugh actually bubbled up.

"What a fucker." Kalina shook her head.

"Yep," I agreed. "What. A. Fucker." I couldn't really muster any enthusiasm for this statement, though.

Kalina was silent for a moment, then suddenly her face lit up like she'd just had a brilliant thought. "So, if we go back to discussing what we were talking about before, am I safe to assume that your sex life has been a bit … lacking, then?"

I snorted. "Well, I assume so. But, I mean, how would I even know?"

"Exactly!" Kalina smiled excitedly. "You don't know! If you've only ever slept with a gay man, then it's like you've never really slept with anyone at all, isn't it!"

"Hey!" I protested. "We had sex. I'm pretty sure it still counts."

"But does it, though?" Kalina asked slowly, as if she'd just stumbled upon a great loophole in the fabric of world sexuality. "You haven't slept with a straight man before. So really, it's like you've almost been with no one. Like you can go out and have sex with a man—a straight man—for the first time."

"I'm not sure Jack's being gay is really going to negate my non-virgin status," I argued, though I could feel something start to lift off my chest, as if even just joking about this was helping alleviate the pain. Plus, Kalina's face was alight with anticipation, and her enthusiasm was kind of contagious in an unavoidable way.

"Just think about how much time you've wasted—or rather, how much you've got to look forward to!" Kalina was on a roll now. "I mean, look, I can't imagine what it was like sleeping with a gay man, but I'm guessing things weren't too hot and steamy in bed. And yet there are so many hot, amazing guys out there. And you are now single and able to experience them all! Like seriously—the things guys can do with their hands now, or with their *tongues*—"

"Oh my God! I'm not ready to even think about this!" I exclaimed, my eyes wide.

"Of course you are! Seriously, Laura—being single is so much fun! You're going to have such a good time!"

I watched her glee, the way she was kind of bobbing up and down on her toes. *Could* it be fun to be single? Could I be one of those people who enjoyed dating randoms?

Kalina reached for two shot glasses. "This calls for a toast."

She expertly created two cowboy shooters and then held hers up. I did the same, slightly alarmed, and tried to ignore the little voice in my head saying shots on a Sunday night were really not a good idea.

"What are we toasting?" I asked, incredulous yet strangely hooked.

"We're toasting the dawn of your new life. You have been deprived of variety and experimentation—"

"Hey!" I protested.

"Your life until now has been consumed only with one man—someone I shall henceforth refer to as 'the deceiver.'"

"He wasn't—"

"And yet here you find yourself, living with a totally amazing, awesome flatmate. Oh, and Ben. Plus, a whole world of fun, delicious men and sex just waiting for you."

"I can't toast to that!"

"Cheers!" Kalina determinedly clinked my glass.

Rolling my eyes in defeat, I drank the shot, too.

"What are we toasting?" Ben asked, sliding back into his seat.

"Laura's newfound independence—no wait—*sexual* independence!" Kalina said.

"No!" I objected, though I was starting to laugh.

"To the exploration of her new self!" Kalina placed a shot down in front of Ben, and refilled our glasses.

"To Laura, the explorer!" Ben said, raising his shot glass.

"Laura—the man explorer!" Kalina echoed, raising hers.

Well, there was no point protesting now. Plus, I was already tipsy.

I raised my glass, clinked it with theirs and we all downed our shots.

# 4

Oh my God, *why* did I drink so much?

Sitting at my desk at work the next day, I had to resist the urge to just lay my head down and press my hands over my ears. All around me I could hear people working away, happily chatting and laughing and answering phones and typing SO LOUDLY on their keyboards.

*Must. Concentrate. On. Work.*

I looked down at the to-do list that I'd been trying to ignore all morning. It had horribly boring things on there such as, "Run audit of 500+ days points balance" and "Source new rewards for people over seventy".

When I took the job in the incentives team for Tiger Finance, a multinational investment bank, I was imagining glamorously testing out all the reward "experiences" and having snooty meetings with vendors in five-star restaurants. In reality, the job wasn't *quite* as I had imagined it, although it was certainly better than the PR agency I used to work for. Well, the pay, at least, was better.

Normally, it didn't bother me too much. Today, though, I honestly could not face my work with such an awful headache. It was so unlike me turning up to work with a hangover. Some of the guys in the sales team, yes, but certainly not me.

I thought back on the previous night, which had become a bit crazy.

After being dubbed "Laura the Explorer" by Ben and Kalina, we'd just kept on drinking. And drinking. And drinking. And then somehow, Ben and I ended up staying back and helping Kalina tidy up the bar, which mostly meant me flopping a dubious-smelling wet cloth over the tables, while Ben shuffled around with the broom doing a rendition of the chimney-sweep act from *Mary Poppins*. I had no idea what Kalina was doing during that time. Possibly having numerous attempts at counting the money and cashing up. Luckily, her boss had never shown up.

But the thing was, the more we drank, the more the idea of Laura the Explorer seemed to take hold. I think Ben and Kalina named themselves my team mascots. Quite possibly, I made a pledge to tell them all the juicy details of my inevitable encounters (although I wasn't really sold on the whole "inevitable" part. I mean really, I'd first have to find some guys who were willing to sleep with me, wouldn't I?).

But I thought—why shouldn't I get out there and start exploring? Having adventures of the kind my mother would be horrified about. That's what single people did nowadays, wasn't it? Single people were expected to go out and sleep with loads of people, and it was just considered normal.

Throughout my late teens and early twenties, the "party days" as other people called them, I'd watched friends go on blind dates, have one-night stands, have multiple boyfriends and adventures, all while I stood by the nice in-a-relationship sidelines. Perhaps part of me was a bit envious, but I'd come to terms with the fact that I would never be one of those single, carefree people who slept around, and was safe in my superior knowledge that they were all just looking for what I already had. Because I had found the love of my life, my soulmate. And how smug I was about it, how secure. Ha!

Fate had such a juicy curve ball waiting for me.

I picked up the phone and dialled Rose's extension.

"Hello, Laura!" came her cheery, somewhat posh voice over the phone.

"Coffee?" I asked.

"Definitely!"

"Coming round now." I hung up and grabbed my purse out of my bag.

Rose worked on the same floor as I did, slightly closer to the lifts, so I swung by her desk to collect her. As usual, I was blown away by how glamorous she looked, her tall, model-esque Swedish heritage allowing her to pull off the most amazing outfits. Today, she was wearing a gorgeous silk pencil skirt with a delicate chiffon ruffled shirt, her long blonde hair pulled back into a perfect chignon, and little jewelled earrings in her ears. Bold pink lipstick, exactly the same colour as her nine-inch stilettos, adorned her lips.

"So, how did the move go? And what are your flatmates like?" she asked once we were in the lift.

Rose was the only person at work fully across my personal life. We got coffee and lunches together, as well as the occasional after-work drink, so we could have gossip sessions about all the other people we worked with. She was also completely across my separation, the breakdown of my marriage, the crying on the floor of my parents' house (everyone else in the office—aside from my manager, Cara, and the HR department—thought I'd had glandular fever) as well as the decision to move to the other side of Sydney and rent with two complete strangers.

"It was good! They're both really nice. In fact, we went out for drinks last night, which is why I'm feeling pretty awful today."

"Really?" Rose looked at me incredulously as we walked out of the building and onto busy Pitt Street. "Laura Baker has a hangover at work?"

"Shh!" I hissed, glancing around the street in case anyone from the office happened to be following us. "I didn't plan on drinking so much. But Kalina—she's one of the flatmates—she works at a local bar and she just kept pouring me drinks. I don't even know if I paid anything at the end of the night!"

"Really?" Rose sounded even more impressed now. "Fab! Drinks down your way soon, then?"

I laughed. "I think they were more just 'pity drinks' than anything."

"Why would she give you pity drinks?" Rose asked defensively.

There was a pause in our conversation as we ordered and paid for our coffees, then moved around to the pickup area.

"Well, the topic of my history and past dating life came up."

"Obviously." Rose smiled.

"And anyway, I revealed that I've only ever been with Jack, who is now gay," I continued in a low voice. "And apparently, Kalina thinks this is a massive deal and that I've been missing out and so I should get out there and start exploring men. In the bedroom."

"Yes, but … well, that hasn't been something you've really wanted to do before, has it?" Rose asked, looking at me in surprise. "I mean, you were perfectly happy being married."

"Yeah …" I trailed off. "But obviously, there was a small part of me that felt like I was missing out. You know when everyone else is dating different people and they have all these stories to tell? I was always the boring one who couldn't contribute to the conversations. You can't really start telling funny stories about your husband, can you?"

Rose got a faraway look in her eyes as I was talking, the ghost of a smile appearing. "Yeah, I remember those days," she said, as if recalling an old friend. "So many dates and boys and sleeping with weird guys."

See, this was the point. Everyone had these memories. These times that they recall fondly about their single days. Well, I never had that, did I? I'd just jumped right ahead to the long-term relationship queue. And look where that got me.

The idea of Laura the Explorer swam tantalisingly through my mind again. Maybe it wasn't too late to have that. Maybe *this* was my time. Sure, I may have done things in reverse. I'd got the marriage out of the way, done and dusted. And what a spectacular failure that turned out to be! Now, it was time for my carefree years. I could be the divorced cougar, preying on younger guys in bars.

The image of that hot volleyball-playing guy on Manly Beach suddenly popped into my mind. His strikingly blue eyes that had stared into mine. How I'd immediately felt lost in them … I just needed to block the memory of me running away from him, camouflaged in a pack of joggers.

"See, this is what I need," I said, just as our coffee orders appeared and we swiped them off the counter. "I need these memories. These experiences. I'm like the sheltered old hag who never did anything fun in her youth."

"You're not a hag!" Rose protested, laughing. "Honestly, Laura, twenty-seven is the perfect age to be single again."

"Single for the *first time*, not again," I argued as we made our way back out onto the street. "I've never even had a proper first date before. I mean, could you imagine being single again now?"

Rose crinkled up her nose thoughtfully. She was two years older than I was, and lived with her totally fantastic futures-broker boyfriend, whom she'd been with for three years.

"No," she said. "But then, I suppose I *have* got all that out of the way. Plus, I couldn't imagine life without Christian now. There's just something so nice about coming home to someone who loves you every night."

An unpleasant sensation shot through my stomach. It must have registered on my face, because Rose's expression suddenly transformed into a look of horror.

"Oh, Laura, I didn't mean to say that!" She looked appalled at herself. "Sorry, I mean, don't worry, you'll have that again! You'll meet someone who is totally amazing and so much better than Jack ever was. You know, for the obvious reasons."

My stomach was twisting, but I forced myself to smile and take a long sip of coffee.

The truth was, the thought of getting to know someone and letting them get to know me was terrifying. Because I knew what would happen, didn't I? I'd open myself up, I'd let them in. And they'd convince me that they loved me, that they really cared. And then right when I was feeling all relaxed and secure, they'd rip it all away and leave me with a giant knife in the heart.

But I wouldn't let that happen again. No. I was far wiser now. I'd cottoned on to the game. I was more observant, more careful. No one would get past the walls while I was on watch.

And maybe that's exactly what I needed to do: simply *sleep* with guys, but not get involved with them. I'd build up my repertoire of stories, the kind that you could entertain others with at parties, or look back on fondly in your old age. Suddenly, I realised that becoming Laura the Explorer wasn't just something that I wanted to do—it was something that I *needed* to do. Not just for experimentation purposes. But because …

I needed to feel normal.

"Well, I'm not looking for a relationship right now," I said, my thoughts crystallising. "I've had more than enough years' worth of relationship that I'm still recovering from. This is going to be purely physical. Just for fun," I told Rose with all the determination I felt.

"Good for you," she said, looking relieved that I didn't seem upset.

"Now, I've just got the small problem of actually finding the men I'm going to sleep with," I said, trying to lighten the mood.

"You know, Christian will be out next Friday night for work drinks." Rose's eyes sparkled with sudden excitement. "How about we also go out after work and chat up some guys? I can be your wingman!"

"That sounds awesome! Let's do it."

"Fabulous!" Rose grinned as we made our way back into the Tiger Finance building, hot coffee in our hands.

** NEW MESSAGE **
**From: Mum at 3.11 pm**
*Hi, darling! How's the new place going? Are you getting along well with Ben? Xxx*

** FACEBOOK ALERT **
**Elle Baker updated her status:**
Feeling Blessed
*Walking the tracks of the ancients* ♡ ♡
– at Machu Picchu, Peru

** FACEBOOK ALERT **
**Hailey Bentley added a new life event:**
Married Pete "Ninja" Belatruse at Doltone House, Sydney

[Future alerts like this blocked]

# 5

The delicious smell of frying onions and garlic greeted me as soon as I opened my apartment's front door that evening. Hip music was playing and I could hear Kalina and Ben laughing about something.

"Hi!" I said as I fumbled my way inside.

"Laura! The new flatmate returns!" Ben announced. He was the one in the kitchen, chopping a load of vegetables with expert precision, while the frying pan happily simmered away.

"Laura!" Kalina echoed, and I saw her sprawled in one of the beanbags, a glass of red wine in hand. "Ben is making us Spanish tapas for dinner!"

"Really?" I asked, looking hopefully towards the kitchen.

"I'm making empanadas, albondigas, and mushroom-and-chorizo salad," Ben said as he diced mushrooms into tiny cubes the way I'd only seen expert chefs do on TV. "Testing out some new recipes."

"Erm … sounds interesting!" I said, though I had no idea what half those things were. Albondiga? Was that a fish?

"Grab a glass, Laura." Kalina raised her own in a small salute. "Ben's forcing us to try some Spanish wine."

"You're meant to be trying it with the food, not beforehand," Ben said.

Kalina shrugged. "Well, I had to start drinking *something*."

"I was only just starting to feel normal again after last night!" I laughed.

Kalina waved a hand dismissively. "Last night is old news. Besides, that was mostly beer, and now we're having wine."

"And shots," I reminded her with a grimace.

"Still not wine."

"Alright, fine." I rolled my eyes, caving.

I hurried into my bedroom so I could change out of my work clothes. My morning hangover was long forgotten, and drinking on a Monday night seemed completely normal in this new environment. Besides, it was Project Fresh Start, the dawn of Laura the Explorer. All thoughts of my marriage, and any lingering painful memories of Jack, were to be blocked out.

I'd forget the Laura who used to come home from work, put on her trackpants and sit on the couch watching TV re-runs until her husband arrived home. Forget the Laura who'd go to Saturday-afternoon barbeques with her other married friends and get drunk on cheap bottles of champagne and be in bed by 9.30. Forget that I had actually been quite happy with my former life. You know, up until my husband announced he was gay and all.

And I'd definitely forget the Laura who had started walking through the baby-clothes section of H&M, staring warmly at newborns or looking curiously at pregnant women. That was so far away from my reality that it was practically laughable.

My reality now was as a single girl. And if I needed any further evidence, I reminded myself that earlier today I'd made myself an appointment for a bikini wax for later on in the week. A *full* bikini wax. This is something I remembered Kalina and Ben arguing about at The Blonde Pony when we were all a few drinks in. About how it's not only expected for women to be hair free, but that men apparently must man-scape, too.

I hadn't partaken in that particular conversation, just sat by and listened avidly. To be honest, I'd never really bothered doing anything when I was with Jack. He didn't seem to care either way, and he certainly didn't do any maintenance himself. In fact, I had no idea men were meant to do maintenance, so there you go. Jack clearly hadn't received the memo, either.

When we were first sleeping together, quite early in our relationship, I did have waxes every now and then. One time I'd even asked for them to give me one of those love-heart shapes. It ended up being just a big blob of uneven hair that looked bizarre (it was also completely off-centre) and Jack had just laughed.

I didn't bother again.

When I re-emerged into the living room, Ben was halfway through a story about his friend Hobsey's relationship woes.

"I told Hobs to just ignore her, but of course he didn't, he went around to her place once again," he was saying, managing to keep up an easy conversation without losing concentration on his food prep.

"Next thing, he's round at Dave's place at two in the morning, because she's kicked him out and locked him outside without his phone or wallet or anything. He's had to walk down the road to Dave's with no shoes on, climb up the tree outside his apartment and break in through the balcony."

I grabbed a wineglass from the kitchen cupboard and poured myself some wine from the bottle sitting on the coffee table. Then I dragged the second beanbag over next to Kalina, and settled in to listen to the conversation.

"See, this is why I don't do relationships," Kalina said, turning to me. "There're too many crazies out there. Just keep it to sex and that's it—then it's really clear for everyone."

Ben snorted with laughter. "Yeah, *that's* why you don't do relationships!"

"Hey, you can talk!" Kalina retorted before turning to me again. "Ben is totally known as Mr One-night Stand—"

"Am not!"

"He's chronically picking up girls in bars, then doing a runner the next morning before they're even awake. That's why you'll hear him arriving home at six in the mornings."

"Well, if you wake up next to a girl, she expects to be taken out for pancakes or something!" Ben said defensively, making Kalina laugh. "Besides, it's not me who does all the one-night stands, it's my brother. As *you* should well know, Kal."

"I'll pin him down one day." Kalina grinned wickedly, then turned to me to explain. "Ben has got the *hottest* older brother."

"Runs in the family," Ben quipped.

"He looks nothing like Ben." Kalina threw him a dirty look.

"Oh, don't start talking about what he looks like naked," Ben groaned.

"He's got the biggest—"

"STOP IT!" Ben shouted, and Kalina laughed delightedly before turning to me again.

"Ben is horrified that I slept with his brother. It was only the once," she threw him another look, "but totally worth it."

"Okay, enough about him," Ben called. "Why don't you tell Laura about the two guys you *are* currently sleeping with?"

"Yes, tell me about them!" I sat up eagerly, delighted and fascinated with the whole conversation.

Kalina rolled her eyes. "What's to tell? They're both equally useful."

"They still don't know about each other, do they?" Ben teased.

"Of course they don't! They both know that I'm not up for anything serious, so everything is just super casual. And when they are here, they're never allowed to hang around long enough to get talking to you, Ben."

"Aww, but I'd have so many great stories to tell them."

"Exactly why you're not allowed to talk to them. Besides, I haven't even seen Ethan in ages, he's gotten all serious and busy at work."

"Ah, so it's just Maverick, then."

"*Maverick?*" I echoed. "Is that really his name?"

"He's a musician," Kalina said, as if that explained everything.

"One of those long-haired, hippie, guitar types," Ben added.

"He's not that bad."

"If he brings his guitar around here again … honestly, Laura," Ben added to me. "He used to come round here and sit on the balcony playing all this shitty emotional music and singing in this awful croony voice. It got so bad we've banned him from bringing his guitar here. We even had complaints from some of the neighbours."

"Seriously?" I looked at Kalina again. "He's banned?"

"His guitar is," she replied. "It was getting pretty annoying, actually."

I laughed along as Ben and Kalina continued to make fun of each other's dating lives. They had a really good friendship going, easy in each other's company and were obviously happy living together. I briefly wondered again if there was anything more than friendship going on between them, but then quickly dismissed the idea. If Kalina slept with Ben's brother and no one cared, then there couldn't be anything between them, could there?

"So, Laura, have you got Tinder set up yet?" Kalina suddenly asked me.

"Erm, no," I replied.

Tinder? Really? Were we up to this already? But of course I should be on Tinder, shouldn't I? It's how all the kids dated nowadays, right? And not just the kids, as a matter of fact. I was pretty sure the formally grumpy single mum who lived across the road from my parents' place met her new boyfriend on Tinder. And they were in their fifties.

"You're not?" Kalina sounded way more excited than she should. "Can I set up your profile for you?"

"Oh shit," Ben groaned from the kitchen. "Watch out, Laura!"

"Hey, I'll make it really good!" Kalina protested. "Don't worry, I'll set it up and then you can check over everything before we make it live, okay?"

I hesitated for only a moment before shrugging and going to fetch my phone out of my handbag. It was just an app on my phone, right? It's not like it was anything serious.

I returned a moment later and handed the phone over to Kalina, who took it eagerly, and set to things with a gleeful look in her eye.

"You're a brave one, Laura," Ben called.

I shrugged. "What's the worst that could happen?"

"Exactly," Kalina piped in, though she didn't lift her gaze from the phone.

I left Kalina to it and wondered over to the kitchen to see how Ben was going. Many delicious smells were happening, and I could see meatballs cooking away in a white sauce on the stovetop.

"Need a hand?" I asked him.

"Sure—can you stir the albondigas?" he said, not taking his eyes off the chopping board and the knife flying around with the speed of a hummingbird's wings.

"The … um … which ones are they?" I asked, looking at the various pots on the stove.

"There." Ben looked around and indicated the meatballs.

"Oh, right!" Well, that was a relief. Albondigas didn't appear to be funky fish. "So, whose choice was it to do tapas tonight?" I asked, stirring the pot with one hand and sipping my wine with the other.

"It was sort of my brother's, actually," Ben replied. "He's opening a bar in a couple of months and I'm helping him put the menu together."

"Really?" I asked, genuinely impressed. "That sounds cool! Where's the bar going to be?"

"Down here in Manly. It's only a pop-up bar, so it will be open for a couple of months over summer."

"Wow. Is that easy to do? Just open a bar?"

Ben laughed. "I have no idea. My brother loves challenging himself and starting all these weird ventures. They normally work out pretty well for him, although I'm still not sure if that's luck or if he really is some sort of amazing business guru."

And this was the guy Kalina had slept with? How intriguing.

"It's pretty nice of you to help out with the food. Although, shouldn't he be hiring, you know, a professional chef? Not that I'm sure your food isn't amazing," I quickly added, as Ben turned around to give me a mock wounded look.

"Aww, and you haven't even tasted my food yet!" he said, feigning injury.

"Well, it *smells* amazing." I said reassuringly.

Laughing, Ben went to the fridge and took out a beer. "I'm probably going to be the chef there, actually," he said as he cracked the top off, and leaned casually against the bench.

"Really?" I said again. God, I was sounding like a broken record.

"Yeah. It's one of those things I've always wanted to try. My brother's pretty good at helping out friends and family with stuff. Plus, let's be honest, I am a totally awesome cook," he said with a cheeky grin.

I eyed the food with mock criticism. "Hmm, well that has yet to be seen. Don't you have a regular job, though?"

"Yeah, but I freelance so I can take breaks whenever I want. I'm an audio engineer."

"Right. I have no idea what that is."

Ben smiled. "I basically work on a lot of video productions, but I do the audio and sound part. I make sure the sound files being recorded are top quality so they can be combined with the video."

"Do you work on movies?" I asked with sudden keen interest. I'd always wanted to work on movie sets! It would be so fascinating to be a fly on the wall and watch the director and the cameraman and the actors all working away. Why on earth hadn't I gone into movie-making as a career? What sad part of me had steered me towards numbers and spreadsheets and working in the finance industry?

"I've done a few movies," Ben said, sipping his beer again. "And some TV shows. They're long contracts, and pretty good work to get. Mostly, I work with other agencies and freelancers, though—we do a lot of ads and video production for corporates."

I was still super fascinated and about to ask more when Kalina interrupted us.

"Okay, Laura!" she called, as she jumped up from her beanbag and came over to me with the phone. "Take a look at this and let me know what you think."

I took the phone from her and had a look at my new profile. I felt a stab of apprehension immediately before looking, but then I was pleasantly surprised. She'd picked three of my nicer profile pictures from my Facebook account, and there was a brief, reasonably witty blurb about me looking for someone "fun" without coming across as simply being after sex.

"I like it!" I looked up at her and smiled.

"*See*, Ben?" Kalina put her hand on her hip and raised her eyebrows at him. "I'm totally great at this stuff."

"You have succeeded in amazing me," Ben replied levelly.

Kalina ignored him and grabbed the phone out of my hand. "Now, we just need to make it live aaaaand … done!" Then she passed it back to me.

"Now what?" I asked, peering quizzically at the phone. I was looking at a picture of "Gerald, 29", who seemed to be an average-looking guy, wearing a straw hat and drinking a beer.

"Now you start swiping!" Kalina crowded in next to me and looked at the phone. "No," she swiped left and Gerald disappeared; "no," David, 30, also disappeared; "no," Hayden, 25, vanished.

"Hey, he looked okay!" I protested. At least I thought the quick glimpse I got of Hayden did.

"Oh sorry, too late. Ooh, yes!" Kalina suddenly swiped right across "Denver, 28", a well-muscled guy pictured on the beach.

"Time to abort, Laura!" Ben called warningly.

"Okay, okay, that's enough." I rescued my phone from Kalina, who looked disappointed at its sudden loss.

"Food's ready now anyway," Ben said, pushing us out of the way so he could get the pan of meatballs off the stove.

"We're out of wine," Kalina lamented.

"You drank both bottles?" Ben asked, incredulous.

"There were two?"

Laughing, I walked to my room and dumped my phone on the bed, while Kalina happily located the second wine bottle. Tinder could wait until tomorrow.

# 6

I jumped out of bed early the next morning, feeling surprisingly alert and awake, and pulled on some of my new active wear. I may have been fuelled by the exhilaration of my new planned life or, just slightly, by the nagging guilt of how much money I'd spent shopping for new clothes— including lots of new workout wear—during my lunchbreak the day before. I decided I wasn't even going to bother checking my credit-card balance (fear had nothing to do with it), but so long as I made the most of my new clothes, then it all would be fine. I mean, if you thought about cost per wear of these items, and I *would* totally wear them loads, obviously, then really they were all a complete bargain. And clearly, Laura the Explorer needed new clothes to go exploring in.

I left the apartment, pleased with myself once again for being one of those motivated, early risers, and headed down to the Manly corso. And yes, seeing all the fit, active people out for a morning run before work, I told myself I was just like them, just one of the locals.

I power-walked along happily (understandably, I had to work my way into running. I couldn't just start jogging straightaway with no practice—I might have given myself an injury), breathing in the fresh ocean air, and felt the warm early-morning sun on my face.

As I made my way past the volleyball nets, I slowed down subtly. A whole crew of people was there again and—yes! He was there; Volleyball Guy with his rippling muscles, tanned skin, tousled hair and sky-blue eyes!

I let my eyes roll right on past him. I was going to be way cooler today. My plan involved a breakfast smoothie, a nice, quiet patch of grass and some morning meditation. And maybe just a *teeny* bit of volleyball-game spectating.

I headed into a trendy-looking smoothie bar that was all wood panelling and ceiling plants, and things on the menu like raw acai bowls and matcha bliss balls.

Checking out the smoothie menu, my eyes were immediately drawn to the banana-honey-vanilla one, but then I noticed two really fit girls sitting in the back corner, casually lounging in their activewear as if they'd already been up for hours and had just finished a morning yoga ritual. They had toned arms and shoulders, skin that was flushed and glowing, and that wavy, beachy hair that made me wonder how it could look so clean if they'd just been working out. And in front of them were two super-sized, bright-green smoothies.

My eyes slid back to the board again. Well, I *had* always wanted to try those green drinks. I saw them all over the fitness blogs and Instagram accounts that I'd spent time stalking the day before (again, probably should have been tackling my to-do list at work, but I'll just make up the time later). Plus, I knew I'd probably feel really good after drinking one. Aren't they meant to be all energising and good for you?

I decided to bypass the light-sounding green smoothies and jump straight to the "Hardcore" one. Kale, spinach, celery—everything on the list sounded green and incredibly healthy. The girl behind the counter was looking at me expectantly, so I stepped up confidently and ordered the large size of it.

*Ha! Look at me now!* I was strolling along the walkway in Manly, in my new active wear, carrying the greenest smoothie I'd ever seen.

Fit person: check. Local: check. Ultra-healthy new Laura: check.

I smiled at a passer-by and took a nice big sip of my drink.

Oh God.

Oh my God.

It was awful.

*Don't screw up your face. Don't spit it out.*

*Maintain facial control. Swallow.*

Ugh! It was so *thick*. And chewy. Why was it chewy?! It was like little bits of plant were in there that hadn't mushed up properly in the blender.

I grimaced visibly but managed to chew and swallow it. Well. I suppose things that are good for you don't necessarily taste nice. Just think about brussels sprouts.

*Are there brussels sprouts in this thing?*

Forlornly, I thought about the banana-honey-vanilla smoothie I'd been planning on ordering and silently cursed those two girls in the shop. No one in their right mind would order this kind of drink. The shop probably paid those girls to sit there all morning, looking all blissed out with their green smoothies, just so they could sell more of them.

But anyway, the aftertaste was beginning to fade. Maybe the second sip wouldn't be so bad. I found a prime patch of grass that gave me a good view of the volleyball nets and took a seat, making sure I looked all Zen and yoga-like. I took a deep breath, crossed my legs and closed my eyes.

Then I opened my eyes, just a smidge, and perved on Volleyball Guy.

Mmm. Now, if only I could meet or hook up with a guy like that. His muscles were rippling as he dived for the ball—oh, and then he got a bit sandy. But then he sprang back to his feet again, and he started doing that semi-squat thing they do when they're waiting for the ball to be served. And the ball got hit out and then he …

Oh no, he started looking at me again. Those eyes, those piercing blue eyes, were staring straight into mine.

I shut my eyes and tried to look all calm and peaceful.

Then I peeked them open.

Shit. He was still looking. And kind of smiling.

I squeezed my eyes shut again.

*Deep breath in. Deep breath out.* I forced myself to count to ten before I opened my eyes again.

Okay. It was okay, he'd stopped looking at me; the volleyball game had resumed.

I stayed in my meditative pose for a few more minutes, surreptitiously watching the game and the players. Then I realised that it was probably time for me to start heading back to the apartment. I did have to go to work, after all. Plus, my green smoothie had started to separate out into dubious-looking "layers" in its cup.

Trying to look like I'd finished my meditation—*should I kowtow to the sun? No, no, that's just weird*—I stood up, collected my off-putting kale drink and started heading home.

I glanced back at Volleyball Guy one more time, but he was focused on the game again.

♋

I was feeling so positive and energised after my morning walk that I found myself flying through my work in the office. However, by 10 am my stomach was rumbling; most of the kale smoothie had ended up down the sink.

I knew Rose had back-to-back meetings this morning, so I grabbed my purse and made my way out of the building alone. I went to my usual coffee haunt and ordered a ham-and-cheese toastie to go with my coffee. Then I moved around to the side counter to wait. The coffee shop was buzzing with a ton of city workers all getting their morning fixes, and I could see a huge list of coffee orders stuck to the machine. Even though two baristas were working at lightning speed, I was going to be in for a bit of a wait.

I took out my phone and opened the Tinder app.

*Hmm… now let's see.* "Brendan, 24" looked pretty cute, but was probably a bit young.

*Left swipe.*

"Pharrell, 31" had some weird hair going on. I quickly looked through his other pictures … but oh dear. Oh no.

*Left swipe.*

"Robinson, 23" looked like a photoshopped picture of a young guy riding a space rocket. His "About" info also mentioned that he liked space travel and fighting intergalactic monsters. I knew I should probably swipe left, but then, with a grin and a burst of spontaneity I swiped right instead.

Next up was "Darren, 26". He looked like a fairly normal, nice-looking guy, with dark hair. His pictures were all candid shots, obviously of him on holidays or with friends. And his "About" section also seemed normal. I hesitated momentarily, then swiped right.

*It's a match!*

Argh! What just happened? God, was he online, looking at my Tinder profile right then?

"Laura?" called the barista, and I snapped into attention. My coffee and toastie were ready, so I stuffed my phone back into my bag and grabbed my order off the counter.

When I got back to my desk, I pulled my phone out of my bag, and I could see a notification from Tinder of a new match and a new message. I glanced surreptitiously around the office, but no one could see me over my desk partitions. Turning my eyes back to my phone, I opened the app eagerly and discovered that Robinson, aka rocket man, had sent me a message.

*Hey theyre grrrl, want 2 tke a ride on ma rocket ship?*

Well, that would be a firm no to Robinson, wouldn't it? Though I wasn't sure what I was expecting. It was probably a group of school boys all sitting in the library together and laughing at their fake Tinder accounts.

My finger hovered over my other match, Darren, and I wondered if I should send him a message. What do you say to someone on Tinder? If Robinson's opening line was anything to go by, then things were not looking promising.

Sighing, I put my phone away and turned to my ham-and-cheese toastie instead.

# 7

"Your job sounds really boring," Kalina said bluntly, before taking a sip of tea.

Kalina and I were sitting out on our small balcony in the early-evening air, and I'd just finished giving her the full rundown on my job. I thought I was making it sound interesting, but Kalina's frank assessment did actually sum it up quite well. It was, as I'd been trying to avoid admitting to myself for some time, very boring.

I shrugged, taking a sip of my own tea. "It pays well, at least."

"There is that, I suppose." Kalina sighed. "Things always end up coming down to money, don't they?"

Kalina frowned and lapsed into silence and I found myself studying her curiously out of the corner of my eye. Aside from working the occasional shift at The Blonde Pony, Kalina didn't appear to have any other employment. And yet, she was hardly living the skint backpacker lifestyle, either. Rent on this apartment wasn't low (unless of course Ben and Kalina had decided to charge the third flatmate an extortionate amount to subsidise their own contributions; and let's be honest, that wouldn't be surprising), and even though she wasn't the kind of girl who was into all-designer clothing, I had noticed that her eclectic assortment of clothes included a lot of upmarket brands mixed in with the high-street labels. Plus, I'd done a full audit of all her cosmetic and skincare items in the bathroom, and they were all brands I'd only buy once in a blue moon as a treat (although, I did enjoy smelling and sampling a lot of them). It made me wonder, not for the first time, where her money came from.

"So, have you been playing on Tinder yet?" Kalina suddenly turned to me with interest, and I snapped myself out of my speculating.

"Sort of. I'm not sure I'm very good at it."

"It's not possible to be *bad* at it. Can I have a look?"

Rolling my eyes at her clearly overexcited expression, I relinquished my phone again.

"You've already got some matches!" she squealed. "Robinson ... um, right. Did you swipe right on him?"

"That was ... um ... an accident. Actually, can I block him now? I don't know how to do that."

"Here, I'll do it," Kalina said.

We sat in silence for a while, me enjoying the evening air, Kalina tapping away on my phone. I checked my watch and saw that it was almost 7 pm. Ben hadn't arrived home from work yet, and rather than attempting dinner, we'd been sitting outside in the vain hope that he'd suddenly roll in and offer to cook for us again.

"I guess it's time to give up hope of one of Ben's dinners," I said with a sigh.

"Oh yeah." Kalina barely looked up from my phone. "He's probably gone to his parents' place for dinner or something. I can cook a meal for us, though."

Before I had time to protest, she'd jumped to her feet and headed inside. I followed apprehensively.

"I'm happy to cook," I offered, even though I was intrigued to see what Kalina would come up with. Obviously I was taking Ben's warning seriously, but in a weird way, I felt like I'd missed out on something special by not getting to try the infamous "fish pie".

"That's okay," Kalina said, opening the pantry and looking inside. "Hmm ... we've got ... a few options."

"Maybe we should just order in. Or go out. How about one of the pubs?" I suggested hopefully, trying to distract Kalina before she became too taken with the idea of cooking.

"Nah, the pubs here don't do food anywhere near as well as British pubs."

"Seriously? But you can get potted pies and grilled salmon here."

Kalina turned to me and wrinkled her nose. "Yeah, but there's nothing quite like a black pudding. Or spotted dick."

"Have you ever *actually* eaten spotted dick?" I challenged.

"I've had my fair share of spotted dicks in my day," she replied loftily, giving me a knowing wink. "Have you never tried *spotted dick*?"

I wasn't sure if we were talking about men's appendages or British cuisine anymore, but I decided to stick with the latter. "I can't say I have tried spotted dick before, no. Although, isn't spotted dick a dessert?"

"There's never a bad time for spotted dick." Kalina arched an eyebrow suggestively, leaning her elbows on the kitchen bench and dropping her voice conspiratorially.

Okay, fine. We were clearly talking male appendages, then. I wrinkled up my nose. "Have you ever seen one that's spotted? For real?"

"I have, and it's called herpes! God, Laura, if you ever see one of those just run! Run away and never go back."

"Eww!" I started laughing. "Did you really sleep with a guy who had herpes?"

"Of course I didn't sleep with him!" Kalina exclaimed, looking at me incredulously. "I draw a very distinct line in the sand at the faintest hint of any STDs."

"How did you know he had herpes, then?"

"Because when he pulled out his cock—sorry, his *spotted dick*—and I saw what was going on down there, I screamed and ran away. In fact, I think I ran into his bathroom first and started scrubbing my hands with soap."

I was really laughing then, having to hold my stomach to try to stop it. "No! Wasn't he offended?"

"Why should I bloody care? He did stand outside the bathroom door for a while, trying to reason with me and saying that 'everyone has it'. I told him if he didn't get away from the bathroom door I'd come out and kick him full in the nuts, turning his already spotted dick into a pulverised mess."

"Wow. That's ... well, I'm quite impressed."

"Yeah." Kalina looked thoughtfully up at the ceiling. "His name was Billy and he was an electrician, I think. Seemed like such a demure guy."

"Okay, well either way I'm certainly not convinced about spotted dick or any kind of British food for dinner. How about we just order a pizza?"

"Okay," Kalina said, picking up my phone again. She made an excited kind of squeal when she looked at the screen, which set off small warning bells in my brain.

"Why are you getting so excited?" I asked slowly.

"No reason." Kalina said innocently. "By the way, are you free on Friday night?"

"Why?"

"Are you?"

"Maybe. Why?"

Kalina looked up at me triumphantly. "Because I've organised a date for you!"

"What? Who with? There's no way I'm meeting that Robinson guy!"

"No! Darren. The one you already had a match with. Although, you've actually got five more matches now."

"What?" I snatched my phone out of her hand. "Let me see that."

Sure enough, there were six little pictures of men whom I'd "matched" with. Robinson had thankfully disappeared.

"I can't go on a Tinder date!" I protested.

"Why not?"

"Because!" I exclaimed vehemently, as if this was all the answer I needed.

"What else were you planning on doing on Friday?" Kalina pressed.

"That's not the point."

"You've got to get out there and start dating eventually," Kalina wheedled. "This way, you're just jumping in and taking the plunge. Like ripping off a band-aid. Besides, Darren looks really cute."

I clicked on Darren's profile again and looked through his photos. He was quite cute, if I was being honest. I read his "About" section again, and there was nothing strange in there. I went back and read over the messages Kalina had been exchanging with him, impersonating me. They weren't too bad, and Darren did come off as rather nice and genuine. I did too, I realised.

"I don't have anything to wear for a date," I said, relenting a little. And it was true, I didn't. My wardrobe had always been more on the practical side of things. "Librarian" or "work" clothing, Elle used to call it. Although, I called her clothing "hippie-sacks".

Kalina took my response as a triumphant win for her. "I can help with that! Come on, let's check out your wardrobe and then we can see what I've got that you can borrow!" And without waiting for me, she was off and racing into my bedroom.

"Let me just order the pizza first!" I called, quickly googling pizza places in the area even as I followed her into my room.

"Get it from Al's!" Kalina called back.

# 8

S hit, shit, shit.

    It was the day of my waxing appointment and I was already having doubts. I mean, who doesn't have doubts, really? You get to strip off and have a total stranger get up close and personal with your nether region, then enjoy the excruciating pain of having every hair ripped out by its follicle.

Maybe it was just because I hadn't had a wax in so long that I was getting nervous. Then again, maybe by now they'd come up with whole new waxing technology, and it wouldn't even hurt at all! Yes, maybe there'd be some sort of special skin-numbing gel or white light that they shined on the area and then you'd feel no pain! That technology existed, didn't it?

Plus, I couldn't chicken out now, since I had a date with Darren from Tinder lined up for Friday night. Yes, that's right. I was going. I'd totally talked myself into it (or rather Kalina had). And I was determined to stay really positive about the whole thing. I wasn't going to allow myself to be *at all* terrified. My first date with a strange guy. My first *proper* first date, in fact. It was going to be fabulous. Okay, maybe not fabulous—I didn't want to get my expectations up too high—but I was at least seeing it as a necessary step in transforming fully into Laura the Explorer, conqueror of men and sexual adventurer.

So, I was *not* going to let myself chicken out. Besides, I was half expecting

Darren not to show up at all.

When the clock on my computer hit 12.20 pm, I grabbed my handbag and headed out of the Tiger Finance building. It was a short walk to the beauty salon, and I smiled at the warm spring weather and the other business people out on their lunchbreaks as I walked down the road.

Arriving at Serenity Beauty, I pushed open the door and entered a cool and minimalist reception area complete with waterfall trickling down one wall, aromatherapy candles burning and gentle, calming music playing.

I let the girl at reception know my name before taking a seat in a plush white leather armchair. I picked up one of the magazines sitting on a coffee table and surreptitiously checked out the one other woman sitting in the waiting area. She was all platinum-blonde hair, long red talon nails and makeup galore over a highly botoxed face. She gave me a weirdly accusatory look, and I hastily dropped my eyes to my magazine. Although, in hindsight, that might have been the only look she was capable of giving.

I hadn't been waiting long before a middle-aged woman in a white uniform appeared in the doorway.

"Laura?" she asked expectantly, and I jumped up and followed her into the inner salon.

She led me into a small dimly lit room that had different serenity music playing, abstract bamboo-tree paintings on the walls and more aromatherapy candles burning.

"I'll let you get changed," the woman said. "There is a modesty towel on the bed for you." With that she closed the sliding door and left me alone in the room.

Hmm. Where was the modesty paper G-string? Didn't salons use them anymore? Gulping, I quickly stripped off my bottom half, dumping my pencil skirt, shoes and underwear in a corner and climbed up onto the bed. The modesty towel was about the size of a face washcloth, but I managed to artfully drape it over myself in a diamond shape.

A moment later there came a soft knocking on the door.

"Ready!" I called, lying down on my back and staring up at the ceiling.

God, I'd forgotten how awkward bikini waxes were. I could feel my heart fluttering nervously as the woman came into the room, sliding the door shut behind her.

*Relax, Laura, just listen to the Zen music.*

"Busy day at work?" the woman got the conversation going as she started mixing up the wax.

"Oh yeah, it's okay," I said vaguely, eyeing the paintings on the wall. "How about you—busy day?"

"Yes, quite busy," she said. "You're already my fourth wax today, and I've also done a massage. So just bend your legs up into the frog position."

I gulped down my dignity and did as requested, staring at the ceiling and trying to ignore the slight breeze I could feel between my legs. A moment later she whipped off the towel, leaving me completely exposed in the dim room, and then I felt the hot, almost-burning sensation of the first spatula of wax being spread on.

"Are we taking everything off today?" she asked. I noticed that she had an accent.

"Yes please." My voice came out a little squeaky. *Wow that ceiling is fascinating, isn't it?*

"So where are you from?" I asked, trying to calm my nerves. If she started talking, at least that might distract me from the imminent hairs about to be torn from my skin.

"South Africa," she said.

"Oh really?" I asked. "Have you been in Australia long?"

"A few years now."

RIP!

I flinched as the first strip of wax was pulled off.

"I moved here with my husband about five years ago and we absolutely love it!"

RIP! RIP!

"The weather is beautiful and the people are lovely."

RIIIP!

"Oh really?" I said, my voice a bit strangled, flinching as another strip was rent off.

"We've now got a gorgeous townhouse in Newtown," she continued as she spread the next section of wax on. "With a little garden out the back where I'm growing herbs. My dog loves it."

Rip, rip, RIP!

"What sort of dog do you have?" I asked, trying to distract myself from the pain.

"He's a Jack Chi," she said and ripped off the last few strips. "That's a Chihuahua and Jack Russell cross. He's the sweetest little dog in the world, so well behaved."

She now had the tweezers out and was peering in with her face about two inches away from my delicate area, picking off the last hairs that the wax missed. Oh my God, I could even feel her breath on my newly bald skin. Did she really have to be that close?

"He's about six months old," she continued, as if we were having a conversation at the coffee shop rather than me lying there half naked and spreadeagled while her eyeballs were mere millimetres from my downstairs. "And he already loves going out for walks in the park. He's a bit scared of other dogs still because he's so small, but he is very inquisitive."

*You seem to be getting a bit too inquisitive down there, honey.*

As I listened to her talk, I tried to ignore the fact that she was running a finger across my skin, feeling for any hairs that had been missed. This wasn't really *quite* how I remembered waxes going.

"Are we doing the back today?" she asked.

The back? Did she mean my butt crack?

"Ah, do most people get it done?" I asked.

"If girls are going full Brazilian, then yes. It's included in the price. If you're going to do it doggy-style with your boyfriend, then it's a good idea."

That was one of the most awkward thoughts in the world. Was I going to be doing it doggy-style with anyone? I almost laughed. I supposed I shouldn't rule anything out, though. The new Laura needed to be channelling her inner Samantha Jones. Plus, if it was included in the price ...

"Okay," I squeaked.

The woman turned back to the waxing pot and turned the heat back on, stirring it up again. I felt little flutters of nerves again. I'd never had "the back" done before, so I wasn't really sure what to expect.

"So, the easiest way to do this," she said, turning back to me with the wax spatula in hand, "is if you flip over and kneel on your hands and knees."

Sorry—WHAT? *Kneel?*

She was looking at me expectantly and I almost said I'd changed my mind. But then—no, no, I could do this.

I awkwardly rolled over on the narrow bed and got myself up into a kneeling position, then onto my hands and knees. And—okay wow, I felt super exposed. Was this normal? I could feel a proper breeze all across my naked butt.

I stared at the wall, face frozen and lips pursed, while she spread the burning-hot wax in between my butt cheeks. I cringed slightly—that wax felt especially hot. Oh God, *please* just hurry up and finish the job.

"Sorry, that wax was a bit hot," she said.

WHAT? *Is she burning my bum?*

"It just needs to cool down a little before I can take it off."

I screamed protests in my mind, but my body remained completely motionless. Lucky she couldn't see my face. And then—oh no ...

WHAT. IS. SHE. DOING?

My body was rigid and I stared at the wall in horror. She was now fanning my bum with her hands. That's right, waving them around at my naked butt, fanning a nice soft wind onto me.

And then—oh no. Oh *no*.

She was now *blowing* on my butt crack.

I couldn't breathe, the horror was just too much. She was blowing at the wax, as if it were candles on a birthday cake.

Blowing and fanning.

Fanning and blowing.

And I was just kneeling there, frozen in a cat pose like I was at some weird spiritual yoga class. Staring in hypnosis at the empty wall. Trying to pretend that someone was not actually blowing and fanning wind onto the hot wax currently smeared in my butt crack.

But I couldn't move, could I? I'd have my bum permanently glued together if I attempted to simply get up and leave. I felt like I was verging on hysterics, having to clench my stomach muscles and not even breathe lest I started laughing like a mad woman. Then, thankfully, she stopped blowing and a moment later, the wax was ripped off, pulling me out of my trance.

"All done!" she said, and I thankfully curled my legs in under me, covering myself as much as possible.

"I'll leave you to get dressed and I'll see you out the front, then." She exited the room and left me, still partly in shock, to get myself up.

I managed to recover marginally as I was dressing, trying to layer my dignity back on again. Honestly, I didn't know how they did things in South Africa, but I certainly wouldn't be agreeing to get the back done ever again.

***

I returned from my lunchbreak later than usual, having stopped off to grab some food and a nice relaxing herbal tea after my waxing experience. I slunk into the office, hoping no one had noticed my long lunch (also hoping that no one had noticed the multiple long lunches I'd taken that week), and arrived at my desk to find a hand-written note on it.

*Call me when you get back—Sandy, 8473.*

Shit, that was Sandy from finance. I checked my calendar and realised I was meant to have a meeting with her twenty minutes earlier so she could help me go over some invoices. I went to pick up the phone to apologise when Belinda, the middle-aged woman who sat behind me, popped her head over the partition.

"Just letting you know Cara was looking for you earlier."

*Double shit.* Cara was my boss.

"How long ago was that?" I asked innocently.

"I think she came past a few times," Belinda said.

*Bugger.*

"Okay, thanks!" I said, and Belinda disappeared behind the partition again.

I dialled Cara's extension, the note from Sandy looking at me guiltily. As the phone rang, I pictured Cara frowning behind her desk. She had a habit of playing with her acrylic nails when she was annoyed about something. And I could just imagine her then, sitting at her desk, doing exactly that.

"Laura," her voice drummed through the phone, startling me.

"Cara, hi! Ah, Belinda said you were looking for me?"

"Yes, I was, about an hour ago," she said brusquely.

"Sorry." *Shit, she sounds annoyed.* "What did you need me for?"

"It's nothing now, I had to send some info to the global office, but it's already done."

"Oh, right. Yes, sorry, I had an appointment at lunchtime," I said lamely, and felt my cheeks heat up.

"Alright, well just let me know next time you'll be out for an extended period," Cara said.

"Absolutely!" I replied, a twinge of guilt in my stomach. "I need to pop down to finance, so if you need me that's where I'll be," I added helpfully.

"Okay, talk later," Cara said, and hung up.

I ended my call with Cara and quickly dialled Sandy's extension.

"Sandy? So sorry I missed you earlier, I was stuck in another meeting!" I lied guiltily. "Are you free now? I'll pop down to you."

# 9

**D**own on level four, I had to walk through the sales department to get to Sandy's office in the financial expenses team. As soon as the elevator doors pinged open, I was greeted with loud talking, laughter and the sounds of people moving around energetically. Normally, I'd find the circus-like atmosphere of the sales department to be irritating, but today it made my spirits lift.

I mean, everyone was having so much fun down there! There were big leader-boards up on the walls, tracking the success of everyone in the team. A dartboard and a miniature indoor golf hole were set up along one wall, so those who liked to keep active while making a sales call could. I'd even heard a rumour that they had converted their tea room to a *games* room, complete with ping-pong table, beanbags and a beer fridge.

As I crossed the floor heading towards finance, two of the sales guys suddenly stood up and high-fived each other.

"That's how it's done!" Charlie said in his booming voice that carried across the floor.

I smiled when he caught my eye.

"Laura!" Charlie called, as he waved me over. "What's someone from the PR team doing down here in boring sales?"

"It's hardly boring down here." I rolled my eyes at him as I approached.

The other guy that was high-fiving Charlie was looking at me curiously. He was new, I realised, not having met him before. As I drew closer to them, I also realised how tall he was—a good foot taller than Charlie (who was more round than tall). The new guy was also large and resembled a rugby player—his bulk consisted mostly of muscle—so much so that he made Charlie seem tiny in comparison.

"Hi," I greeted him.

"Laura, meet Pete," Charlie said, giving Pete a friendly clap on the back.

We shook hands and I felt like mine was a tiny child's hand in his grip. I didn't normally feel short around other people either, but I found I had to crane my neck back to look at him.

"Nice to meet you," he said amiably.

"Pete's just made his first sale, so we're going to celebrate with a round of pong!" Charlie said. "Come join us!"

"So, it's true that you really do have a ping-pong table down here?" I asked.

"Yes, but sshh!" Charlie dropped his voice to a dramatic whisper. "It's only for cool people to play on."

"And I'm cool, am I?" I asked, also dropping my voice.

"Absolutely."

"Come play a round, it'll be fun," Pete said, watching me curiously.

"I'd love to, but I have a meeting with finance now."

"They're actually boring in there," Charlie said, although he looked like he was only half joking.

"It'll be much more fun hanging out here," Pete said, his voice verging on suggestive.

"Maybe afterwards," I said, and managed to break away from the conversation.

As I walked towards finance, I glanced back at the sales team and saw Pete watching me. He gave me a big, genuine smile, which made my stomach flip over. I smiled back then turned away quickly, feeling my cheeks flush as I rounded the corner.

⁓๏⁓

Once my meeting with Sandy was done, I made my way back across level four towards the lifts. And then I found my feet slowing. Not just because it always seemed like party central in the sales department. And not because the thought of doing my own work was making me feel like I was wading through cement. But because it was after three in the afternoon and Cara thought I'd be in finance for a while and, well, the sales guys were just *fun*.

I headed instead to their tea room, and sure enough there was Charlie, Pete and two other guys from their team playing ping-pong, with open beers sitting on the tables around them.

For a minute I stood in the doorway watching, then as their set ended Charlie spotted me.

"Laura!" he boomed. "You're up!"

Smiling, I walked in and one of the guys who was partnered with Pete handed me his paddle.

"Here, you can take over from me, I'm getting smashed," he said, before picking up his beer and moving to the sidelines.

"Thanks!" I replied.

"We're two sets down, partner, but I feel a change coming." Pete grinned at me and I grinned back.

"We're not going to go easy on you!" Charlie joked from across the table.

"Don't worry, Pete and I are about to kick your butts, so you watch out!" I responded, as I took up my serious "game" stance.

The ball was served, and for a tense half-minute we parried it back and forth before it bounced out on our opponents' side.

"Yes!" Pete and I cried in unison, and he held his hand up for a high five. Trying not to laugh again, I whacked his hand with mine.

"Beginners' luck," Charlie said, as he retrieved the ball.

"How's the game going?" someone said behind me and I turned to see that a few of the girls from the sales team had also turned up to watch.

"Want a go?" I asked them, offering my paddle (I was actually terrible at ping-pong, so it really *was* beginners' luck that we'd won the last set).

"Sure!" one of them said, and I handed over my paddle.

"Here, you too," Pete gave the other girl his paddle and we squeezed out to the back of the room to join the other spectators.

"Want a drink?" Pete asked me.

*Beer at work?* People didn't really do that up on level five.

"Sounds great!" I said rebelliously, as we walked over to the fridge.

"Grab whatever you like." Pete gestured to the contents. There were different sorts of beer, white wine and champagne, but then also a few whole shelves of energy drinks, sports drinks and soft drinks.

To my surprise, Pete reached in and took a coconut water for himself.

"What, no beer?" I asked incredulously, my eyes glancing around to where everyone else seemed to be drinking alcohol.

"Nah, I don't drink during the week, it messes with my training," he said.

"Really?" I grabbed a coconut water as well. "What are you training for?"

"I do power lifting," he said. "Though I train for general fitness and strength as well. It's a really intense but underrated sport."

"Right," I said, eyeing him again. Standing next to him, his height seemed even more apparent, as I was only really eye level with his bicep.

"How about you, what do you do for fitness?" he asked.

"Oh, ah, well I'm just getting back into things at the moment, actually," I said. "I've just moved to Manly and I've started running in the mornings."

Well, I was sure I'd make it into a run soon.

"That's cool. Do you do any weight training?"

"Not really. I wouldn't know where to start with that!" I laughed.

"Yeah, lots of girls find it intimidating. But you know, weight training is actually really important for everyone. Especially as you get older, it's really important to have a strong core of muscle to keep your body healthy. Women especially need to do it to prevent their bone density dropping. How old are you?"

"Er ..."

"Thirty? Thirty-one?"

Oh God, did I seriously look that old?

"Just turned twenty-seven," I replied with as much dignity as I could muster.

"Right, so you probably haven't really experienced any of the noticeable ageing effects yet. Once you get over thirty, you'll start to notice a difference."

Oh, would I now? Well thank you, Mr Sour Grapes.

"And how old are you?" I asked snarkily. "Thirty? Thirty-five?" (This was me trying to be mean. He only looked about twenty-four.)

"I'm twenty-five." Pete grinned, failing to take offence at my comment.

"So how do you know so much about ageing, then? And the *negative effects.*"

"I'm a personal trainer. Well, sort of part-time personal trainer now that I'm working here."

I supposed that explained things. Sort of.

"You know, I could help train you if you want. Give you some pointers on where to get started and where you need to tone up."

I raised an eyebrow haughtily at him, but he just smiled invitingly. Failing, again it would seem, to pick up on my annoyance.

"I need to tone up, do I?" I was starting to feel irritated.

"Everyone needs to tone up," he replied, still giving me that weird, genuine, open smile.

And oh! I finally got it—he was doing the *sales* thing on me. Of course, he was trying to get me to sign up for personal-training sessions with him.

"I really can't afford personal training," I said more kindly, now that the penny had dropped.

"Nah, you wouldn't have to pay. Just come over to the gym with me after work and I'll give you some pointers."

Interesting. I thought he was trying to line me up to be a client. You know, do the whole "knock-down, build-up approach". But why would he offer to train me for free?

"Um … are you sure?" I asked, frowning. "Isn't that sort of a bad business model, to train people for free?"

Pete shrugged. "It'd be a favour. And a chance for me to hang out with you."

*Oooohhh, okay!* So he *was* trying to pick me up, then? Was this modern-day code for asking someone out? I mean, he was being a bit mean and insulting to start with. But then he said he wanted to "hang out" with me? What did that mean?

"Right. Well, I'll think about it," I said evasively. I turned my attention back to the ping-pong game while I tried to process what his offer actually meant.

*Was* he asking me out? It seemed kind of weird and coincidental, didn't it? I mean, there I was, single and trying to get into the "game" and suddenly someone asked me out? But I was probably just imagining it. All that talk about being Laura the Explorer and all. I mean, he'd only offered to take me to the gym, hadn't he? It wasn't really date-worthy. But still, there had been something kind of suggestive in it …

Maybe it was caused by the bikini wax I'd had earlier today! Somehow, it was sending out weird, beacon-like signals to all the single guys around me, saying something like, "Laura Baker is now open for business …"

"Hey, Pete, you're up!" one of the ping-pong players suddenly called out, proffering a paddle.

Snapping my awareness back to the present, I gave myself a little mental shake. Clearly, my vagina was not a beacon. I knew that. Vaginas didn't send signals independent of the people they were attached to.

"Right, then! Game on!" Pete dropped his empty coconut water bottle in the recycling bin and crossed to the table.

I glanced down at my watch and felt a little trill of guilt—it was almost 4 pm. I quickly finished my own drink, then waved my goodbyes to the sales team and headed for the lifts to take me back to my floor.

As the doors pinged open on level five, a wave of boring normality washed over me, cancelling out all the fun, elated feelings I'd been having on level four. Why couldn't everyone at Tiger Finance be more like the sales team?

As I reached my desk, I saw the little red message indicator flashing on my phone. I dialled my message bank and felt a stab of unease as Cara's voice spoke into my ear.

"Laura, hi, it's Cara, can you give me a call when you get this? I need the top-ten incentives from last month ASAP. I'm heading out at four today so I'll need them before then. Thanks."

*Oops.* I checked my watch and saw that it'd already gone four. I dialled Cara's extension, but it rang out and went to voicemail, meaning she'd probably already left. I quickly pulled the report and sent it to her anyway, though the unease didn't abate at all.

Honestly, though, if it really was that urgent, she should have asked me earlier, shouldn't she?

# 10

My mum called while I was on the ferry home.

"Hi, darling!" her overly cheerful voice greeted me loudly in my ear.

"Hi, Mum, how are you?" I responded, as I squished down in my seat.

"Oh, I'm lovely! So, how's the new flat going? How are things with Ben?"

"Things with Ben—and Kalina—are all fine. We're just, you know, getting along as flatmates do."

I wasn't really sure what I meant by that. How *did* flatmates usually get along? Mum didn't seem to notice, though.

"Good, good. So all settling in? Been going out much?"

My mum was clearly fishing for something, I could tell. The question was *what*.

"Yep, all settled. And yes, went out the other night, actually," I replied guardedly.

"Oh good!" Mum sounded too excited. "Did you meet any nice boys?"

Aha! I should have known.

"Mum, I only moved out last weekend!" I protested indignantly. "And I'm still technically married, you know."

"Oh, honey, it's been six months since things ended with Jack. Don't let your technical marriage status get in the way of finding someone new. It's not important."

"Well, according to the Australian Government it's still important! I'm not allowed to get a divorce until March."

"You don't need to *tell* anybody that you're still married. It's all just finer details."

"Mum, I can't believe you expect me to rush into another relationship!" I hissed angrily, squishing down further in my seat and dropping my voice. A couple of girls sitting nearby looked over at me curiously. "You know what a rebound is, don't you? I need to give myself proper time to, you know, get over Jack properly."

"Time? Laura, sweetie, you're twenty-seven. A year ago, you were looking to start having babies. I don't want to rush you into anything, but you really need to get a move on if you still want to have children. You *do* still want kids, don't you?"

"Mum!" I cried indignantly as I felt my anger start to rise.

"You know the risks, darling! I'm only saying this for your own good. I'd hate to see you go through what I went through." Mum's voice had gone all soft and apologetic and I felt my anger crumple. She wasn't deliberately trying to be mean and pushy, she actually thought she was being reasonable.

I sighed. "I know, Mum," I said kindly. "But just because you had problems, doesn't *necessarily* mean that I will. Plus, there're all kinds of things nowadays—you know, IVF and all that."

"Sweetie, if you do have the same problems as I did, IVF might not be able to help. By the time I was your age, I'd already had you and we'd given up hope of ever having a second child."

I dug my fingernails into my palm and felt my throat go tight. I knew the story all too well. I'd grown up knowing the story. Maybe it had even contributed to me getting married and wanting to have kids at an age that many people would consider being too young.

My parents had wanted a big family. They'd both wanted at least four kids. They'd been high-school sweethearts too, and had married when they were twenty. Mum had me when she was twenty-one and everything seemed to be on track for them. But then after me, she hadn't been able to fall pregnant again. For years and years, they'd tried. They saw doctors and specialists, but there wasn't really that much technology around back then to help, or at least not anything they could afford. They'd long given up hope of ever falling pregnant again when Elle suddenly appeared, six years later. It was a miracle, the doctors called it. And after Elle they'd kept hoping for more miracles, but of course no more ever came.

"I know, Mum, trust me I know," I said and turned to stare out the ferry window at the sight of the sea water rolling past.

"How's your friend Louise doing?" Mum asked, knowing she'd already made her point. "She must be six months on now, mustn't she?"

A painful stab went through my stomach. *Louise*.

"Yeah, she'd be six months. She basically fell pregnant the same time Jack ended things, remember?" I said flatly.

"Have you seen her recently?" Mum pressed hopefully.

"Not recently." Truth was, I hadn't *wanted* to see her.

"Well, don't cut yourself off from your old friends," Mum said stiffly. "She was a good friend to you when things got messy, remember?"

I pursed my lips in annoyance. Yes, Louise had technically been a good friend, but she'd also been a bit insensitive, hadn't she? I mean, there I was, having just been dumped and humiliated, and her solution was to take me out shopping for baby things with her because she was all pregnant and happy and glowing. Didn't she realise how hard that was for me?

Then again, I thought with a pang of guilt, I hadn't been a very nice friend either, had I? I should have been happy for her—she was my friend, after all. I should have been able to put my own problems aside and support her. Instead, there'd been that horrible "incident" between us in the baby section at David Jones … which, obviously, Mum knew nothing about.

"Look, Mum, I've got to go. I'm on the ferry," I said, suddenly just wanting this conversation to be over.

"Okay, darling. Well talk soon, then," Mum said brightly.

"Yep. Bye." I hung up and stared moodily at the water and the passing coastline again.


Talking to Mum had brought up all kinds of memories that I'd been trying to block out. Like how earlier this year I'd gone in to see my health-insurance provider and upgrade to a family-level plan. Like how I'd bought prenatal vitamin tablets and started taking them every morning. Like how I'd sat on the bathroom floor crying and staring at that packet after Jack had informed me that we would be getting a divorce.

I could feel that big hollow space in my chest opening again. And I knew it wasn't just pain there, it was shame, too. The same shame I felt every time I bumped into an old family friend in the supermarket and they stopped to ask me how I was doing. How they pretended to look all concerned and caring, even while they were sympathising with Jack, saying how hard things must be for him.

For *him*.

And I just had to nod along, even while my chest grew tight, because that was the correct thing to do, wasn't it? The friends meant well—they always meant well—but I could always see that trace of pity in their faces. That look that said, *How could you not have known?*

73

# 11

The air was warm and pleasant as I left work on Friday night, walking towards the city bar where I'd be having my first proper date.

Catching sight of my reflection in a passing window, I gave myself a reassuring little smile, trying to calm my nerves. It was just a date, after all. Just a *Tinder* date, to be exact. Did people even call those things dates anymore? I mean, I was just meeting up with some strange guy whom I'd only ever communicated with through an app for a drink. Just one drink.

Was I ready for that? It had all felt so far away and surreal when Kalina was setting it up. Was I really going to go and sit down with a strange guy, in a bar? A guy who wasn't my husband. We'd have to talk. And *flirt*. Shit, would there be flirting? Was I expected to flirt?

Somehow, my steps were slowing down and then I'd completely stopped walking. The streets were busy with people passing by and I was jostled as someone brushed past me.

My heart was racing and I was starting to find it difficult to breathe. And suddenly, it had become really hot here, hadn't it? I was distantly aware that I was just standing in the middle of the pavement hyperventilating, so I reached into my bag and pulled out my phone. Then I tried to focus on just looking really casual, standing to the side of the walkway, staring at my blank phone screen, even though I wasn't really *seeing* it.

What was I *doing*? How had my life come to this? I was so conscious of the fact that in a few minutes I'd be face to face with a completely strange man. And what for? What was even the point? So we could talk about mundane things? So he could look at me and judge me?

I had the horrible feeling that somehow he'd *know*. He'd know that someone had pretended to love me for so long. He'd work out that I was barely more than a pity case, married to someone who was hiding from himself the whole time.

Three girls suddenly walked past me, laughing loudly, and I snapped my eyes up to them. They all looked stunning in high heels and lovely dresses, their hair cascading down their backs and lifting slightly in the breeze. And there I was, huddled over my phone, having a panic attack.

*Oh, stop it, Laura.*

Yes, I needed to stop it.

*Enough with the pity party.*

Okay, okay. I gave myself a little mental slap and stood up straighter, forcing my lungs to take a deep, slow breath of air then let it out just as slowly.

*I can do this.* I wouldn't dwell on the past. Just because one man—my husband—rejected me, didn't mean everyone would. Besides, I wasn't even that interested in this guy, was I? Not in *relationship* terms anyway, because that's not what I needed. I was there purely for physical gratification, wasn't I? That was the plan. It didn't matter what his personality—or mine—was like. I was simply going to be sizing him up as a potential sex partner.

That's right, *sex partner*.

That sounded crass, didn't it? But really, I wasn't hoping to meet Mr Right. I thought I'd married Mr Right, didn't I, and look how well that turned out.

Do you want to know a secret? Although it's not really a secret; laughable maybe, but not really a secret. Well, here it is: Jack and I hadn't even had sex for three months before he ended things. I know, I know, I probably should have seen it coming. But well, we just weren't having that much sex by then. And we'd never really been having that much sex to start with. I thought that was just normal, though. I mean, I hadn't had anything else to compare it to, had I? And perhaps I'd simply thought that we'd moved into the "comfortable" stage of our relationship. You know, where you'd rather have an engaging conversation than have sex.

God, *how* did I not see it coming?

But anyway. The point was, I hadn't had sex at all in over nine months. So, if nothing else, it was high time I found someone to sleep with.

I took another deep breath of air and looked again at the retreating backs of the three girls who'd passed me. I could be just like them. I wasn't married, boring Laura anymore. I was Laura the Explorer.

I was fearless.

I resumed walking down the street towards our chosen location, feeling more in control. Tinder Boy (aka Darren) and I had arranged to meet at Las Senoritas, a Mexican-themed bar which had only recently opened on York Street.

As I stepped inside, I couldn't help but be impressed by the decor. There was Day of the Dead paraphernalia all over the place, from corpse brides to skulls and paintings. Brightly coloured tiles adorned all the tabletops and created a fantastic mosaic behind the bar. Everywhere, people were sitting on wooden stools or benches with vividly patterned pillows, drinking margaritas or Coronas with lime, little bowls of guacamole and corn chips in front of them. A kind of spicy, salsa-ish smell filled the air.

I spotted a guy sitting alone at the bar, and there was a moment of, *is that him?*, before Darren looked around and waved at me. He'd saved me a seat next to him, which I slid into, albeit a little shakily. Those nerves, or adrenaline, or whatever it was, were annoying, weren't they?

"Laura? Hi, nice to meet you," he said and gave me a casual kiss on the cheek. It was surprisingly not too awkward, and I allowed myself to relax a little.

"Nice to meet you, too." I smiled and examined his face for the first time. He looked just like his Tinder photos (which I may have studied numerous times), but he was definitely livelier in real life. He smiled back at me, and I quickly looked away, casting around for something else to say.

"This place is great!" my voice was a little over-enthusiastic as I gestured around at the bar.

"Yeah, a friend of mine works here," Darren said, seeming nowhere near as nervous as I was. "They do a really good sangria if you're interested?"

"Oh yes, sangria sounds perfect!"

After ordering a jug, we started chatting and I discovered that he was a really sweet guy. He was studying at a business college in town while working part-time at a cycling store, and was a Darlinghurst local. I briefly outlined my job and my living situation in Manly, making it sound as if I'd flatted there for years.

We'd almost finished our first jug of sangria (which seemed to have disappeared *really* quickly) and were nibbling on some jalapeño poppers when Darren broached the relationship topic.

"So, how is it that a gorgeous girl like you is single?" he asked casually, leaning his elbows on the bar.

"Oh, you know. Just am." I shrugged, embarrassed by his exaggeration. I mean, gorgeous, really? I looked at him sideways under my lashes, but he had his eyebrows raised, waiting for more.

"I split up with someone recently," I continued cautiously, not wanting to go into details. "Not *recently*, not like last week. But, um, well, a few months ago." I hastily reached for my drink, feeling my cheeks warm up.

"Lucky for me, then." Darren grinned, and I sipped my drink in relief, thankful that I was off the hook and didn't need to elaborate more.

"And how about you?" I asked. "Why is it that a guy like *you* happens

77

to be single?"

Darren shrugged. "Just haven't met the right girl, I suppose. Plus, I do heaps of travelling. Last year, I was away in Europe and Asia for most of the time, and spent the summer working in a bar in Mykonos."

"Wow! What was that like?"

"It was great! Mykonos is such an awesome place to be over the summer, and the beaches there are unreal."

While Darren filled me in on his amazing time in Greece, I found myself studying him closely. He was talking animatedly, getting quite excited by his own memories, and my eyes started roving over his arms and shoulders when he wasn't looking.

He was pretty good-looking. I mean, he was no Chris Hemsworth, let's be clear, but in a *normal* way, he was pretty hot. Could I imagine sleeping with him? Or rather, I wondered if he wanted to sleep with me? Our arms had brushed up against each other a few times while we'd been reaching for the sangria jug. Was that a good sign? His arms were kind of hairy— not super hairy, but enough to tickle my skin a bit. I guess that was manly, wasn't it? It's weird, but I don't really remember Jack having much arm hair. I suppose he did. It just wasn't something I noticed.

Oh, God, did Jack shave his arm hair off and I never noticed? Was that one of the signs that I missed?

*Stop overthinking it, Laura.*

I suddenly had this funny sense that I was in a David Attenborough documentary, and there was a weird kind of voice-over running through my mind narrating the interaction between me and Darren.

*The male of this species tries to impress the female in a confusing display of masculine bravado. The female, meanwhile, is too timid to respond directly, so she politely watches the display.*

I wondered how the logistics of us actually having sex would work? I mean, obviously I had an apartment, but I didn't want to take any strange boys back there. I think Darren had mentioned he lived with a friend, so maybe we'd go to his place? Just so long as "friend" wasn't code for parents.

I realised that Darren had stopped talking and there was an awkward silence between us. Oh shit. I'd better get things back on track.

I sat up a little straighter. "So—"

"So how—" Darren said at the same time. We both stopped and grinned at each other.

"You go," I said quickly.

"I was just going to say, have you been on many Tinder dates?" Darren asked.

"Oh! Um, no actually, this is my first one."

"Really?" Darren looked like he didn't believe me.

"Yeah. I only installed the app this week," I said. "Why, how many have you had?"

"A few." Darren shrugged. "Though you're one of the first normal girls I've really met."

"How do you know I'm normal?" I teased.

Unfortunately, that comment went down like a lead balloon. Darren shifted uncomfortably. "Well, I mean," he mumbled. "You at least look like your pictures."

"Oh, right. Yes," I said, and quickly gulped down some more sangria.

There was another awkward silence between us, and I noticed that our second jug of sangria had been depleted. I was also feeling a bit tipsy, I realised. Those jalapeño poppers we ate weren't exactly dinner.

I briefly wondered if I should suggest getting some proper food, but the conversation had already fizzled out. *Better just pull the rip cord.*

I did an exaggerated glance at my watch and feigned surprise. "Gosh is that the time!" I said (it was 7.30; we'd been there for an hour and a half). "That's gone so quickly. I wish I could stay longer, but I have to get going."

"Really?" Darren sounded disappointed.

"Erm, yeah." Shit, should I have stayed longer? Had I just blown things by ending the night too early? Did he think I hadn't had a good time? "I've had a really nice time," I said, signalling for the waiter to bring us the bill.

Darren finished the last dregs of his sangria and we both stood up. Our bill arrived and we inelegantly shuffled around with money until we'd put in half each. Then we left the bar together.

Outside on the footpath I turned to face Darren, wondering what to say next and how to end the night. But then he surprised me by stepping forward and kissing me. And—okay, wow. Yes, I know, I probably should have been expecting that. I thought our night was ending kind of dismally, but then this kiss was a bit different!

I immediately felt like I couldn't breathe. My lungs were frozen as his mouth—soft and scratchy at the same time—moved against my lips. He tasted like sangria and salt and it was a heady mix.

I was startled by how nice the kiss felt, how my stomach tightened and how I was instantly aware of his body so close to mine. I thought I'd be imagining Jack when I kissed someone else, comparing how different anyone else was to him. But God, Jack hadn't kissed me like this for years! It was nice, surprisingly nice, and passionate.

I felt his hand on my lower back, pulling me up against him, and then our bodies were also pressing together, the kiss deepening.

My body felt electrified.

Seriously, how was it that I barely knew this guy and yet he was able to make me feel like *this* straightaway! What on earth had Jack and I been doing? Were we that bored and familiar with each other that sex had begun with someone reaching into the bedside drawer for the bottle of lube?

"Get a room!" someone called near us. Or maybe they were far away. I couldn't tell.

Darren broke the kiss and I felt almost dizzy as he stepped away from me. I took a huge, deep breath of air as if I'd just surfaced from a free dive.

"So, when can I see you again?" he asked, giving me a smug, satisfied smile.

I quickly recovered myself, and we discussed who was going to call whom. Then before he walked away, he pulled me towards him and kissed me passionately again. And oh my God! This kissing was brilliant! I mean, surely Jack and I used to kiss like this, at least in the beginning? But this kiss with Darren—it was sending all kinds of sparks and flashes flying through my body, like I was a keg of fireworks that'd been dormant for too long. I could barely breathe and yet feeling Darren's mouth on mine, his body pressed against me, his hands on my back, it was all a thousand times worth the lack of oxygen.

Eventually we broke apart, and then with a few self-conscious laughs we said goodbye and parted to head home in our own directions.

As I made my way towards the ferry wharf, I was feeling a whole new sense of adrenaline rushing through me and I couldn't seem to wipe the smile off my face.

** LINKEDIN ALERT **

**Congratulate Helena Marshal on the new role!**

Business Development Director at Fortesheim Technical LTD.


** LINKEDIN ALERT **

**Helena Marshal posted a new article:**

How Critical Thinking Analysts can supercharge your Business' technological capabilities.


[LinkedIn Alerts blocked]


** FACEBOOK ALERT **

**Elle Baker added a photo to the album "South America":**

*"Another miscellaneous meat dish for lunch. Think <u>Marrika Bentley</u> is going to cry soon."*

Laura Baker Commented:

*You didn't seriously eat that Ellie?? You know what you're going to be starting!!*

Elle Baker Commented:

*I know!! Mum will make us eat her weird kangaroo stuff now* 😫

Cath Baker Commented:

*It is not weird! Kangaroo is very healthy. Everyone else eats it all the time.*

Elle Baker Commented:

*We refuse to eat the national animal!* 😂

# 12

A huge smile spread across my face the second I woke up. I'd kissed a guy last night! Darren was … well, he'd seemed fairly normal, even if the conversation had been a little stilted. But he'd kissed me! He'd actually *wanted* to kiss me. And he had.

And okay, you're probably wondering why I was so amazed by this. But when Jack rejected me, I'd been faced with the reality that the whole time we were together he was simply pretending to love me and want me. While I wanted to hope that the experience hadn't permanently scarred me, I couldn't help the thought crossing my mind that Darren could also be pretending.

But no, I squeezed my eyes shut and shook my head. Surely it was virtually impossible that *that* could happen again. Odds-wise, that was. The likelihood of that had to be small, right? Besides, the *way* Darren had kissed me! It was so demanding, so full of desire. The smile returned to my face and I reached over to the bedside table for my phone, opening the chain of messages between Darren and me again.

He'd texted me last night, just after I'd arrived home, saying he'd had a great evening and he couldn't wait to see me again. We'd exchanged a few texts and arranged to see each other again tomorrow. His flatmate was going to be away, so he'd offered to cook me a Sunday dinner at his place.

I felt almost giddy as I looked up at the ceiling because I knew that it was going to be a totally blatant opportunity for us to have sex. And who cared if that was all Darren wanted? It was all I want right then, too. Plus, I figured I might as well utilise the bikini wax while everything was still smooth down there.

Another thought suddenly struck me—would he be able to tell that I'd only ever slept with one person before? And that that person turned out to be gay? Would it be obvious that I was really quite inexperienced? Oh God, what if I really didn't know how to have sex properly? He'd know, and then it would be awful, and I'd end up either lying there like a starfish or being too enthusiastic and knocking out his teeth.

I shook my head, threw my phone back on the nightstand and jumped out of bed. I knew it'd drive me crazy if I obsessed over it all day, so instead I turned my attention to what my flatmates and I had planned for the day: an afternoon of sun, fun and wine.

Ben and Kalina had told me about how awesome the Mudgee Food and Wine festival was each year. Apparently, many of the vineyards and wine producers from Mudgee arrived in Sydney for the weekend and set up little wine stalls all along Balmoral Beach. Then you could go along from stall to stall with a special wineglass and taste the different wines they had to offer.

I made my way into the bathroom for a shower, and when I emerged Ben was already in the kitchen, cooking Mexican-style eggs.

"Is this a recipe for the bar as well?" I asked.

"Nah, no one wants to have eggs with beer. I'm just making them because they're awesome. And spicy," he said with his ever-ready grin. "Want to try some?"

"No thanks, I'll stick with yoghurt," I said, as I pulled my favourite Greek yoghurt out of the fridge and located a breakfast bowl.

"Suit yourself." Ben fried off some chilli to add to his eggs. "Actually, Kalina normally likes eating these. Hey, Kal!" he bellowed that last part loud enough to wake all the neighbours, let alone Kalina.

"I'll go see if she's up," I offered, mostly so Ben wouldn't attempt to deafen our entire apartment building again.

I padded quietly up to her closed bedroom door and knocked softly. "Kalina?" I called. "You want Mexican eggs?"

There were some shuffling noises from inside and then the door swung open, but it wasn't Kalina standing in front of me. Rather, it was a shaggy-looking guy wearing nothing but boxers, his long hair and long beard making him look rather homeless.

"Oh, ah, hi!" I squeaked in surprise and took a step away from him.

"Hi, roomie," he purred in a low, husky voice.

"Er, is Kalina there?" I asked, as if I'd just knocked on a stranger's door.

"She's indisposed still," he said, giving me a half-smirk while his eyes lazily looked me up and down.

"Shut up, Mav and put some clothes on!" Kalina barked from inside.

"Bye," Maverick said to me, before shutting the door in my face.

*Well. Okay, then.*

I walked back into the kitchen, shrugged helplessly to Ben, then resumed eating my yoghurt. A moment later, I heard the bedroom door open again and then Maverick walked into the kitchen, this time wearing denim shorts (which looked like they used to be denim jeans that he'd cut off himself to create shorts) and a t-shirt with rips in the front.

"Mmm, that smells great," Maverick said, walking over to the stove and eyeing Ben's breakfast. "I'll have some of them."

"Oh, sorry, wish I'd known you were here," Ben said, his voice insincerely regretful. "Not enough for you, I'm afraid."

Kalina appeared in the kitchen wearing one of her oversized Disney nighties. "Mav's just leaving, though I'll have Mexican eggs, thanks, Benny. Mav's got a huge day of rehearsals to get to, don't you?"

"Yeah, big day," Maverick echoed, sticking a finger into the frying pan and scooping out some of the egg mix.

"Eh, get out of it, mate!" Ben whacked his hand away.

Maverick wandered back out of the kitchen and over to Kalina, wrapped her in a big bear hug and kissed her neck loudly until she squealed. I looked away, trying not to laugh.

"Alrigh', alrigh' now get out," Kalina said, pushing him away playfully.

"Later." Maverick exited the apartment.

"Another Maverick night, eh?" Ben asked, as he plated up the two breakfasts.

Kalina shrugged and walked over to the kettle and flipped it on. "He was in the area last night." She scooped a teaspoon of instant coffee into a mug.

"You didn't tell him about the wine festival, did you? That's just what we'd need, him turning up with his hippie-shit guitar and starting to play you love ballads in the middle of Balmoral Beach."

"That happened the one time!" Kalina retorted, as she spooned sugar into her coffee mug. "I've told him I don't want to hear any more love shit from him."

"What happened last time?" I asked curiously.

"He rocked up at the beach when I said I was going there to sunbake for the day and started playing all these love songs right near me. And he made it so obvious that they were for me, too—it was such an embarrassment."

"I thought it was just a casual, nothing-serious thing between you?" I teased.

"Well it is now," Kalina replied. "Though you know musicians, they act like every girl is going to be the love of their life."

"At least you've become a source of great inspiration for him," Ben chimed in. "I hear his latest music is all about she-devils and girls who use guys for sex."

"It is not!" Kalina whacked Ben on the shoulder. "Wait, have you

86

actually heard his stuff? Is that what it's about?"

Ben laughed. "As if I'd listen to it! He's got stuff out on Spotify, though. I thought *you* at least would have listened."

"Why would I listen to it?" Kalina sounded affronted. "I'm only interested in sleeping with him, not in being musically entertained."

"What's his artist name?" I asked, pulling up Spotify on my phone. "Let's have a listen."

"Oh no!" Kalina groaned, but then she seemed to reconsider. "Alright, it's 'Maverick and the Lyricists.'"

I quickly did a search and they appeared straightaway, with five songs available.

"This one sounds good. 'British Girls in the Sack.'"

"WHAT?!" Kalina screamed and ran over to look at my phone. I'd already hit "play" and a moment later we all froze as an enthusiastic guitar solo began, only to be quickly followed by erratic drumming and a piercing saxophone.

"Oh my God, it's even worse than I imagined," Kalina said faintly.

The drumming and saxophone diminished to a quiet background track as the singing began and Maverick's unmistakable crooning voice emerged from my phone.

*"Those British girls they get you in, they sure know how to make you grin, and when they get you in the sack, well I hope you know that you don't mean JACK to them!"*

"Ha-ha! I was right!" Ben yelled and started laughing.

A drumming/saxophone cacophony played briefly, then diminished again to leave Maverick's voice to take centrestage.

*"Those sexy girls they take your mind, and when they leave they leave you blind, but we all know that we can't resist, yeah those British girls they'll leave you PISSED!"*

"Turn it off!" Kalina pleaded, her hands held over her ears. Ben was doubled over with laughter.

I hit "stop" and the affront ended, Ben's snorting the only remaining sound.

"Well, I can see now why you don't want to listen to his music," I said, also trying not to laugh.

"That ass," Kalina huffed, returning to her coffee preparation. "He's got a lot of explaining to do before he comes around here again."

"But then you'll have to admit that you've listened to his music," Ben admonished.

Kalina gave a non-committal shrug. "I can pretend to be really pissed off, then he'll have to make it up to me in the bedroom." She winked at me. "Got to give him something to use as inspiration, don't I?"

☙

It was midday when we disembarked from the bus at the top of the hill leading down to Balmoral Beach, where the wine festival would be underway. The streets in the area were filled with beautiful old houses mixed in with modern architectural ones, and some of the most impressive old trees I'd ever seen lined the road, casting a dappled shade across the footpath. Smiling at finding myself in such a gorgeous area, my steps felt light as I followed Ben and Kalina down towards the beach.

The closer we got to the water the more people started to appear around us, also making their way towards the festival. And when we rounded the last corner and the beach came into full view, I felt a little thrill of excitement—the place was buzzing! All across the grass area above the sand, there appeared to be almost fifty stands, all with different vineyard names proudly displayed on the tops. Winemakers and salespeople stood inside the tents, chatting to festival-goers and topping up their wineglasses with small samplers.

I almost lost Ben and Kalina because I'd stopped to survey the area, while they'd walked on ahead, but I caught up to them and we joined the line to buy our souvenir wineglasses and tasting tokens.

"What are you guys going to try, reds or whites?" Ben asked us, peering eagerly over the heads of the people in front of us to the beginning of the queue.

"I'm going to find some sparkling if anyone has it," Kalina immediately responded, her eyes roving across the nearby stalls. "Followed by rosés. Ooh, and I wonder if anyone will have any dessert wine?"

"What about you, Laura?"

"I have no idea," I answered honestly, my eyes darting around to all the different stalls. There was so much to choose from, how could I even decide what to start with?

"Well, I'm doing reds," Ben said. "And I'm going to make it my mission to locate any Spanish or Italian varieties. So, if you spot any, let me know."

"Right," I said, though I had no idea what Spanish or Italian varieties were.

We reached the front of the queue and each paid our money, and were handed a little strip of ten tasting tokens and a miniature wineglass that had "Mudgee Wine Festival" printed on it. Once I was done paying, I stepped out of the line and realised that Ben and Kalina had already disappeared, though I then saw Ben over at a stall talking enigmatically with the stall-holder.

I wandered along, eyeing the stands from a safe, noncommittal distance, then decided to stop at one called Benhallon's Estate. It was the label that'd caught my attention really—a little pig jumping over the moon was incorporated into the design, his curly little tail merging into one of the letters in the name, and a bunch of grapes draped around his head like a Roman crown.

Adorable. I was such a sucker for cute marketing. I cautiously approached the winemaker.

"Hello!" The man smiled at me nicely. "What sort of wines are you after today?"

"Something white?" I asked, no doubt sounding as unsure as I felt, but I eagerly eyed the extensive wine list.

Full disclosure: I know hardly anything about wine. Whenever Jack and I would go out for dinner, I'd let him choose the wine, and if I was sent in to a bottle shop on my own, I'd just pick something at random, usually based on the price tag or the label rather than the variety.

"Are you after something fresh and citrusy? Or maybe something a bit more buttery?" he asked.

"Um ... citrusy?"

"I've got just the one!"

Thankfully, he didn't ask me any more questions. I gave him my glass and he poured me a tasting of something.

"Thanks!" I said. I quickly handed over one of my tokens and then turned away. But as I spun, I bumped straight into someone else walking past. I managed not to spill my wine, but I did take a step back hurriedly as the man who'd just walked into me caught my arm to stop me from falling.

"Watch out!" he said, and I looked up into his face.

*Oh. My. God.*

It was Volleyball Guy!

"You!" I exclaimed before I could stop myself, or think of anything better to say.

He looked at me quizzically, scanning my face, and those striking blue eyes made my knees feel weak.

Oh shit. Of course he didn't know who I was. What was I meant to say—that I was the weird stalker girl who liked to watch him play volleyball?

"I mean, I've seen you around in Manly," I covered quickly. "Playing volleyball?"

I looked at him hopefully and felt my face heat up, and then a look of recognition crossed his face.

"Ah yes, I remember you."

He was totally lying, I could tell.

"You're the one who meditates in the park."

Shit, he wasn't lying. I was the meditation girl, was I? Served me right for pretending to meditate in order to perve on him, I supposed.

"Ah, yeah, I've only done that once, you know, just to try it out," I hurriedly said.

"And how was it?" He asked.

"How was what?" Perving on you? Did he *know*?

"Meditating. Any good?"

"Right, the meditating." Good, he didn't know. "It was … interesting. Actually yes, I think I did find some spiritual enlightenment. Really connected with myself. And the beach, of course."

*What* had I just said? *Stop now, Laura, stop while you're ahead.*

"Really? I think you were only doing it for about half a minute?" He was looking sceptical.

"It was, um, power meditating. It's a new thing. You have to be really experienced to be able to do it and get the same level of, um, enlightenment in a short time."

My cheeks were on FIRE.

"Plus, I had to go to work," I added lamely.

"Right. So, you were trying it out for the first time, but you're also really experienced?" he asked. There was a teasing smile on his lips, and his eyes sparkled slightly.

"Erm … well, I was trying the *power* meditating for the first time. But you know, meditating in general is a, um, standard practice."

*I sound like a fruitcake, don't I?*

"Ah, I see." He nodded. "Well, good luck with the *power* meditating."

And then he turned and walked away.

He *walked away*.

Oh good one, me. A really hot guy that I'd been perving on happened to bump into me, I happened to have a conversation with him (which, granted, had made me sound like a weirdo), and then I'd just let him walk away. Honestly, was power meditating the most intelligent thing I could think of to say? What *was* power meditating? What if he went away and googled it and discovered that it wasn't even a real thing? I'd be revealed as a fraud. A power-meditating fraud.

Brilliant.

# 13

I found Kalina at the Chamberlaine Vineyard stand, chatting to the winemaker, also a Brit, about pubs they both knew of in the Cotswolds area that had names like "The Stag and Hound" or "The King's Horseman".

"Ah, The Clever Fox, that was my favourite!" Kalina was saying, swinging her wineglass around in enthusiasm. "The one up on the hill above the cemetery in town there, wasn't it?"

"Yes, that's the one. I used to pass a few good afternoons there, always eating their famous beef-and-mushroom pot-pie," the winemaker said wistfully with a heavy Geordie accent.

"I don't think I had the pie there. Think I had the bangers and mash."

"Hello!" I broke into their conversation and placed my wineglass down on the counter.

"Laura!" Kalina affectionately wrapped an arm around my shoulders. "This is my flatmate," she said happily to the winemaker.

"What'll you have, love?" he asked me, indicating the array of bottles spread out on the counter.

I pointed confidently to a random white wine and he poured me a healthy "tasting" amount, then topped up Kalina's glass of rosé. While we drank them, we talked with the winemaker for a while, and he told us all about his move to Australia with his Aussie wife, followed by their subsequent divorce. He was already in love with the country by that point, mostly due to the weather, he said, so he stayed anyway and bought himself a vineyard in Mudgee.

Eventually, Kalina and I were pressed out of the Chamberlaine stand as other eager festival-goers squeezed in around us to get a taste of the wines, though not before Harry the Brit topped up our glasses again. And I mean topped up—those pours definitely weren't the thirty-millilitre tasters we were meant to be getting.

Both feeling a bit buzzed, Kalina and I linked arms and marched around the festival, attempting to locate Ben. We failed to find him, but we did spot the Mudgee Cheese House stand and discovered that not only could we taste a range of their cheeses (all delicious), but that we were also able to purchase a cheese platter with biscuits to take away and eat.

Within minutes, we'd procured our own cheese board and a cold bottle of chardonnay from a nearby stand, and were setting up a private little picnic on the grass in the midst of the festival.

We sat in the warm sun, sipping our wine and nibbling on cheeses, and chatted and laughed about nothing in particular. Ben eventually appeared and joined us, filling us in on which wine stands he'd visited so far. And it was then, while Ben and Kalina were talking about nothing in particular, that I noticed a really strange feeling wash over me.

It was *happiness*.

Right then, I was actually, genuinely, feeling happy.

The feeling was so weird, so long forgotten. That tight ball of pain that had been residing in my stomach for the past few months seemed to have magically vanished. It was like I could breathe properly again.

But how could I be happy? It wasn't like the last decade of my life could be changed. Jack's impact on my life could never be reversed, and nor would everyone who ever knew me magically forget what happened.

As if on cue, that tight feeling squeezed in again, nestling back in where it was comfortable, sitting in my insides. In fact, I probably just imagined that it'd ever left in the first place. It was probably just the cheese and wine. And the sun.

"We should definitely find a few good bottles and take them back to the flat to drink tonight," Kalina was saying. "What do you think, Laura? You got any plans for tonight?"

I snapped my attention back to my friends. "No, nothing tonight," I replied.

Ha, like I'd have any plans! I was single, wasn't I? Single people didn't have plans, they didn't have people to do things with. And yet ... I was meant to be changing that, wasn't I? Wasn't that the point of my fresh start, to get out and try to find my feet again? I did have that second date with Darren tomorrow night, but was that enough? Should I have been doing more?

Absently, my eyes started scanning the crowd around us. I wondered where Volleyball Guy had gone? Maybe if I bumped into him again, then my evening plans could be a whole other matter ...

"Who are you looking for?" Kalina asked curiously, her keen eyes not missing a beat.

"Oh, just a cute guy I bumped into earlier."

"Really?" Kalina sounded intrigued. "Where is he?" She also started scanning the crowd, as if he might suddenly jump out at us.

"I can't see him." I turned back to my friends with a dismissive shrug. "Oh well."

"*Oh well?*" Kalina repeated, sounding outraged. "That's not the attitude, Miss Laura the Explorer! What happened to your mission?"

"I'm still taking it seriously! In fact, I already have a second date lined up with Tinder Boy tomorrow," I said proudly.

"Nice one!" Ben said.

I laughed, feeling a little giddy thrill run through my stomach. Yes, it was exciting, wasn't it? I was on track—I was doing what single people should be doing.

"Great!" Kalina said. "But seriously, if there's a cute boy here, go and find him and talk to him!"

I sipped my wine, considering, playing for time. I mean, I *did* want to talk to Volleyball Guy again. Maybe I could think of something a bit cleverer to say the second time. And after all, what was the worst that could happen? My life had basically already ended once, so it wasn't like things could get worse. Plus, the image of him on the beach with no shirt on was an appealing incentive. And his eyes. Those amazing, sky-blue eyes.

I looked back at Kalina and Ben, who were both watching me with expectant grins on their faces.

"Alright!" I announced, rising to my feet in one fluid motion. "Challenge accepted!" I raised my glass and saluted them, and Kalina and Ben both raised their own glasses from where they were lounging on the grass in return.

"God speed!" Kalina said seriously.

"Go get 'im, tiger!" Ben added.

Turning around, I marched off determinedly into the throng of the festival, my heartbeat jumping into a marching pace.

❧

Actually locating Volleyball Guy was more difficult than I imagined it would be. Why on earth were there so many people there? And why was the festival so large? Everywhere I looked, stands just seemed to keep appearing—it all just went on and on.

And people weren't sticking inside the invisible bounds of the festival, either. They were wandering off and setting up picnics all over the place. Couldn't they be fenced in? How was I meant to locate someone when he might have already wandered off on his own free will?

Another thought suddenly struck me. Maybe he had a girlfriend? He could be curled up somewhere nice and cosy on a colourful picnic blanket right then, feeding her chocolate-coated strawberries and drinking champagne with her.

I was ready to give up looking when the crowd suddenly parted, as though my eyes were pushing people aside like the red sea. And on the other end of that strange people tunnel: there he was.

He was behind the counter at the Middlebrook Vineyard stand, serving wine and talking to a middle-aged lady, indicating the bottle he was holding as he spoke.

Wow. I hadn't expected him to be a winemaker. Weren't all these vineyards from Mudgee? What was he doing working at a Mudgee vineyard when he played volleyball in Manly?

The crowd abruptly merged back together and I lost sight of him. Well, at least I now had a good reason to go and talk to him.

I surreptitiously poured out my half-full wineglass onto the grass and started making my way through the crowd towards the Middlebrook stand. I had to lurk dubiously nearby while I waited for him to finish talking to the woman; there was a second person behind the stand, an older woman who was looking out at the crowd and waiting to serve someone. Well, I didn't want her to serve me.

Eventually, the customer Volleyball Guy was speaking to left, a bottle she'd purchased in one hand, and it was time for me to make my approach.

"Hi there!" I said brightly and gave my most charming smile.

"Hi." He smiled back, and I saw the recognition flare in his eyes.

Then there was silence.

*Oh no. Why didn't I think of something to say, some lines to use?* I was just smiling at him like an idiot.

As I felt my cheeks heat up again, I gestured around at the stand. "Is this your vineyard?" I asked.

"Well, this isn't a vineyard, it's a wine stand," he replied, amusement shining in his eyes. "But no, Middlebrook is my aunt and uncle's winery."

The other woman at the stand took an interest in our conversation, and I realised this must be his aunt, the winemaker.

"Yes, we've had Middlebrook for over twenty years now!" she said warmly, coming over to join our conversation. "Have you tried our wines before?"

"Erm, no, no I don't believe I have," I replied, annoyed that she was butting in. How on earth was I meant to flirt with Volleyball Guy with his aunt there?

"Hopefully it's to your taste!" she continued. "We planted a very specialised semillon grape when we first bought the vineyard, and last year was the first time we had a really good yield from it, so if you try the 2017 semillon or the semillon chardonnay blend, which is a mix of grapes that we sourced from the Hunter, then ..."

As she prattled on about the wine, I found myself nodding my head and trying to look engaged, but she might as well have been speaking French. I glanced over at Volleyball Guy and saw that he actually seemed interested in what she was saying, listening intently and nodding as she spoke. But then his eyes slid over to mine and he smiled.

I had the sudden feeling that he knew I'd come over specifically to talk to him, and the fact that his aunt was now intervening was amusing him. Thankfully, I was saved from the aunt by another eager wine-goer who turned up at the stand and started eyeing the wines expectantly.

"I'll leave you to help this young lady," the aunt said, touching Volleyball Guy briefly on the shoulder before going over to the newcomer and greeting him.

"So, what'll you have, then?" Volleyball Guy asked me. "Did the sound of the semillon-chardonnay blend appeal to you?"

"Why don't you tell me what your favourite wine is and I'll try that?" I countered.

"My favourite wine," he leaned towards me slightly, dropping his voice, "is not actually from here."

"Oh? And where is your favourite wine from, then?"

"Well, I have a few." He grinned. "Every time I find a really great specialised or boutique wine producer, I try to add them to the list of wine companies I rep. But don't tell my aunt that," he said with a wink. "She thinks she's my best client."

"Your secret's safe with me." I attempted a wink as well. "So, you rep wine companies, then?"

"Yeah, some of the time. I do lots of different things." He smiled at me confidently.

I waited a moment to see if he was going to elaborate. Our eyes were locked together, and I was aware once again of just how blue his eyes were. How was it possible for eyes to even *be* that blue? He probably had so many girls drooling over him. Which was ... exactly what I was doing.

I cleared my throat and dropped my gaze as I realised that he wasn't going to say anything more on the subject.

"So then, um, out of *these* wines, which would you recommend?" I asked, feeling myself flush.

He made a show of examining the choice of wines on the counter top. "I'd recommend trying the shiraz. It's a winner." He picked up the bottle, looking at me expectantly.

"Shiraz it is," I said, handing over my glass.

As he poured the taster, I tried desperately to think of something else to say which would prolong our conversation, but my mind had gone blank. Should I backtrack and ask what other "things" he did? But then that seemed a bit desperate, fishing around in a past topic. Why couldn't I think of something witty to say?

"So, how often do you play volleyball? Are you part of a club or something?" I blurted out.

"Most mornings at the moment." He handed me back the wineglass, a deep, rich-looking red now swirling around inside. "We've got comps starting in a few weeks and my teammates are pretty committed."

"Cool," I said a little lamely, and made a show of smelling the wine (that's what people did, wasn't it?).

"And how about you? Meditate often on the beach?" He quirked his brow, and I knew he was teasing me.

"Fairly often. In fact, I might be doing it more often in the mornings now. It really helps to settle the mind before work."

"A quick power-meditation session?"

"Er, yes." *God, why did he have to remember that?* "Actually, you should try it some time. It might help with the volleyball."

"Do I need help with volleyball?"

"Well, you know, everyone can do with a bit of extra help, can't they? It might give you a bit of an edge over the competition."

"So, what, a quick power meditation before the game and I'll be a better player, will I?"

"Yes, absolutely! I'm sure there've been studies on it. Or at least, it can't hurt to try."

"Ah, so it's not guaranteed to work, then?"

"Nothing is ever guaranteed, is it?" I was warming up to my topic by that point. I could almost fool myself that I really was an expert on power meditating. "For example, just because I'm drinking wine here, I'm not guaranteed to get drunk, am I?" I gestured with my wineglass to emphasise my point, but a bit of wine sloshed over the side.

*Oops.*

He smiled slowly. "I'd say that getting drunk from drinking a lot of wine is pretty guaranteed."

Oh no, I was *drunk*. The realisation hit far too late. Why hadn't I noticed the effects of the wine before that point? And so now, not only was I the meditation girl, I was also going to be the drunk girl.

"Yes, you're probably right on that point, Ninety-Nine," I said. Oh dear. What, was I quoting *Get Smart* now?

I also realised that some other festival-goers were fronting up to the stall and were waiting for me to leave so that Volleyball Guy could serve them.

"Well, I'll let you get back to it," I said and turned away before he could see the colour rising in my cheeks.

"Hey, wait!" he called, and I froze mid-step. *Ha! This is it!* He totally wasn't ready to end our conversation yet. *I'm witty when I'm drunk, aren't I? Who wouldn't want to talk to me?*

"Yes?" I turned back to him, a coy smile on my face.

"I need to grab one of your wine tokens," he said, totally deadpan.

And there was my answer: no one. I guess I hadn't been that witty, after all.

I pulled out one of my tokens and passed it to him. As he took it, our hands brushed against each other and I looked up into his eyes.

"See you round." He grinned at me, his eyes twinkling, before smoothly turning away and greeting the couple who were examining the Middlebrook wine list, giving them the exact same charming smile he'd just used on me.

I turned on my heel and quickly left. To be honest, I wasn't sure what I was expecting to come out of that encounter. I probably should have had a bit of a game plan put together before I approached. Something like:

Step 1: Distract the aunt and isolate the target (aka Volleyball Guy).

Step 2: Be extremely witty.

Step 3: Commence flirting.

Step 4: Seductively write phone number on bar napkin and thrust it in his face.

Hmm. In hindsight, I wasn't sure a game plan would have helped me. But at least I tried. He saw me drunk and thought I was totally into meditating. So, it was only *slightly* humiliating.

# 14

**D**eep breath in. Deep breath out. Now, just reach forward and *press* the buzzer.

My hand was shaking. It was hovering a few centimetres away from the button, seemingly unable to bridge that final airspace. Why was I so terrified? I'd spent the day psyching myself up for this moment. Kalina had spent the day psyching me up. I was ready, wasn't I? This was how I was going to move forward in life. I was going to date new people. I was going to go to their houses. And I was going to sleep with them.

And then ...

No, there wouldn't be an "and then". There'd be no relationships. No *feelings*. No risks.

I pursed my lips together, pulled back my shoulders, and pushed the buzzer for Darren's apartment with as much aggressive determination as I could muster.

*No turning back now.*

Well, it wasn't like I was being forced to sleep with him tonight. It could just be another date, and end with nothing more than a goodnight kiss.

And yet ... I really had been psyching myself up all day to sleep with him. After all, it'd been nine months since I'd had sex with anyone. Jack was still the only man I'd ever slept with. And I was never going to get past that fact until I just took the plunge and slept with someone else. It would be like ripping off a band-aid—I just needed to get it done.

Plus, Darren was a nice guy. And he was good-looking. And, if that kiss on Friday night and the messages he'd sent me since were anything to go by, then he definitely was interested in sleeping with me. So really, it was the perfect time, the perfect opportunity, wasn't it?

"Hello?" Darren's voice suddenly came over the intercom.

"Hi, it's Laura!"

Okay, it was time to focus. It wasn't like I was going to walk in there and straightaway say something corny like, "Shall we get this show on the road?" No, there'd be dinner first, and I could make sure I was a hundred percent comfortable with everything before we proceeded. The alcohol would help with that. I clutched the wine bottle in my hand a little tighter. Good old emotional support package.

"Come on up, it's the second floor," Darren said and the lock on the door clicked open.

I entered the apartment building and climbed up to the second floor, the familiar smell of cooking that frequently haunted carpeted stairwells greeting my nose.

Darren pulled open the door and I was a little taken aback by his appearance. He was wearing what I could only presume were nice pants and a shirt, but they were obscured by a brightly coloured kitchen apron that had pictures of farm animals all over it. And ruffles all around the edges.

Trying hard to supress my natural reaction to the offending garment (he *couldn't* be gay; that was almost statistically impossible, wasn't it?), I stepped inside. It was … nice. A typical boy's apartment. Although as I looked around the mess in there, I could suddenly understand Ben's aversion to living with other guys. But anyway. I decided to assume his absent flatmate was the messy one.

"I brought wine," I said, holding up the bottle.

"Oh, cool," Darren replied. "I'm drinking beer, but I can pour you a glass if you like?"

"Right. Yes, a glass would be great." What, did he think I brought it just for show and tell?

I sat on one of the stools at the kitchen bench and Darren poured the wine. Then we started chatting, discussing how our weekends had been so far and what we'd been up to since we saw each other last. While we were talking he kept fiddling with the kitchen stove, but I wasn't sure what he was trying to do. There was a pot of water simmering away, and I think I glimpsed a Latina Pasta packet sitting in the fridge.

As dinner was being prepared, I couldn't help but wonder if things were going well. Were we going to sleep together? Or would it end up being a total downer of a night and neither of us would want to sleep together by the end of it?

Once dinner was ready, Darren took off his apron (thank God) and we took our plates and drinks over to the small dining table, which had been set with candles and everything. I tried not to laugh as Darren put on some music and fetched the packet of parmesan cheese out of the fridge. He actually seemed way more nervous with me at his house than he had when I'd met him on Friday. It was kind of endearing.

"This looks great," I said as I slid into my chair.

Darren seemed to relax. "Yeah, I don't cook very often as you can probably tell!"

"That's okay, I don't think my cooking skills are much better! I already have one housemate who thinks of himself as a chef, I'm not sure I could handle being around another person like that."

"You live with a chef?"

"Oh, he's not really a chef. More just an amazing amateur cook. He's designing a menu for a new bar at the moment. Spanish themed, I think."

"Really?" Darren perked up eagerly. "Spain is the best! I spent ten weeks travelling around there last year, I even walked the Camino de Santiago, which is this amazing historical pathway ..."

And he was off on a story about travelling again. I dug into my food, thankful that I wasn't required to contribute to the conversation, and just enjoyed listening to him talk.

⁓ꙮ

By the time we'd finished eating, I was feeling a nice warm glow from the wine (I'd drunk most of the bottle). My eyes were skimming across Darren's chest and arms every time his own gaze dropped, and I'd been trying to work out what he'd look like without his shirt on.

Oh God—was I ready for this? Did I want to run my hands over his chest, which would probably be sticky with sweat and/or rough with hair?

I took another gulp of wine, smiling and nodding at what Darren was saying (I think he was talking about scuba diving in Thailand). I glanced down at my plate, which was still half full of pasta, but I couldn't face eating any more. My stomach was doing some nervous flip-flops, and I didn't want a belly full of food if we were going to be having sex.

Which, I mean, *were* we? That was the question, wasn't it? And why was it so hard to work out? Should we have been clearer when we were setting up the date?

"Are you finished?" Darren asked, his eyes dropping to my plate.

"Yes, thank you! I guess I'm a light eater," I said with a laugh.

Darren nodded, and started clearing away the plates.

Okay, the moment had arrived. Action time! Or was it? I wondered if I should stay sitting there at the table or if I should help him clear up.

"Um ... I might just pop to the bathroom. Is it ...?"

"Just down the hall there," Darren said as he indicated with his arms full of dishes.

106

I escaped to the bathroom, momentarily avoiding my previous dilemma. I peed quickly and then checked my makeup and made sure there was no food in my teeth as I washed my hands. Then I found myself adjusting my dress, fluffing my hair and giving myself my best semi-drunk, frank assessment in the mirror.

*I was looking pretty good*, I thought! My cheeks had a bit of a glow happening from the wine, and my hair was still looking great (Kalina had spent an hour curling it into soft waves for me). I grinned as my eyes travelled down across my dress, a new one I'd bought a few days ago. It was ruffled and flirty, with big flowers printed across it in pastel greens and oranges. The neckline was low, but the skirt skimmed almost to my knees, so it balanced itself out.

I raised my eyes back to my face in the mirror. So: question time. Were we going to have sex?

A loud clattering sound came from the kitchen, and I realised I'd been in the bathroom for a while. Shit. I didn't want him to get the wrong impression about what I was doing in there. Time to reappear lest he started to get suspicious.

I walked back into the kitchen, where Darren was stacking the last of the dishes in the sink.

"Hi." I smiled as he looked up at me.

He seemed momentarily stunned at my appearance, then he dropped the pot he was holding with a shake of his head, and, with a sly grin, he sidled over to me.

"Hi," he responded, his voice almost a purr.

He was standing so close to me that my heart started to race. His eyes dropped to my lips and I sensed him inhale deeply before he raised his eyes and met mine. I shifted towards him, giving what I imagined to be the go-ahead signal, and then I had just enough time to take a quick gasp of air before he moved forward, his mouth finding mine in a soft kiss. Which quickly became an electrifying kiss.

And yes! The answer to the question was yes! Whatever doubts I had were quickly being burned away as I felt his body gently press up against mine, his arms wrapping around my waist. My body was responding immediately and I kissed him back like a starving person receiving their first meal.

Darren broke our kiss and leaned away fractionally, a satisfied look in his eyes.

"So," he said, his hips still pressed against mine. "Can I interest you in some dessert?"

He was totally not referring to dessert.

"Definitely," I said with a wicked smile, my voice coming out low and husky.

Darren dropped his arms from around me and took my hand instead. "I have just the thing," he said as he led me towards the bedroom.

I was breathing quickly as we walked down the hallway, my skin feeling hot and tingly with both the memory of his body pressed against mine and the anticipation of more to follow.

We walked inside and I went to pull him towards me again, wanting to feel his mouth on mine, but he resisted and instead turned to his chest of drawers.

"Do you want a tart?" he said, his voice low and seductive.

A *tart*?

"Sorry, what?" I said, unable to hide my confusion.

"A tart," he repeated, and next thing he'd dropped my hand and was picking up a plate from the drawers that had a strawberry tart sitting on it. And he held it out towards me, a little ... what? Shyly? Hopefully?

"Right! A tart." I recovered myself. To be honest, I thought we were done with the food. Wasn't he just being suggestive when he asked if I wanted dessert? Had I misinterpreted? Had I been the only one thinking that "dessert" was code for "sex"?

"I'm actually okay for now," I said cautiously.

Should we take the strawberry tart back out into the dining room and cut it in half with a butter knife? But if that was the case, then what were we doing in the bedroom? And why was dessert *in* the bedroom? I could still feel the ghost of his lips on mine—*that's* all I wanted right then, not a pastry.

"Oh, okay," he said, looking disappointed. Thankfully though, he put the plate down and stepped back towards me.

And ah, yes! This was what I'd been wanting, what I'd been psyching myself up for all day. Our mouths were pushed together, and I arched my body against his, trying to get as much of myself pressed against him as possible. For a good minute we stood like that, kissing passionately, hands pulling the other closer. My eyes were closed, and in that darkened state, with my dominant sense gone, my brain took off on its own monologue:

*Well, this is different! He was much scratchier than Jack ever was, wasn't he? And his mouth had that slightly beery taste to it, but not in a bad way.*

*Funny, I thought this would feel a bit like cheating, like I'd be doing something wrong. But there was no guilt here, was there? Excellent! And really, why should there be? Jack was long gone, long over. This was my body. I could do whatever I wanted with it. And just look at me! Look at what I was doing!*

Darren pushed the straps of both my dress and bra down off my shoulders while our mouths were still exploring each other, and I shivered as his hands brushed over my bare skin. Our mouths were still hungrily locked together, and I pretended not to notice as I felt him reach around and unhook my bra (after about five unsuccessful attempts).

I decided it was altogether too bright in the room, so with a smile I flicked off the bedroom light, the glow still streaming in from the hallway giving us plenty of visibility. Darren seemed to take this as confirmation that sex was definitely on, because in a flash he had his shirt unbuttoned and coming off.

And mmm … yes! There was something deliciously erotic about bare skin. I let him remove my dress, shivering slightly again, and then we were all skin on skin, my chest pressed against his, our hands on each other, our mouths together.

*Ooooh, lovely! He's all warm and solid. And he smelled a bit like … what was that? Issey Miyake? Paco Rabanne? Gosh, I didn't realise how much I'd missed the smell of men's cologne.*

I fumbled around with the belt on Darren's pants, my hands a bit shaky, until he took over and got it undone, stripping off his pants quickly. Then we were both on the bed, hands and mouths exploring, breath coming faster. And then our underwear was being removed.

*Okay, this was it! The big event! It was about to happen. Did I need a cheer squad? Something like:*

*Yes, you can!*

*Get it done!*

*Condom on!*

*Legs apart!*

*Go, go, go!*

"I have a condom in my bag," I said.

"I've got one here." Darren retrieved a packet from the drawer and efficiently shielded himself. Then he was above me once more and I pulled his mouth back to mine, keeping my eyes closed and going entirely by feel as our bodies pushed together.

We got into things quickly, our skin rather sweaty, our breathing both ragged. There was an unspoken agreement that we weren't really looking at each other, so I took the opportunity to close my eyes again and tried to really get into the zone. Or you know, whatever it was that you were meant to think about while having sex with someone for the first time.

*Ha! Ha-ha!* Shit, I almost started laughing. *Stop it, brain, this shouldn't be a funny situation.*

Well, it was not specifically a non-funny situation, and I couldn't help it if I wanted to laugh. Because this was a funny—sorry, *fun*—enjoyable situation. This was … you know, this was supposed to be what all the hype was about. Didn't people spend their whole lives just trying to find someone to have sex with? Trying to find this? Isn't that why we go to bars, why we go on dating websites and apps? Sleeping with someone for the first time was meant to be the most exciting moment, wasn't it?

Darren was certainly becoming rather enthusiastic, and I was just wondering if I should suggest switching positions when I realised it was imminently too late for that. He made a few high-pitched, grunting, satisfied sounds before collapsing on me, his whole weight crushing me. I wheezed a couple of choked breaths, not sure if it'd be rude to ask him to move, before he finally lifted himself, grinning down at me and kissing me again. Then he climbed off and I managed to get a nice big breath of air, quickly pulling a sheet up over me.

And there—look at that! I'd done it! I'd just had sex with a new guy! And honestly, it wasn't bad. It was good, in fact. I mean, I think it was.

Darren looked at me, a goofy kind of smile on his face, and I smiled back, a little shy. Then he sat up and turned on a lamp.

"Do you want a tart now?" he asked.

Was he serious? Right, well at least he wasn't concerned with the sex if he was back to thinking about dessert.

I sat up as well, holding the sheet around my chest, and was about to say no when I suddenly caught sight of what was around his bedroom. It was strawberry tarts. Delicate little individual pastries, no bigger than my fist, with a halo of glazed strawberries sitting atop the custard filling.

And the strawberry tarts were *everywhere*.

There was a tart on the bedside table. There were two tarts on his desk. There was a tart sitting on the chair of his desk. There was even a tart peeking out at me from inside the wardrobe.

What the hell?! What was this? Did he have a tart fetish? How had I not seen those tarts before?

He picked up the tart sitting on his own bedside table (I hadn't even noticed that one!) and offered it to me.

"I'd love to watch you eat one," he said huskily, looking at me with desire in his eyes again.

Oh. My. God.

"Oh, um," I said, awkwardly looking around the room. Shit, what was I meant to say to this? Did he make the tarts? What was he expecting me to do with one? Rub it all over myself or something?

The tarts were all staring at me accusingly. As if they were saying, *Didn't you know what you were getting yourself into? What, you were just going to use Darren for sex and then pretend to be surprised that there were baked goods all over his bedroom?*

I looked back at the tart he was holding, his face looking hopefully at me. The tart was raised like it was an offering.

Look, it wasn't that I didn't like strawberry tarts. My grandma made them all the time, and they were delicious. But really, a post-sex strawberry tart? While he watched me?

"I'm lactose intolerant," I blurted out. "Can't eat the custard—sorry."

His face fell in disappointment while I felt an acute wash of relief.

"Some of the strawberries, at least?" he asked, and in horror I saw him go to pick one of the strawberries off the top.

"No!" I said hurriedly. "Um … the lactose, it might have soaked in."

He looked at me with concern. "Are you that allergic? Shit, there was cheese in the dinner, I didn't realise."

"Was there? Oh no!" I put my hands to my neck dramatically. *As if I didn't notice the cheese!* "Oh, that explains this—I think I'm having an allergic reaction!"

"What?" he said, aghast.

"Yes, I-I'd better leave."

"Should I take you to a doctor? Or the hospital?"

"No, no, I have an epi-pen at home, I just need to go and get that." I jumped out of the bed and dressed swiftly, suddenly wanting nothing more than to get far away from there. I tried not to look at the strawberry tarts that were all around the room, the glazed fruit and crumbly pastry beckoning me.

"Let me take you home," he said, getting out of bed and reaching for his pants.

"It's okay! You've had too much to drink to drive anyway, I'll just grab an Uber."

I finished dressing but felt a little guilty when I saw the worry written on his face. Allergic to lactose, really? And an epi-pen? God, they weren't even good lies.

"Thanks for dinner," I said lamely as I started backing towards the door.

"That's okay," he replied, looking confused.

"Well, bye!" I made a rush for the front door.

I heard him start to call something out to me, but I was already hastily exiting the apartment, the front door swinging shut behind me.

Oh my God. What was that?!

I paused for a moment in the nice empty corridor and let my breath out slowly. Had I just had a panic attack? I leaned against the door, closing my eyes, and I had a sudden vision of a strawberry-tart army marching towards me, their little evil strawberry mouths huskily saying, 'Eat us, Laura.'

My eyes flew open, and all I wanted was to get away from there. I dashed down the stairs and out into the fresh air, my fingers flying across my phone as I requested a car.

Trust me to have the first guy I sleep with post-Jack to be a weirdo.

# 15

I think I was expecting something to be different after sleeping with a new guy. Like, something would have changed fundamentally and now I'd feel like a whole new person. Or I'd somehow magically have levelled up in terms of maturity. But I still just felt like me—regular, sitting-at-her-desk, going-over-boring-spreadsheets me. Even Belinda this morning hadn't notice anything was different. She'd just gone on and on for ages about how one of her cats got stuck at the top of the wardrobe.

I sighed, and tried to get my attention back to what I was meant to be working on. I mean, it wasn't that double-incentive schemes for high-spending clients *didn't* excite me. But really, as if I'd be able to concentrate on work after the night I'd had. With a goofy kind of smile on my face, my mind strayed back to my Sunday evening.

The dinner and bottle of wine. Listening to Darren talk about his travels. Having sex with a guy I barely knew.

And the strawberry tarts.

WHY were there strawberry tarts all over his bedroom? And why had he wanted to watch me eating one?

I screwed up my face, trying to re-imagine the memory, hoping it would seem less weird, but all that happened was that images started flashing through my mind of what *could* have happened:

Me slowly peeling a strawberry off the custard and placing it on my tongue.

Me delicately nibbling at a tart so that crumbs fell all over my legs.

Or me picking up two tarts and smooshing them, custard side down, onto my boobs and then doing a little dance in front of him to a Beyoncé song.

*Stop it, Laura.*

With a shake of my head, I picked up the phone and dialled Rose's extension.

"Coffee?" I asked when she answered.

"Yes!"

I collected Rose and we headed out of the building, into the warm, fresh air.

"So, how did your date on Friday night go?" Rose asked as we strolled down the street.

"It was pretty good. In fact, I saw him again last night."

"You … what, really?" Rose looked at me incredulously.

I smiled smugly and raised an eyebrow, waiting for her to work it out.

"Wait." Rose stopped walking and grabbed my arm, her eyes turning wide. "Are you saying … did you sleep with him?"

"I may have done."

"Oh my God!" Rose was still staring at me in shock and her grip on my arm tightened. "Wow, that's … I mean wow!"

I laughed delightedly, and we started moving again down the street.

"Are you surprised?" I asked.

"I am." Rose finally seemed to recover herself. "I mean, not that I'm surprised you'd sleep with someone. It's just that I've never known you as a single person."

I grinned, glad I could shock her. "So, how was your weekend?" I asked.

Rose scrunched up her nose. "It was okay. Pretty standard weekend, I guess. I went shopping on Saturday while Christian was at home hungover. Then I had a go at him for just playing Xbox all day, so we went out for dinner. And Sunday was pretty much the same, although Christian was out golfing all day with clients rather than hungover."

"He seems to spend a lot of time with work people, doesn't he? Does that bother you?"

"It's just his job," Rose brushed off my question lightly. "And really, I quite like having the house to myself when he's out."

She smiled at me confidently and I got the weird feeling that she was hiding something. I'd known Rose for a long time, ever since I started at Tiger Finance and we'd become friends in my first week. Back then, Rose was the definition of a socialite, always going out for fancy dinners or cocktails. She loved talking to people and being surrounded by others. In fact, I was pretty sure she used to say that she despised sitting at home alone.

"So anyway, fill me in on your dates! Are you going to see him again?" Rose asked, changing the topic back.

As I told her all the juicy and sordid details from my two encounters with Darren, we arrived at our regular haunt. The fresh smell of coffee assailed us, and we were immediately surrounded by the familiar babble of people talking, coffee brewing and waiters shouting. We made our way up to the front counter to order and there was the usual swivel of men's heads as their eyes seemed to home in on Rose. She was like a Swedish goddess walking into their midst, all long limbs and blonde hair. She even did that thing where she seemed to stand a little straighter and walk more confidently, even though I knew she pretended not to notice the attention.

There was a brief pause in my story as we ordered then moved around to the collection area, and soon I had Rose in hysterical laughter.

"What did he want you to do with the tarts?" she whispered gleefully.

"I didn't hang around to find out!"

"I'd forgotten about all the weirdos that are out there!" Rose chuckled.

"Yes well, you're lucky you don't have to experience any of it anymore," I said.

"Yeah," Rose said vaguely. An odd look crossed her face, then her eyes suddenly lit up and she turned animatedly to me. "Hey, did I ever tell you about the football player I dated?"

"I don't think so ..."

"He was so bizarre! He started asking me to wear his jockstrap on my head every time we had sex!"

"Eww, no!"

"I mean it was clean," Rose clarified. "But still, it was a bit strange, don't you think?"

"Definitely strange."

"Yeah," Rose repeated, sounding wistful.

"Rose? Laura?" One of the baristas called us, placing two coffee cups on the collection counter.

We picked up our coffees and squeezed our way back out of the shop. The bobble heads followed Rose's departure.

"So, do you have any more Tinder dates lined up?" Rose asked me once we were back out on the street.

"No." I scrunched up my own nose. "I'm not so sure how I feel about Tinder after Darren."

"You know, there're plenty of cute guys at work at the moment. *Single* guys," Rose added. "In fact, there's a new guy in the sales team. He actually looks really big, like a footballer ..."

"Pete?" I prompted.

"Yes, that's him! Have you met him? I passed him the other day and I thought, wow."

"Really?" I laughed. "Don't you think he's a bit, you know, meaty?"

"Oh, I'd take them big and chunky any day!" Rose wiggled her eyebrows at me wickedly.

"I *suppose* he's kind of hot ..."

"Kind of? He's tall, muscly. But you know, if he's not your type ..." Rose trailed off with a shrug.

I didn't respond as we made our way back into the Tiger Finance building. After waving goodbye to Rose at her desk, I thought over what she'd said about Pete as I returned to mine. I mean sure, he was single, so there was that. But was he really hot? Did "gigantically proportioned" automatically mean attractive? Did I find him attractive?

And *did* he ask me out the other day? Or had I just imagined that?

Then suddenly, it was Volleyball Guy floating through my mind. At the wine festival. The delightful smell of red wine and grass in the air. The tanned skin on his forearm highlighting toned muscles as he poured me a glass a wine. His bright-blue eyes looking into mine, that teasing, knowing smile on his lips.

And our conversation. How embarrassing.

At least Pete had offered to take me to the gym. Which was more than any other offer currently on the table. Well, aside from Darren, who had texted me a few times since last night. But, you know. Strawberry tarts.

Maybe I *should* take Pete up on his gym-training offer. In fact, maybe I just needed to go down to level four and take another look at him. Because I hadn't been in the best mood when we'd met the last time, and I'd thought he was being really rude and insulting to begin with. I must have been on the back foot, and *that* was why I didn't find him as hot as Rose did. Because he must be hot, right? If Rose thought so?

"Laura?"

I half jumped out of my chair as if someone had just jabbed me in the back with a cow prod. I swivelled around and found Cara standing behind me.

"Hi!" I said, my voice rather higher than normal.

"Are you okay? You were staring off into space for ages," she said, her eyes sliding to my computer screen, which was still in sleep mode.

"Was I?" Shit. "I was actually just trying to, um, remember what the best forty-plus incentives were that we had last year."

Cara lifted one of her perfectly groomed eyebrows. "Have you tried looking it up in the system?"

"That's exactly what I was about to do!" I turned back to my computer and hastily unlocked it, then brusquely opened up my files, quickly selecting the filter option and starting to input criteria.

"Well, just to let you know, I'm heading out for a meeting in Bondi and I won't be back this afternoon," Cara said after a moment of watching me work. "I'm on email and phone if you need anything."

"Okay great!" I said cheerily and peeked over my shoulder. To my relief, Cara was moving away and going to speak with some other people in our team.

Argh, why did she always appear when I wasn't really doing anything? And now I'd have to find something useful to do with that report I didn't need.

But at least she'd be out all afternoon. And if Cara wasn't going to be around, then ... well, perhaps I could go pay Pete a visit.

❧

Once I was sure Cara had left the building, I picked up my notebook and popped my head over the partition to where Belinda was sitting at her desk, surrounded by about five different pot plants and various photo frames of her cats.

"I'm heading down to finance if anyone is looking for me," I told her.

"No worries!" she replied, barely looking up from her work.

Smiling smugly to myself, I headed over to the lifts and pressed the button for level four.

*Here I go.* Time for the next objective for Laura the Explorer. I wasn't going to let one weird experience affect my mission. I needed to find another man to sleep with. One without a fetish for baked goods. And instead of dreaming uselessly about a hot volleyball-playing guy from Manly, I'd totally convinced myself that Pete was going to fit that bill. Plus, if it turned out that he wasn't actually interested in me that way, then at least I might get some free personal-training sessions.

The lift doors pinged open in the sales department, and I was greeted by the buzzing sounds of chatter and laughter once again. I was half expecting to see paper aeroplanes flying through the air, since this was clearly where all the fun in the building had migrated to.

As I made my way through sales, I noticed that many of the desks were empty, the noise being made by only a handful of the sales team who were still there. I wandered over to Pete's desk and was glad to see that he was one of the few remaining. I eyed him critically as I approached; still footballer-proportioned. He was holding the phone up to his ear and I was somewhat astonished it could even make the distance because there was *so much* bicep in the way.

"Hey, Pete," I said, just as he ended the call.

He looked up and surprise washed over his face before he greeted me warmly. "Hey, Laura!"

"It's quiet down here. Where is everyone?" I gestured at all the empty desks.

"Ah, most of them are out at meetings this afternoon."

"They're not off playing golf or something, then?" I teased.

"Not that I'm aware of," Pete said, deadpan. "There're a few big deals on the table at the moment."

"Oh right," I replied vaguely. I didn't really pay much attention to the Tiger team's sales activities as a general rule. Unless there was something really major going on, in which case marketing became involved early.

"So, how's your training going?" I asked him, leaning against his desk. "Have you been lifting … heavier weights?"

"Hell yeah!" Pete enthused, his face lighting up. "I had a great session on Saturday, got a P.B. doing raw lifts. I'm getting up to comp level now, though if I can drop a division I'll have an advantage."

"Uh-uh." I nodded seriously, feigning interest. (Did P.B. stand for peanut butter?)

As Pete spoke he swivelled his chair around to face me, his huge frame seeming to dwarf the tiny chair and desk. I was momentarily distracted from thoughts of food as I caught sight of his shirt straining across his arms and chest. He really was massive, wasn't he? I wondered if all the girls who worked at Tiger Finance thought he was hot. Did they all walk past his desk and stop by for a chat?

I rolled my shoulders back and stood up a little straighter. "Well, I've decided I really need to start getting into fitness more," I said confidently. "Ever since you mentioned how important it was for girls to tone up and, um, well to do weights and things …" What else had he said?

"Really?" Pete looked impressed. "That's a great idea!"

"Yes!" I smiled. "So, um, I suppose I just need to work out what to actually do now. Because it's all a bit new to me …" *Go on, take the hint.* "And I'll probably feel really lost wandering around in a gym by myself … with all that equipment …"

Pete just sat there looking at me blankly. Was I really going to have to ask?

"And they do say you should train with a friend," I continued slowly. "Except none of my friends really go to a gym …"

"You can come with me if you want," Pete offered finally, as if he'd just thought of this himself, again.

"Great!" I said with relief. "That would be fantastic! What day would be the best? Do we just go straight after work?"

"Yeah, I go every day after work, so whatever works for you. How about tomorrow?"

"Tomorrow sounds perfect! I'll bring my gym gear and meet you after work, then."

"Cool." Pete smiled. His desk phone started ringing and he glanced at it and then looked hastily back to me. "I'd better ..." He gestured at the phone.

"Of course! See you tomorrow."

# 16

I was watching the clock on Tuesday afternoon, my eyes moving constantly from the giant pile of papers on my desk, to the open document on my computer screen, to the tiny clock in the corner. Honestly, how was I meant to concentrate on "age vs points balance correlations" when I knew that in just over an hour I'd be at the gym doing who knows what?

I hadn't set foot inside a gym since ... well, since a very long time. The last time was when I was still at uni, and then it was just me and a girl from my course trying to kill time between lectures by pretending we were really into squash.

My eyes glanced down to the duffle bag sitting under my desk and I smiled smugly. At least I was going to look super cute at the gym in my new workout clothes. I'd spent a good half-hour the night before laying out all my options on the bed and choosing the coolest outfit. Because I figured that if I looked the part, then no one would notice how physically unfit I was.

When the time hit 4.25 pm, I logged out of my computer and swung my bag over my shoulder.

"I'm heading off, see you tomorrow," I said to Belinda as I started to make my way past her desk.

"You aren't staying for the conference call?" she asked, and I froze.

Shit. I'd forgotten about that.

"Oh, no I can't this afternoon," I muttered. "I have an appointment."

Damn, and now Cara would get all judgy at me for missing the call. But honestly, they weren't that exciting. I was sure I didn't *really* need to be there.

"Can you fill me in on it tomorrow?" I asked, warding off the guilt creeping over me.

"Sure," Belinda said, a trace of annoyance in her voice.

"Thanks!" I hastily walked away.

It wasn't like I needed official permission to leave work early on occasion. I mean, that's what "flexible hours" were meant to be, weren't they? And I really had been planning on getting to work early that morning to make up for it. Except, I'd missed the early ferry so had spent the extra time at the Wharf Cafe eating a yoghurt and muesli cup instead. But I was *totally* planning to come in early the next morning. Most likely.

I made my way to the lifts and took one down to the lobby. As the doors opened on the ground floor, my eyes were immediately drawn to Pete's huge figure, which seemed to be dwarfing everyone else around him. He was standing near the exit doors, a gym bag slung over one shoulder, drinking a protein shake.

"Hi!" I said as I walked over to him.

"Hey! All ready?" he asked, eyeing my gym bag.

"Definitely! Let's do it!"

We pushed our way outside to the street and I followed Pete as we headed towards UNLEASH Fitness, the huge city gym that was a few blocks away.

"How long have you been going there?" I asked as we walked along the street.

"A few years," Pete said. "I live pretty close, so it's the most convenient. Plus, it's the biggest gym around and has the best equipment."

We arrived at the complex and walked into a well-lit reception area with hip young people in gym uniforms behind the counter and trendy couches and ottomans forming a small lounge on the other side. Pete had a chat to one of the guys at reception, and before I knew it, he'd winged me a free guest pass. I filled in and signed a release form, then walked into the main area.

As I looked around at the immense structure that we were in, I was pretty blown away. I'd heard from various people aside from Pete that it was the biggest gym around, but wow! The street entrance definitely did not prepare you for just how large the place was. I wasn't even sure how this thing could fit into a building in the middle of Sydney. Where did the space even come from? It must have been some kind of parallel universe where space was not an issue.

Maybe it was even the real Diagon Alley! Yes, or it could be just like platform nine and three-quarters, where a space existed that no one would think was there. Except of course we weren't *actually* in *Harry Potter.*

"The girls' change rooms are that way," Pete's voice snapped me back to reality, and I looked over to see where he was indicating. "I'll meet you in the weights section when you're done, okay?"

"Alright!"

The "girls' change room" was like walking into a giant spa complex. There were lockers all over the walls and beautiful white shiny tiles across the floor, with wooden changing benches in the middle. A sign pointed to an exit to the pool on one side, and another pointed to the "sauna and steam room" next to it. Near the showers (which had those amazing roof shower heads that made you feel like you were standing in a tropical downpour), was a bench with salon-looking hair dryers and GHD hair straighteners, plus a little caddy of hair treatments and sprays.

Once I'd changed and my bag was safely stored in a locker, I did a quick fly-by of the pool area (stunning!) and also popped my head into the steam room—there was a fat man in there sweating profusely and he gave me a grumpy look as I peered in at him.

Leaving the locker rooms, I made my way out to the gym floor and towards the weights area. I passed a big glass wall closing off a separate room, the sign by the door reading 'FREEDOM Dance Studio', and I paused to have a look. Just like the rest of the gym, it was stunning inside. It had wood-panelled floors, floor-to-ceiling mirrors and ballet barres all down the walls.

There was a class on right then and I hovered outside for a moment watching. It looked like a Zumba class, the room filled with regular-looking people trying to follow along with the teacher. There were a few really good ones at the front, who knew the dance moves before the instructor even said them, and then a few slightly overweight ladies at the back who were giggling and seemed to be generally overwhelmed by their situation.

Pulling myself away, I kept moving to the weights area, scanning around for Pete. I spotted him on one of the benches and he saw me at the same time, and began waving me over.

"This place is so nice!" I said, looking around at the interior again in awe.

"Yeah, it's pretty good," Pete said noncommittally.

My eyes fell onto a guy in the corner who had the most enormous arms and shoulders. In fact, his shoulder muscles were so big that his whole neck had basically been swallowed up. He had giant dumbbells in his hands, and as I watched he started doing arm raises, his whole neck straining, veins popping out all over the place, and his face turned a beetroot-red colour.

"So," I said to Pete, turning away from He-Man. "What should I start doing?"

Pete put his own weights down on the floor next to him and then looked at me appraisingly. It was quite good with him sitting down—our eyes were almost level.

"Well, what is it that you want to achieve?" he asked after a moment.

"To get fit?"

Pete smiled. "I guess you just want to look good in a bikini, right?"

"How did you know!" I joked. "But actually, yes."

Pete rolled his eyes. "That's what all the girls say."

Did they? "Have you had many female clients before?" I asked.

"Clients?" Pete looked confused.

"Yeah. Training clients?"

Still, he looked confused.

"Didn't you say you were a personal trainer?" I prompted.

"Did I?" Pete scratched his chin vaguely. "Oh well, yeah, I've *trained* loads of people."

There was an awkward pause and I wasn't sure what to say. Pete was staring off at something on the other side of the gym, a look of concentration on his face. I followed his gaze …

Oh, right. He was staring at a super-fit girl with enormous fake boobs. And she was doing squats. And, okay, seriously, who wore makeup to the gym? Didn't it just sweat right off? And look at her outfit—coordinated leggings and crop top in an aqua leopard print. She was making my carefully selected outfit look so *boring* in comparison.

"So anyway." I turned back to Pete, who was still staring openly at the Amazonian girl. Okay, really. *I* was the one standing right in front of him. I shifted to the right in an attempt to encroach on his field of vision.

Finally, he turned his attention back to me. "Sorry, what was I saying? Oh yeah, so weights. Let's go."

Pete stood up off the bench and I immediately had to crane my head back to look up at him. I followed him around the gym as he set us up on a little circuit with three machines—apparently, I was doing "back and arms" to start with. Four sets of fifteen reps each; it sounded easy enough.

We moved through the sets quickly, switching machines every minute or so. I *may* have dropped my weight level each time, but you know, I had to start small, didn't I? Besides, I don't think Pete noticed. His eyes had been focused on Leopard-print Girl ever since she had started doing box jumps. To be fair, I couldn't help but stare at her, too. I mean, I'd never seen boobs that big that didn't really *move.*

Once our arms-and-back circuit was done, we moved to a different set of machines and Pete set us up with a leg circuit followed by an abs-and-chest circuit. Eventually we finished them all (and Pete didn't even mock me when I had to do bench presses with a bar only, not even a meagre two-kilo weight on each side!), and I was surprised to find that an hour had already flown by.

"Are we doing anything else?" I asked Pete.

"Nah, that's it for today," he said. "You did really well!"

"Thanks." I smiled. Leopard-print Girl had left a little while earlier, so Pete had actually been paying a tad more attention to me.

"If you want the training to have an effect, you really need to be doing weights at least two to three times a week," Pete said as we started to walk towards the change rooms. "I'm here most afternoons, so you can come and train with me again if you like."

"Thanks! I might just take you up on that offer." I beamed up at him.

"You'll need to do something else for cardio fitness, though. You run, don't you?"

"Um, sort of," I said. "I mean, I've been *meaning* to start running."

Pete raised his eyebrows at me. Evidently, he could tell I wasn't much of a runner.

"Well, it'd be good to go running on the days when you're not doing weights. Although you can run on the same day, just break it up into morning and afternoon sessions."

We arrived at the change rooms and split up to collect our bags. As I was getting my stuff out and washing my hands, I felt a new workout resolution settling in my mind (though it was probably just the endorphins). Yes. Yes,

I would start running. I'd train with Pete twice a week and I'd run along the beach every other morning (well, except weekends). And possibly I'd run into Volleyball Guy and he'd be so impressed with my obviously toned arms that he'd start running along with me. And then we'd get chatting and I'd be super witty and dazzling and our conversation would be so awesome that we'd end up spending the whole day together, night included.

I spotted my own goofy smile in the mirror and rolled my eyes at myself. *Honestly.* Could I get any more pathetic right then? But I was still grinning as I left the change rooms and met up with Pete again at reception.

"Well, thanks so much for today!" I said. "It was so good having someone to train with!"

"No worries," Pete said. "It's fun for me too having someone to train. Like I said, let me know if you want to do this again."

"Definitely!" I said.

"Right, well see ya round."

"Bye!" I called as we left the building and headed in different directions down the street.

# 17

I was determined to stick to my new exercise regime. Although, was it a regime if it was only day two? How long do you have to do something before you can call it a regime?

I rose early with the sun (this was *so* hard; how did people manage to put so many sunrise pictures on Instagram? What was wrong with them?!) and pulled on a selection of my new activewear. I then headed down to Manly and commenced a slow jog along the walkway. And you know what? Once I was actually up and outside, being awake that early felt fantastic! I had oxygen pumping through my lungs, and the air was crisp and cool with the promise of a warm day to come.

And there were so many fit people around! I was blown away once again by how many active people were out and about, some running, some power-walking, some with strollers and dogs in tow. Along the grass above the beach, there was a little group of people doing morning tai chi, while down on the sand a scary military man was leading a group of horrified-looking people through a boot-camp session.

As I approached the volleyball nets I slowed down, straining my eyes to try to see if Volleyball Guy was amongst the players down there. Surely it would be unlikely that he'd be there, wouldn't it? I mean what were the chances—

Aha!

Oh, wait, no. That wasn't him.

Bugger.

My eyes scanned all the people playing—and the ones spectating—again, but he was definitely not among them.

Boo. I felt my chest deflate, and I was surprised at the level of disappointment I felt that he wasn't there. I mean, it wasn't like I got up early just to see him, right? Because really, that would be a bit pathetic, wouldn't it? There was no reason to feel disappointed. I was out for an early run purely to get some exercise, get some fresh air, and start my day off on the right foot.

As if my little pep talk was actually convincing me, I broke out into a faster run. Because yes, this was why I was here! It was for the wind in my hair, and the beating of my heart and the ...

Ow. I got a stitch.

Okay, I needed to slow down.

Stopping at the side of the path, I did a few side stretches and found myself checking my watch. Hmm. I did get up *rather* early this morning, didn't I? I didn't need to be back getting ready for work for almost an hour.

As I twisted around to stretch my muscles, my eyes roamed across the street. There was that nice cafe over there that I'd been meaning to try ...

Before I knew it, I'd crossed the road, my morning run basically forgotten, and I was stepping inside a funky breakfast bar that was all industrial furnishings and hanging gardens, the delicious smell of roasted coffee in the air, the buzz of early-morning chatter filling my ears.

I squeezed past a large group of people to get to the counter and ordered a coffee and a berry-chia breakfast bowl, which sounded interesting. Once I'd paid and received my number, I squeezed back past the large group, heading for a table near the front. I was almost there when my eyes caught on a guy standing near the coffee pick-up area.

And … okay, you were going to think I totally planned this or something, but … it was Volleyball Guy! He was there, in this cafe! I almost choked on my own air, and quickly covered it with a cough.

He was talking to another guy who had a shaved head and a big tattoo across his shoulder and down his arm, both of them standing in board shorts and singlets with bare, sandy feet. I paused by the doorway to survey them—Volleyball Guy was laughing at something the other guy said, his eyes crinkling with amusement.

God, I wished he'd laugh like that at something *I* said.

Argh, okay, I was being pathetic again. And was probably doing that creepy, starey thing, too.

I slid onto a bar stool right by the door, putting my number down on my table. I took out my phone and pretended to be looking at it, even though my eyes were spending far more time on the cute guy I couldn't seem to forget. The large group who'd been taking up most of the room in the cafe moved out the front of the shop and commandeered a few tables together on the pavement. In their wake, a large space opened up, and the distance between Volleyball Guy, his friend and me suddenly became a lot smaller.

"Tom? Lucas?" the barista called, and Volleyball Guy and his friend turned to pick up takeaway coffees.

"I've got to run. See you later, mate," the friend said, and he made a quick exit out of the shop and jogged off down the footpath.

Volleyball Guy took a bit longer, putting sugar into his coffee and stirring it. Then he thanked the barista, turned and started walking out more slowly, his attention down on his coffee as he made sure the lid was in place.

And, oh no! He wasn't going to see me! He was going to walk right past …

"So, is it Tom or Lucas?" I said rather loudly.

His head jerked up and his eyes locked onto me.

"Hi." I smiled and did a little wave with my hand. (Fuck—what was *that*?)

"Hi," he said, looking surprised but—what, pleased, maybe?—to see me.

"I don't think I'd pick you for a Tom," I said, pretending to assess him.

"You sure? I think I could pass as a Tom," he replied with an amused look, and walked the few steps over to my table.

"Hmm, no. I'm going to guess your name is Lucas," I continued, and watched as he smiled.

"Good sleuthing, Ninety-Nine," he said.

Was that ... did he just use my same lame joke from the wine festival?

"I can't help but think that you're stalking me," I said, somehow acting way cooler than I felt. "I mean, I bump into you here, I bump into you at Balmoral Beach. Really, what does a girl have to do to get away from you?"

"Well, you know, I've lived around here all my life and I've never seen you here before. So if anything, I'd say you were stalking me," he challenged.

While he was speaking, Lucas placed his coffee cup and phone down on my table and slid into the empty chair as if it was the most natural thing in the world. His knee brushed against my leg and I could swear my heart did a weird little flip-over.

"Me, a stalker? I hardly think so. Actually, I've only just moved here. To this area, that is, not the coffee shop, obviously."

"Obviously." Lucas nodded.

"So, um, were you playing this morning? Volleyball?"

"Yeah, we've just finished up. Getting my morning caffeine fix now."

A waiter appeared in front of us and put my coffee and breakfast bowl down on the table in front of me, scooping up my number and whisking it away.

"That looks interesting," Lucas said, his mouth quirking up in a half-smile as he stared down at the breakfast bowl.

And okay, yes, it did look quite interesting. Sort of like a purple sago pudding with a few berries on top.

"Yes, it's ... well, it's not *quite* what I thought it would be. But I'm sure it'll taste delicious."

"Absolutely." Lucas nodded, picking up his coffee and watching me.

I took a mouthful of chia goop and told myself it was wonderful.

"So, did you find any nice wines?" Lucas asked, a half-smile still on his face as he watched me attempting to chew.

"Sorry?" I gulped, managing to swallow the gelatinous mouthful.

"At the wine festival? Find anything good?"

"Oh right! Yes, um, I think so. I mean, I definitely had a lot of nice wine on the day."

"You did seem to be enjoying yourself." He grinned slyly.

"Hey! It was a wine festival. You're supposed to have a bit to drink at those things, aren't you?"

"Most people do."

"Well, I suppose if you weren't working then you would have been drunk, too, right?"

"Me? Oh no, I never get drunk."

"You expect me to believe that someone who reps wineries doesn't ever get drunk?"

He laughed. "Shit, I forgot I'd told you that. Okay, you win. I'll admit I probably drink far more wine than I should."

"Aha. Hopefully, next time it will be me seeing you drunk, and not the other way around."

He considered me for a moment, his amused eyes assessing mine. I felt my breath catch, but I held his gaze, making it almost a challenge.

"So, does it taste better than it looks?" Lucas asked, dropping his gaze to my breakfast.

I made a show of taking another small spoonful and judging the mouthful, squinting my eyes in concentration, as if I was doing a proper food tasting.

"I can definitely say," I replied after swallowing it whole. "That it tastes just about as good as it looks."

"So, like crap, then?"

I choked slightly, a laugh that came out the wrong way. "Don't say that!"

Lucas chuckled. "Why not?"

"Because the cafe workers might hear." I glanced around to make sure none of the staff were in proximity.

"The walls can't hear anything," Lucas said, his voice teasing.

"Of course they can't. But you know, the *staff*. They might get offended."

"Well, if it's not good, they should know about it."

"I didn't say it wasn't good. It's just … not really my thing."

Lucas raised an eyebrow.

"Okay fine, it's not good. But I wouldn't say it tastes like *crap*. Caviar, maybe. Has the same texture."

"Delicious fish eggs for breakfast?"

I dropped my spoon on the table. "That's it, you've put me off it."

Lucas laughed quietly. "You don't want to finish your fish eggs?" he asked innocently.

I stuck my tongue out at him. "I'll stick to coffee, thanks."

"Did you seriously just stick your tongue out at me?"

"No, you imagined that." I hid my smile behind my coffee cup.

He narrowed his eyes, but I could see his mouth tense as if he too was trying hard not to smile. Then he shook his head and stood up from the table. "I'm not sure my company has done much other than put you off your breakfast."

My heart started racing again. Shit! Was he leaving?

"Sorry about the … ah … food," he said, looking down at the bowl that had all of two spoonfuls taken out of it.

"Wait!" I said, as he picked up his coffee cup.

He paused, his gaze on me again.

"Um ... well, it just seems silly that we keep bumping into each other. I mean, maybe we should actually organise a time where we *intentionally* meet, you know? And we can eat some food that's more appealing than this."

I finished speaking and looked up at him, a hopeful smile on my lips. *Did I seriously just ask him out?*

He looked back at me, but he *hesitated*, and I thought I saw a shadow of doubt flicker across his face. I felt my heart sinking, already sure of what his response would be.

"That's ... I'm not sure that's a good idea."

Just like a punch in the guts.

He evidently clocked the disappointment, or probably the embarrassment, on my face, because he drew breath to speak again, running his hand through his hair.

"I mean, I'm just not really dating at the moment," he said, sounding almost uncertain. "It's nothing to do with you, I promise."

"Right." I swallowed, unable to meet his gaze now. "Sorry, I just thought ... I mean, you've probably got a girlfriend, don't you? Or ... or a boyfriend?" I added quietly, holding my breath.

Lucas let out a small laugh. "I definitely don't have a boyfriend. Or a girlfriend. It's not that, it's just ... I've got a lot going on right now."

A lot *going on*? What kind of excuse was that? Although at least he wasn't gay. A tiny bit of tension released from my stomach with that confirmation. I didn't think I could handle ...

I suppose I should have felt rejected, but he looked so remorseful that I almost laughed. "Look, it's okay. You don't have to make up an excuse. I can perfectly handle that you're simply not interested."

*Or at least I'm going to tell myself that I can handle that.*

"I wouldn't say I'm not interested."

My eyes darted back to his. For a moment, we regarded each other in charged silence. Then he closed his eyes, shaking his head minutely as if giving himself a mental kick.

"I'm just trying to be nice here," he said. "I'm not really the best news, and you'd probably be better off *not* getting to know me. Plus, I'm really flat out with work."

"You don't think I can handle you?"

He smiled apologetically.

"I think I should be the judge of that," I went on, feeling emboldened. "Besides, what makes you think I'm looking for good news? Maybe I'm just looking for someone to have a drink with sometime. That's all."

Lucas considered me, placing his coffee cup back down on the table. My eyes dropped down to his bare shoulders and arms, and I had the overwhelming urge to run my hands up them. I could see the outline of his muscled chest beneath his shirt, and I felt myself biting my lip. Then I snapped my eyes back to his face, feeling my cheeks heat.

His eyebrow raised just the tiniest bit, as if he knew exactly what I was thinking. And okay, it might have been my imagination, but I *think* his eyes were sparkling.

"I wasn't lying. I've got a pretty hectic schedule. But if we *can* find time for a drink ..." he trailed off.

"Excellent!" I reached for his phone, which was still sitting on the table, in an attempt to cover my embarrassment from so openly ogling him. "I'll just put ... oh, you've got fingerprint lock on."

Lucas chuckled and shook his head as he unlocked the phone for me.

"Okay, take two. I'll put my number in here, and you just let me know when you're free. I mean, *I* might not be free. I also have a pretty hectic schedule," I finished loftily. I was about to hand the phone back to him when I had the sudden fear that he wouldn't call, or that I was giving him all the power, so I quickly hit "call" on the contact I'd just created. Once I was sure it'd rung sufficiently, I hung up and handed the phone back to him. "And now I've got your number, too."

He took his phone back and glanced down at my contact. Then he picked up his coffee again, meeting my eyes one last time. He rested a hand on the table, leaned in ever so slightly, and his eyes stared right into mine as if he was sussing me out somehow.

"Laura." He sort of growled my name in a quiet voice, the faintest hint of a smile on his lips.

*I was melting!* Melting in those pools of blue, feeling like the heat from his body was so close and my heart was racing, and if we just leaned in a bit closer …

Then he shifted away, giving me a teasing look as his eyes sparkled, before turning and walking out the door, disappearing from my sight.

For a second, I stared at the empty doorway and the street beyond, which was now devoid of Lucas, my mouth hanging open. And then I suddenly became aware of everything else around me, as if someone had just turned the volume back up. I shook my head, jarring myself back into reality, and back to some semblance of sanity. But I couldn't prevent the smile from splitting across my face as I discovered there was a nice, warm feeling sitting in my stomach, which was definitely not from the coffee.

# 18

I gazed up at the facade of the building Rose and I had just arrived at. It was one of those really old Sydney buildings with sculptured sandstone patterns out the front and tall arch-shaped windows. The late-afternoon light was washing the building in a beautiful golden glow and sparkling across the sign above the large doors which read "Renwick Hotel".

"You'll love this place," Rose said as we made our way inside.

Rose and I were out for our planned Friday-night drinks, having spent the prior half-hour in the work bathrooms glamming up. I was already feeling the effects of the Friday-afternoon buzz—that giddy feeling you get when you know that you're going to have a whole weekend of freedom before you have to return to work on Monday morning.

I was also buzzing because of the super-successful week I'd had. Not only did I exercise three times (weights with Pete on Tuesday, then morning runs on Wednesday *and* Thursday), but I also had Lucas's number sitting in my phone, like a warm little secret. Not that he'd messaged or called me yet. And neither had I messaged or called him. But, you know, it'd only been two days. I was totally going to play it cool and see how long it took before he caved and called me. Or I called him. Either way, I may have brought his contact up on my phone a few times over the last couple of days and just had a little look at it.

I followed Rose into a luxurious lobby that just oozed five-star sophistication: there were black marble floors and columns, stylish antique-leather armchairs and huge glass vases filled with white roses.

Rose, of course, looked completely at home in the foyer, wearing a stunning designer white sheath dress that highlighted her amazing figure and set off her perfectly tanned skin. I, by comparison, well, I'd done my best to make the "office to drinks" transition, wearing the new Cue dress I'd bought last week. And I must say I did look particularly good tonight, though I wasn't sure it would really count for much when standing next to Rose. I knew she thought she was going to be my wingman—bless her— but I wasn't convinced any guy was going to look twice at me when I was standing next to her.

Rose nodded confidently to the concierge, who stared with mouth agape at her, then we crossed over to the lifts. I followed her into the elevator and she pressed the button for level six, which had a small copper sign fixed next to it that read, in swirling letters and quite unimaginatively, "Bar Six".

"This place is the best," Rose said.

The lift doors opened to a luxurious corridor, and we could hear lounge music coming from the right. I followed Rose down the corridor, and as we rounded the end we arrived in a sophisticated industrial-styled bar that was all exposed brick walls, and wood-and-metal furnishings.

The place was already buzzing with a stylish after-work crowd. Everywhere I looked, clusters of suave men and women were sipping cocktails, wine or beer in tall glasses, chatting and laughing together. The bar counter ran parallel throughout the whole place, the entire side wall behind the bartenders filled with a huge display of every type of spirit imaginable.

Rose led me straight towards the bar and we made a beeline for two empty stools in prime position.

"Perfect!" Rose said as she slid onto one.

I sat next to her, feeling elated as I took in how popular this bar was.

"How are we, ladies?" A hipster bartender with a neat beard and a sleeve of tattoos on one arm was on to us already. "Are we doing cocktails this evening?"

Rose grinned at him. "Absolutely! I've been telling my friend here what amazing cocktails you do."

"I'd better not disappoint, then. Is there anything in particular you had in mind?"

"Surprise us!" Rose said, giving him one of her dazzling smiles.

The bartender nodded, and I watched as he began muddling, mixing, shaking and creating the most elaborate cocktails I'd ever seen.

"This guy is the best cocktail maker," Rose leaned in and whispered to me. "They're really different creations as well. I always just ask for a surprise and I've never had a bad one."

In what seemed like no time at all, we were sipping some truly spectacular cocktails and observing the rest of the room.

"Do you come here much?" I asked Rose. She looked completely at home, one arm resting confidently on the bar. Aside from the initial wave of heads that had snapped to attention when we entered the room (staring at Rose, obviously), she was still getting the occasional long look from a male admirer, which she pretended not to notice.

"Christian and I used to come here all the time on Fridays," she said, sounding wistful. "We haven't been in a while, though. It's all still the same—same groups of people, same crowds."

"I never would have known this place was here," I said, eyeing a group of businessmen who were laughing rowdily.

Rose shrugged. "Christian knows a lot of places. He always has to take clients out for drinks, and they're always going to the latest, fanciest bars."

"Do you get to go to them, too?"

Rose's eyes moved down to her cocktail. "Not so much. But I mean, it's *work* for him."

"That's a shame," I said. I could tell from Rose's expression that it bothered her more than she said.

"But anyway, this is great!" She sat up straight again. "We haven't been out together for a girls' night in ages!"

"I know!" I smiled. "And last time we went out I was *married*. How weird is that? Although, well, I still am technically married."

My eyes dropped involuntarily to my left-hand ring finger, which was bare. I'd taken my wedding and engagement rings off for good a few weeks after Jack and I split, and for a while there'd been a lingering pale line around my finger, a mocking tan line reminding me of what used to be there. It had completely disappeared now; looking at my finger, it was as if I'd never worn any rings there before.

"That's just legalities," Rose said with a dismissive wave of her hand. "Although, speaking of your former husband, have you heard from him at all?"

"No. Not since we spoke to the lawyers and sorted out the house. And I suppose I won't really need to speak to him again until March now, when we can actually file for a divorce."

"Does that bother you? That you haven't seen or heard from him?"

I thought about Rose's question for a moment, searching my mind (and heart, I supposed) for a reaction. It was no great surprise that I hadn't heard from Jack. The last time we'd seen each other, when we'd said goodbye for the final time, he'd made a vague "I'll call you" remark. To which I'd said to him, quite firmly, to please not. Then there'd been that look shared between us—mutual hurt, regret—before he'd nodded.

"It's been good," I said, looking up at Rose and knowing it was true. "I think it's really helped me move past things by just cutting him out."

"Do your other friends still see him?" Rose asked.

Which sent a pang of guilt through me.

*Louise.*

How long had it been since I'd seen or even just spoken to Louise? I didn't have a clue if she and her husband, Simon, had kept in touch with Jack. I really should call Louise, I thought. I should call and apologise, and put the water under the bridge. But jeez, the *incident*. I could still clearly see Louise's shocked face staring at me open-mouthed amongst the racks of baby clothes, while that other mother rushed her little child away …

"Who knows?" I shrugged, giving myself a little mental shake. "But anyway, let's not talk about *him* and my before-divorce life. We're here for a girls' night!"

Rose hesitated for only a moment before accepting that I wanted to change the topic. She took a deep breath and sat up a little straighter, turning to survey the room again. "You're right! Now, let's see if there are some cute boys we can chat to!"

For a moment, we both scanned the crowd in silence.

"How about that guy, there, with the red tie on?" Rose indicated a bulky-looking guy. "He actually looks like that guy from sales."

"You mean Pete?" I turned to Rose with a grin, ignoring her choice of man across the room. "Did I tell you he took me to the gym the other day?"

"What?" Rose turned to me in surprise. "I thought you weren't interested in him? How did that happen?"

I laughed. "It was no big deal. He's offered to help train me after work."

"No big deal?" Rose raised her eyebrows in disbelief, her voice flat.

I shrugged. "Well, I don't know. I can't work out if he's interested in me … in that way, or not."

Rose looked uncertain. "Right. Well, what did he say about it?"

"That's the thing, he's sort of hard to read …" I trailed off. Rose was looking at me with a weird expression on her face. "What?" I asked.

Rose started as if I had prodded her. "Oh, nothing. I mean, good for you! Hanging out with a hot, single guy. That's exactly what you need to be doing." Rose picked up her cocktail, suddenly seeming very interested in it. There was something very odd in her expression, so I cast around for a change of topic.

Over on the other side of the room, one guy in particular caught my eye. He was wearing a dark-grey suit with a black shirt underneath. He had dark hair and broody eyes, and I wasn't sure what it was about him (it could be the way he was standing or the way the girl he was talking to seemed to be fawning over him), but he possessed a certain charisma that pulled my eyes towards him.

"Okay, that guy over there." I nudged Rose, drawing her attention back to our previous topic. "*He's* pretty cute."

She looked over to where I was indicating and then inhaled sharply and abruptly grabbed my arm. Her whole posture immediately changed as well, from slightly slouched to straight and alert again. "Oh my God!" she whispered dramatically. "That's Derek Windsor!"

"Who is that?"

"He's, like, a major player. Christian's spoken about him before, and he always points him out to me when we see him. Apparently, he's got a yacht and a penthouse apartment in Rose Bay and he's always having these massive parties with heaps of models and things."

"Seriously? No way!" I said, looking at him again.

"Yeah, it's true! Christian's met him a few times, but I think he really wants to get in with Derek's inner circle and be invited to more of the parties. I've spoken to a couple of girls who've been on the yacht—one girl even reckons he has one of those *Fifty Shades of Grey*-style S&M rooms in his penthouse!"

"No! People don't really do that, do they?" I couldn't help but laugh.

Rose shrugged. "Who knows? He's pretty secretive, actually. It's all just rumours and gossip. Although, it would be amazing to spend a night with him and see what all the fuss is about. No commitment, just sex in a penthouse!"

"Rose!" I admonished, laughing. "You couldn't do that!"

"Oh, not me!" Rose turned to me with a wicked smile. "Obviously I'm not single. But for someone who *is* single." She gave me a suggestive nudge with her elbow. "Maybe he really does have all the kinky stuff like whips and handcuffs!"

"That sounds awful!" I said, but my eyes were sliding speculatively over him again. "Anyway, looks like that girl he's talking to is already fishing for an invite," I said and we both eyed her.

"Well, another drink?" Rose asked, turning back to the bar.

An hour later Rose and I had become a lot louder, and our arm gestures were also becoming a little wild. Rose, of course, still looked stunning, and I think she was deliberately trying to draw more attention to us. Or to her. I couldn't really tell.

"Who am I?" Rose said, flipping her hair about in a dramatic impersonation. "Oh no, no, no, darrrrling! That font is Helvetica and I specifically said Helvetica *Light*!"

"Isabella! You're totally Isabella!" I squealed, and we both laughed uncontrollably.

"Another round, ladies?" our bartender (whose name, we had discovered, was Trevor) was back, and I looked down to see that both our glasses were empty, once again.

"Yes!" I enthused. "Another one of those peach cocktails you made—they were delicious!"

"Coming up," Trevor said, and started whipping together a new concoction.

"I'm just going to run to the ladies." Rose climbed to her feet and rearranged her dress. "Back in a minute!"

"Okay." I turned back to watch Trevor creating our drinks. I was so engrossed in watching him (I was also a little drunk, so I wasn't actually paying that much attention to what was going on around me) that I barely noticed as a man appeared at the bar beside me.

"Looks like you and your friend have been enjoying the best cocktails all night," said a deep voice next to me.

I looked up, a little startled, to find Derek Windsor standing next to me. And he was really hot up close.

"Oh, yes!" my voice came out in a little squeak and I had to clear my throat.

Derek smiled. "I'm Derek," he said, holding out his hand.

"Laura." I smiled back and shook his hand. It was warm and firm but a little rough underneath.

"I've seen your friend around before, but not you," Derek said, leaning on the bar.

"Do you know Rose?" Ha, I'd have to tell her that Derek knew who she was.

"No, I've just seen her about. I have a photographic memory, so I never forget a face."

"Oh," I said, not really sure what to make of that. I glanced around and saw the girl Derek had been talking to earlier staring daggers at me. I sat up a little straighter and turned back to him.

"My friend and I are out celebrating tonight, and so hopefully you'll remember us as being completely fabulous." I gave him my most dazzling smile and tried a little hair flick.

"Indeed? And what are you celebrating?" I noticed that his eyes were very intense. It was like they were glued to my face, which was a little unnerving.

"We're celebrating … um …" What? My new single life? My exploration of the male species? The fact that I was trying to have sex with as many straight men as possible? "New beginnings," I finished a little cryptically.

A drink appeared on the bar in front of Derek and he lifted it in a silent cheers towards me. "To the two of you, then," he said. "And your 'new beginnings."

And then he was gone.

I turned back to the bar, feeling a bit giddy. Well, look at that! Chatting to a strange man! And not just any man—a super-wealthy playboy, apparently.

"Were you just talking to Derek Windsor?" Rose hissed as she slid back into her seat.

"A little. He was chatting to me while waiting for a drink," I said. I glanced over Rose's shoulder to where he was back standing with his friends, facing away from me.

Rose also looked appraisingly at him, a frown on her face. "Well." She turned her attention back to me. "One of my girlfriends just texted. She's down the road at Tokkuri's with some work friends. Do you want to head over there and meet up with them? They do really good Japanese-style tapas, and she said there are loads of cute single guys there as well."

"Yes!" I enthused, boosted with confidence both from the cocktails as well as my little chat with Derek.

"Great! Let's finish our drinks and go," Rose said and we both did exactly that before standing up.

As we exited the bar, I looked towards Derek Windsor, just to see if he was noticing us leaving. He was talking to a friend, and even though he was mid-sentence, his eyes shifted and caught mine.

A triumphant jolt went through me, which may have been partly because he was one of the only men whose eyes had come to rest on *me*, rather than Rose as we walked out. I smiled at him, maintaining eye contact just long enough to be suggestive. An image of a rich, luxurious penthouse and a red S&M room appeared in my mind, and I found myself wondering what it would be like to go home with Derek Windsor.

But then I left the bar with Rose, leaving Derek behind. Oh well, it was all just fantasy, wasn't it? That sort of stuff didn't *really* happen.

We headed back down the lift and out onto the street, Rose directing us towards our next destination. Barely a block down busy George Street, we arrived outside another uber-cool-looking bar, complete with bouncers out the front and a long line of people waiting to get in.

Rather than joining the queue, Rose walked confidently up to one of the security guards while I trailed dubiously behind.

"Hi there!" she said on approach. "How's your night going?"

The bouncer seemed to assess her briefly before responding. "It's pretty good."

"Is it busy inside?" she asked casually. "We've checked out a couple of other places, but the music has been terrible."

"It's starting to pick up." He glanced at me. "Is it just you and your friend?"

"Yes, just us two." She beckoned me over and I stepped in closer.

The bouncer nodded and then detached the little rope barrier and held it aside for us to enter.

"Do you know him?" I squealed as we walked inside, not quite believing that we'd managed to skip the line.

"No." Rose said. "I just don't line up."

As if that statement were enough, Rose strode assertively towards the bar and I followed her in awe.

After ordering two drinks, Rose did a sweep of the room with her eyes. "There they are," she said, indicating a group of people in one of the corners, half of them standing around and chatting while the other half sat on swanky ottomans and couches.

"Do you know them all?"

Rose surveyed them closely before answering. "I've met most of them before. My friend Sophie is the Korean girl with the long hair. We used to work together a few years ago."

We paid for our drinks then headed to the group. There were lots of hugs for Rose and exclamations of, "Oh, daaarling it's so lovely to see you again!" before I was introduced to everyone (and I forgot almost all their names as soon as I heard them). After the introductions, I found myself talking to a guy (whose name I think was Justin) and he'd already launched into a story about his work.

"Of course, I didn't need to take the new role because it's a lot more work than what I was doing before, but since they created the role specifically for me, I would have felt like a prick turning it down," he said, gesturing with his glass of scotch at the same time.

"Oh, right." I nodded, though I was struggling to work out what he was talking about and why I should care.

"Plus, it also means that I'm moving into one of the offices that overlooks the street. You know, one of those really big offices in the Denzel Building?"

"Er …"

"Fifty-six Martin Place? The Denzel Building? It's one of those sweet offices up on level five. Nothing at all compared to what they have on level three—have you seen level three? It would be like working in a dungeon in there."

"Ahh, yeah." I nodded again as if I was completely on board with how horrible level three at the Denzel Building was.

"Anyway, so there was this woman—Rosanne—who was in that office before. But she really hasn't been performing well lately, so it's her own fault that she's being moved out."

"Poor Rosanne!" I couldn't help saying.

"Of course, it wasn't my decision to take over her office," he continued defensively, throwing me an unimpressed look. "Obviously, I don't want to kick her out. I suppose I *could* get her a card or something, you know, just to show that there's no hard feelings from me. Hmm." He pulled out his phone and typed something into it before putting it back in his pocket.

"Sorry. Where were we?" he asked, his brows furrowed pensively. "Ah yes." He smiled, his face clearing. "So, the big move is happening on Monday, which is why I'm ready to celebrate tonight!" He downed the rest of his scotch in one gulp, ramming the empty glass down on a nearby table once done.

"Another drink, then!" he said, rubbing his hands together and walking off to the bar without a backward glance.

I blinked and looked around me, glad that Justin was gone, though it had left me devoid of anyone to talk to. Luckily Rose saved me, appearing next to me and handing me a full glass of champagne.

"Cheers!" she grinned, and I clinked my glass with hers.

# 19

Around 10 pm I realised I was pretty drunk. An almost never-ending stream of champagne had been appearing in my hands for the past few hours, although I had managed to temper some of the effects with morsels of delicious finger food that somebody ordered. (And Rose was right—the food *was* amazing.)

I'd just teetered up to the bar again when a familiar presence sidled up next to me.

"Here you are again, at a different bar. I'm starting to think that you're following me," said Derek Windsor.

I looked at him and raised one eyebrow. "I believe I left Bar Six before you did, so if anything, I think it is you who's following me," I countered.

Derek raised an eyebrow. "Perhaps I am following you."

"Oh? And why would that be?" I turned to face him, putting my hand on my hip. "Do you want to tie me up and spank me?"

He looked genuinely surprised, and for a moment I think we were both a little stunned. Had I really just said that? Oh God, maybe he wasn't actually into that *Fifty Shades* stuff like Rose's friend had said, and I just looked like a weirdo.

But then Derek seemed to change slightly. A sparkle came into his eyes and he drew himself up taller and leaned towards me, in a way that was quite ... dominating.

"Would you like to be tied up by me?" He smiled slowly, his eyes staring directly into mine.

I felt a little shiver of excitement go through me and I was forced to break eye contact. "I'm not sure about being *actually* tied up," I said, my face flushing. "But, um ..." What could I say? That the thought of kinky sex games freaked me out ... and yet, that perhaps I was just a tiny bit intrigued?

Derek leaned casually against the bar, bringing himself back into my line of sight. "So, I take it your friend has been telling you stories about me?" he said.

"She may have filled me in on some details," I answered vaguely. "Does that mean it's true? Do you have an S&M room in your penthouse apartment?"

Derek considered me before answering. "Would you like to find out?" he asked.

"How?"

"Well, I do have a new toy that I haven't tried out yet."

"Is that so? And what might this new toy be?"

"A swing."

I laughed loudly, thinking he must be joking. "Seriously? What, like a swing set?" I asked, imagining the kind of thing that children play on.

"No." Derek smiled slowly again. "A sex swing. You could be the first person to try it out." As he said this, he moved closer to me so that his leg brushed against mine.

I suddenly had a vision of that scene from *Sex and the City* where Samantha goes home with the guy who has a sex swing, and I felt another thrill of exhilaration go through me.

*Oh my God, that could be me!* A guy with a sex swing had invited me home for kinky sex! Was this really happening? Could I do a Samantha?

"Let me get this straight," I said, facing him properly. "You're offering to take me back to your apartment and show me your S&M room and we can, ah, try out the swing, what—together?"

Derek's smile widened. "If that's what you'd like to do," he said.

I started visualising myself lithely straddling Derek as we swung gracefully back and forth through the air, the pressure from the different angles hitting all the right spots.

I wasn't sure if it was the alcohol coursing through me, or the fact that I was on a pre-set mission to explore as much as possible (or, let's be honest, it could be that whole it-happened-in-*Sex-and-the-City*-so-I-need-to-try-it-too justification), but either way, the only thought running through my head was—why not? A gorgeous, (apparently) rich man had just invited me to try out his new sex swing. It wasn't like this opportunity presented itself every day.

And okay, yes, I know about the whole stranger danger, one-night-stand risks. But then, Rose knew this guy, didn't she? Or at least Christian seemed to know him. So, he wasn't *really* a stranger.

I took a deep breath, picked my clutch bag up off the bar, then turned to him and simply said, "Let's go, then."

One of Derek's eyebrows quirked upwards, but then his eyes sparkled with pleasure and he turned to go, a hand pressing lightly on the lower part of my back to steer me out with him.

I felt a taught, electric feeling between us as he led me out of the bar. I didn't even stop to look for Rose, thinking of nothing other than letting Derek steer me and the way his hand felt so large and warm through my dress.

We left the bar and Derek hailed a passing cab. He opened the back door and helped me in, but then, to my surprise, he got into the front seat next to the driver. He gave the directions to his apartment and our cab pulled away.

I could feel my heart racing a mile an hour, and I felt giddy. Had I seriously just climbed into a cab with a total stranger who was taking me back to his apartment for kinky sex? What if Rose was wrong and Derek wasn't some mega-playboy who lived in a penthouse apartment. Although, she said Christian had been to his place, didn't she? And was there seriously going to be a sex swing there? How on earth was one actually meant to use a sex swing? What if I couldn't use it properly, or I was too heavy, or—

"How's your night been?" Derek asked the taxi driver, and then they became immersed in a hearty discussion about late-night passengers and what funny things the cabby had witnessed in his time.

I couldn't care less about their conversation, and since Derek wasn't making any effort to include me in it, I pulled out my phone and sent a text to Rose.

*Have left bar and going home with Derek Windsor. He has sex swing & going to try!! Enjoy the rest of your night! xx*

I looked out the window at the city passing as we cruised along the busy roads, and felt a grin splitting my face. Look at me now! I almost wanted to laugh. Laura the Explorer was certainly living up to her namesake, wasn't she?

I leaned back in my seat and took a few deep breaths as the cab sped along towards Rose Bay. Derek was still confidently chatting to the cab driver like they were old friends. I wondered that he wasn't at all curious about the strange girl in the back seat that he was taking home. But then, well, he probably took strange girls home all the time. This undoubtedly wasn't a big deal for him at all.

My phone chirped with an incoming message from Rose.

*WHATT???? OMFG that is so crazy! I want deets later, get a pic of his penthouse if you can!!*

I put my phone away, already wondering at the stories I was going to have to tell, the fun I was surely about to have. Because that was the whole point of going home with Derek Windsor, Sydney Playboy, wasn't it? We'd go inside his swanky apartment, he'd pour us a glass of wine in the kitchen which we'd sip, and then we'd start making out and undressing each other and of course I'd know exactly what I was doing.

"Just past that red car will be fine," Derek said to the cabbie, and I realised that we'd arrived.

*Shit! It's happening.*

Derek paid for the cab and helped me climb out of the back seat, then took my hand and led me inside to what was a really posh, fancy lobby. As we stood waiting for the lift, he was still holding my hand, and his thumb was making little circular motions across my skin.

I looked up into his eyes and could barely breathe. He was staring down at me with that intense gaze, a small smile on his lips.

"Feeling alright?"

"Yes," I said, too quickly. "You?"

"Excited."

I felt my stomach clench. *I'm about to have sex on a sex swing!* my little internal voice was saying, and my heart raced a bit faster.

The lift door opened and we stepped in. Derek swiped a small disc on his keyring across a security pad and then pressed the "P" button.

P for Penthouse. It looked like Rose was correct.

*That's so cool.*

When the doors opened at the top, we stepped out into an amazing apartment full of art-deco furniture. It was the biggest, most impressive apartment I'd ever been in, although on closer inspection I noticed that there were clothes lying around everywhere, the kitchen sink was full of dishes, and there was a whole bunch of magazines and notebooks piled up on the dining table.

Oh well, so he wasn't the tidiest person, then. It wasn't like I was imagining he was going to have a butler or anything. Not really.

"Wow, this place is amazing!" I said enthusiastically (honestly—mess aside, it was amazing).

"Pour yourself a glass of wine—there's a bottle in the fridge," Derek said. "I just need to get things set up." He gave my hand a quick squeeze then disappeared off down the hallway, leaving me standing somewhat awkwardly in the middle of the living area.

Right, so straight down to business, then. So much for a bit of getting-to-know-you conversation before we jumped into things.

Not really sure what else to do, I went over to the fridge and found an open bottle of pinot grigio inside. I looked around for a wineglass (there were two dirty wineglasses next to the sink, but I didn't really want to think about who else he might have been entertaining here recently) and managed to find a clean one in one of the cupboards.

As I was standing alone sipping wine in Derek Windsor's kitchen, things were feeling a bit surreal. What on earth was I doing there?

I was about to have kinky sex, that's what.

Was I the kind of person who had kinky sex?

If there was ever a time to find out it was now.

But was this really a good idea?

Yes. Yes, it was. Completely no-strings-attached, casual sex. Just what I needed.

Trying to distract myself, I strolled over to the dining table and checked out the magazines lying there. They were mostly financial and business titles and my eye wandered over them disinterestedly.

"Hey—can you give me a hand in here?" Derek called out from down the hallway.

Yes, this was it! Sex swing time!

"Sure!" I called back.

As I started walking down the hallway, some new thoughts suddenly flew through my head. *I should have chewed on a piece of gum! I probably smelt like Japanese food and vodka!* And argh, what underwear did I put on this morning? I think I picked the nice ones, but I did remember considering the old-daggyies in the drawer there, too.

I reached the door and pushed all the negative thoughts out of my head—now was the time for suave, sexy Laura to walk through the door to …

… find Derek squatting on the floor balancing four huge poles with what looked like a sort of hammock strung between them as he tried to connect the pieces.

"Hey!" he panted, looking around. "Here, grab that end and clip it into the base mount there."

"Er, right." I quickly got over my surprise and tottered forward in my heels to help assemble the sex swing.

I mean, really? He hadn't even set it up! I bet Samantha didn't have to assemble the bloody sex swing.

It took longer to assemble than I would have liked. Instead of swinging around having wild sex, I found myself sitting on the ground (my shoes having been kicked off a while ago) reading out the instructions on how the swing should be assembled, while Derek tried to connect all the pieces—which just didn't want to connect as they were supposed to in the picture.

Honestly, this was worse than IKEA stuff. And I could feel my drunken haze starting to wear off. Was I going to be able to have wild, kinky sex if I wasn't tipsy anymore? My back was starting to hurt, and I was imagining my pyjamas and bed at home in a wistful way.

*No, stop that, Laura. You are going to stay and have kinky sex before returning home to your comfy bed.*

After all, I was setting up the bloody swing, so I might as well use it.

"Right, it's done!" Derek suddenly exclaimed and stood up.

"Are you sure?" I squinted at the picture and then eyed our structure dubiously. There was now a big freestanding frame on four legs, with a range of different-sized straps hanging down from various hooks. "I don't think—"

"It's perfect!" he said in a slightly manic way. "Come on, let's get another glass of wine." He held out his hand and pulled me up off the ground.

As he led me back into the kitchen, I felt the anticipation return and suddenly I was wide awake again. This was it! Really this time!

Derek poured us each a glass of wine, and as he handed me mine our eyes met.

"Well, then …" He took a sip of wine, his eyes never leaving mine. Very slowly, he put his wineglass down on the bench. I quickly took a few gulps of mine before following suit. Then he stepped in close to me, our bodies only centimetres apart but not touching.

"Are you ready to have some fun?" he asked softly, his face only millimetres from mine, his eyes intense.

"Yes," I breathed, tilting my face up towards his.

For a moment we were still, our eyes locked together, our bodies almost touching. And then we both moved at the same time, grabbing each other roughly, kissing fiercely. Our hips were pressed together and I could feel that he was hard already.

Derek lifted me up onto the bench and I wrapped my legs around his hips. His hands were down the back of my dress and I felt my bra being undone. I reached for his buttons and started undoing his shirt. His torso was muscular and firm, and there wasn't a trace of a hair on his chest. Although, I could feel the *teeniest* bit of stubble when I ran my hand over it, but you know, I couldn't really complain. I mean, no one actually expected my legs to be Veet-smooth all year round, did they? At least I'd got that bikini wax last week. And unlike Tinder Boy, Derek might even get to appreciate that I'd had the back done!

Things were starting to get intense on the kitchen bench and I began to wonder how we were going to move this act into the sex room. Surely, he could pick me up and carry me in? I wasn't that heavy, plus my legs were already locked around him. I squeezed my legs tighter and tried lifting my bum up off the bench, but he didn't really get the hint. Instead, he stopped kissing me and pulled away a bit, letting me slide off the counter onto my feet again.

Bugger. It would have been so cool if he'd carried me in.

Derek's eyes were alight as he took my hand. "Ready to try out the swing?"

"Ah, sure," I said, and he led me back down the hall.

When we entered the sex room again, Derek switched off the lights—but then he flicked another switch and suddenly there was mood lighting everywhere, and lounge-style music as if we were in a really cool bar. I also only just registered that this *was* the sex room, as it was more sparsely furnished than I would have imagined. There was a big cupboard on one side and a basic bed and a few chairs on the other, and most of the floor space was now taken up with the swing. It was only really the lamps and a few arty pictures that gave the room any atmosphere.

"Wow," I said dumbly. Was that a lava lamp over in the corner? Were they still in?

Derek rubbed his hands together and I noticed that he was eyeing the newly erected sex swing gleefully, as if he'd just received the most awesome Christmas present. "Let's try the flying lotus position first!" he said excitedly, and then he stripped off his shirt and—oh wow, his pants were coming off, too.

I just stood there, ogling him.

He grinned at me and looked pointedly at my clothes, before pulling a strip of condoms out of a drawer and putting one on.

*So … I guess I'll just undress myself, then?*

I felt a little self-conscious as I removed my own clothes. I mean, not that I minded—it wasn't like I was expecting a really intimate undressing by this man I'd only just met. But you know. You don't really expect to be undressing yourself, do you? Especially not when the man who was supposed to be undressing you was currently strapping himself into a giant sex swing, his erect penis already covered with a bright-red condom.

"Ready!" Derek said eagerly.

"Er ... Okay." I stepped forward gingerly (now I was really glad about the mood lighting in here) and removed the rest of my clothes.

"Put one leg over here." Derek pointed. "And then the other one over there."

"Ah, okay." I managed to get one of my legs up and through the strap that he was indicating, but then I couldn't quite work out how to get my other leg up and over.

"Put your weight on me," Derek said, but since he was already suspended in the straps when I tried to put my weight on him, we started swinging.

"Ahhh!" I squealed as I almost lost my balance, one foot still stuck in a strap.

"Here." Derek unhooked my first foot. "Grab that chair from the corner. You probably just need a bit more height."

Oh my God, I felt like I was in a gymnastics class, not attempting to have sex! I could feel my face burning as I went and fetched the chair. Was kinky sex supposed to be this hard?

Once we had the chair's assistance, I was able to get my legs in the right position (after accidentally kneeing Derek in the face) and he held my hips and guided me onto him.

To be honest, it wasn't bad.

We started to swing back and forth between the poles (I managed to kick the chair away) and it was actually quite fun. I started leaning into the swinging motion and the pressure was good—each angle was hitting a different spot.

Yes! Now this was more like it! This was what I was imagining!

"Let's swap positions," Derek said. "I'm not getting much from this one."

What, seriously? After it took so long to get into this position?

He lifted me off and back down to the floor then got himself out of the straps. "Here, you get into them," he said, and next thing I knew I was airborne, holding on to the straps up above my head with my ankles and thighs strapped into other straps.

I was basically hanging in the yoga "bow" pose, my back arched and my legs up in the air behind me.

"Okay?" Derek asked as he stood behind me.

"Yeah, this is great!" I said positively, my voice a bit strained.

Derek stroked his hands down over my hips and then—okay, yes, we were going again.

If I concentrated on the actual sex, then it was fab! I really was suspended at the perfect angle and he started nice and slowly, getting the speed right. He also had his hands free, and he stroked them down across my hips, sending a shiver through me.

I just needed to concentrate on the awesome sex, that was it. Just ignore the fact that the straps were cutting into my thighs painfully. And my arms were starting to shake a little as I continued to hold my upper body weight. God, I was quite heavy, wasn't I? How on earth did those aerial acrobats make things look so elegant and weightless? To be honest, right then I was feeling about as heavy as an elephant. And about as elegant as one, too. I mean, would anyone feel elegant, hanging suspended in an awkward spread-eagled position while a man did you from behind? It was a good thing Derek hadn't tried to carry me into the room. I really must make more of an effort to get fit. And maybe go back to green smoothies instead of the banana-honey ones.

I was starting to pant a bit with the exertion and I heard Derek respond, obviously thinking that I was just enjoying myself so much. And I was enjoying myself. Really. It was great. It was just not exactly the most *comfortable* sex I'd ever had. My back was starting to hurt. And I wasn't sure you were supposed to hold a backward bend for this long in yoga. One time I bent my back a bit too far during one of those super-hot Bikram yoga classes, and the next day I couldn't move my neck at all. I'd walked around looking like Uncle Fester all day.

"Can we switch?" I gasped out. "My back is really hurting."

"Oh!" Derek exclaimed, and I could hear he sounded disappointed. He pulled out though and helped me back out of the straps.

"Let's try the Bear Hug position," I quickly suggested, spotting it on the diagram still lying on the floor. It looked like the easiest pose. I was meant to put the straps around my legs again, but then I could wrap my legs around Derek and face forwards this time. I was also quietly thinking that I'd be able to put most of my weight on him, rather than the straps, and that I could curl my back the other way and straighten myself out a bit.

We got going again, and that position really was much better. Derek even grabbed hold of the straps and put his weight on them, too. And oh yes, that was much, much better.

We were both really enjoying ourselves then, and I could run my hands over his back, and up through his hair, kissing him at the same time. Plus, we could swing comfortably—I mean really swing, and it was great! I was finally experiencing what a sex swing was really made for, surely! It had all the fun of swinging in a park, but a much more adult version.

We started to really take off, the backwards and forwards motion rubbing the perfect spot, and I leaned my head back and arched my back a little. But it was at that point, just as we were both really getting into things, that there came an awful cracking sound from above us.

We both froze and tensed simultaneously, looking at each other in horror even as we kept swinging.

"Did—" I started to say, but the rest of my question was cut off as a second later I felt the swing collapse.

"Ahh!" I screamed, grabbing onto Derek's shoulders, my legs still wrapped around his hips.

We dropped straight to the ground with a heavy thud, the swing straps snapping away from the structure around us. As we landed, Derek made a choking, pained sound and I quickly tried to pull away from him, disentangling the straps from around me.

"Are you okay?" I looked at him in alarm.

He was curled over, his hands in his crotch. Another pained sound escaped from his throat.

Oh my God. Did we just break his penis?

I looked around at what was left of the sex swing and marvelled that the metal beams at least hadn't collapsed on us—it was just the straps that had snapped out of their anchors.

"Ah … do you need some ice?" I offered.

He shook his head, his eyes squeezed shut, and another pained groan escaped.

"Can I … get you anything?" I asked awkwardly.

He just shook his head again, his eyes screwed closed.

Well shit, this certainly didn't happen in *Sex and the City*. What was I supposed to do?

I kept kneeling next to him, while he just lay there in a ball. Hmm. Should I … get dressed? Offer to try to fix the swing? Turn the lights back on? The lounge music was still playing, an almost comical mockery of our current state.

Derek finally opened his eyes and sat up, his face drained of colour.

"Are you okay?" I asked again, leaning forward and self-consciously trying to cover my nakedness a bit.

"I think so," he gasped, and he managed to take a few deep breaths of air.

We both looked around at the remains of the swing in awkward silence, then our eyes met. And then we both broke out into peals of laughter (although his laugh sounded a bit pained still).

"I think I'll go," I said when I'd managed to stop laughing.

"Okay." Derek nodded, calming down a bit, too, though his eyes were watering.

I quickly got dressed, while Derek slowly stood to his feet, grunting and doubled over. He grabbed his shirt up off the floor and pressed it against his groin as if it was a tourniquet.

"So ... ah ... sorry about that," I said vaguely, having dressed as swiftly as possible. I headed out of the room and Derek managed to follow me (limping) out towards the lift.

"Not to worry," he gasped out, waving his hand nonchalantly as he tried to muster up some dignity. "I'll be fine."

"Well ... bye," I said, hastily stepping into the elevator and pressing the button for the ground floor.

He smiled at me ruefully, a look of—regret, mixed with pain?—on his face as the lift doors closed between us, and then I felt the lift descending, taking me away from the penthouse and my bizarre evening.

Well, at least I could cross "sex swing" off my bucket list.

And also possibly "breaking a guy's penis".

** TINDER ALERT **
*Congratulations! You have 4 new matches!*

** TINDER ALERT **
**New Message: Andrew, 29**
*Hey, you having a good night?*

** TINDER ALERT **
**New Message: Ewen, 27**
*Hey hows your nite going?*

** NEW MESSAGE **
**From: Mum at 11.17 am**
*Hi, darling! Guess what—I was having lunch with Mrs Gilbert, and Annalise is pregnant with TWINS!!! You remember her, don't you? She's turned out so lovely, nothing like the shy thing she was in primary school!! Plus, her mum already has six grandkids, so this will make it eight!! She must be very busy!! Xxx*

# 20

I woke slowly, the sharp light peeking in through my blinds telling me it was well past sunrise.

For a moment, I was disoriented and thought I must be late for work. But then, no, I realised it was Saturday. And thank goodness for that—my head was pounding with a headache.

And then I remembered the previous night.

My mind did a quick blow-by-blow over everything that happened in reverse time: getting a cab home after midnight, breathing in the fresh, cool air out the window and trying to clear my head; breaking Derek's penis (?) and awkwardly leaving his penthouse; sex in the sex swing; assembling the sex swing; deciding to go home with Derek; drinks with Rose.

A huge smile took over my face. *Ha!* I thought, hugging my quilt to my chest. My eyes were wide with wonder as I stared up at the ceiling. I was in awe. I was in awe of *myself.* I also wondered if Derek was actually alright? I felt a bit bad; even if I hadn't broken his penis, we had at least broken the sex swing.

I pawed at my bedside table until I located my phone and quickly opened a text to Rose:

*Hey, Rosey Posey! How did your night end up? Mine was v. interesting—will have to tell you about it on Monday! Also does Christian have Derek's mobile number? Xx*

I tossed my phone back on the nightstand and lay in bed for a bit longer, feeling pleased with myself.

Eventually, the faint sounds of talking and pots and pans rattling around in the kitchen roused me out of bed. I padded my way down the hallway as delicious smells wafted around the apartment from whatever Ben and Kalina were doing in the kitchen and hit the shower straightaway.

After I was refreshed and dressed, I wandered into the kitchen to see what they were doing.

"Morning," I said.

"Morning!" they both responded brightly.

"You guys are up early. What are you cooking?" I came around and sat at one of the kitchen stools to observe.

Food that'd been partially prepared covered one entire side of the bench, and Ben was at the stove frying something off. Kalina, meanwhile, was standing in front of a collection of jugs and glasses at the other end of the bench, each jug filled with a different-looking drink. Around her were wine bottles, a brandy bottle, and a chopping board covered in cut fruits. I also noticed that there were a few notebooks and notepaper lying around, scribbled notes and lists on them all.

"It's creating time!" Kalina enthused, gesturing around at the mess.

"Right. What are you creating exactly?"

"We're designing the final menu for my brother's bar," Ben offered from where he was turning something in the frying pan.

"And I'm making a sangria recipe," Kalina said proudly.

"Which may or may not be featured on the menu," Ben said, giving me a sideways look.

"Hey, he's going to love this. Plus, it's kind of like my CV. Because he's totally going to give me a job in his bar when he tries this," Kalina said.

"You're going to work there, too?" I asked in surprise.

"Absolutely!" Kalina said, although I saw Ben rolling his eyes. "I mean, why would I keep working with the competition when I can get a job with the family?"

"You know you don't need to audition for a job, Kal," Ben said. "He'd give you one anyway."

"I know. But this is more fun." Kalina grinned at me.

"Well, that's one way to impress him." I gave Kalina a knowing look. If she was looking to rekindle things with Ben's hot brother, then working for him would be a great start. I wasn't sure she noticed my look, though, as she was too busy measuring orange juice into a jug.

"How much wine did I just put in?" she asked, scrunching up her nose thoughtfully and looking at me. I shrugged.

"Shit." She frowned down at her jug. "I'll have to start a new batch now. Want to drink this one?"

"No, thanks." I grimaced at the thought of whatever Kalina had concocted. My body definitely didn't need any more alcohol. "But I'll happily taste test whatever Ben is cooking over there," I added hopefully, my mouth already watering.

"What, no Sangria on a Saturday morning? Laura, you disappoint me," Kalina joked.

"Nah, she just prefers my stuff to yours." Ben shot Kalina a sly look.

"You are in charge of the menu, so your stuff had better be good!" Kalina shot back, making me laugh.

"I'm sure the Sangria will be great. I just had a bit much to drink last night," I said.

"Ah yes! How was your night?" Kalina suddenly looked up at me with interest. "You got home pretty late."

My responding grin must have answered her question.

"Okay—details!" Kalina leaned forward eagerly.

Laughing, I filled them in on my night with Derek Windsor, renowned

Sydney playboy.

"Oh my God—that's awesome!" Kalina shrieked when I was done.

"Where do you buy a sex swing from?" Ben wondered aloud.

"That's now, what, two points on the board for Laura the Explorer?" Kalina said. "You're doing fantastically!"

I felt a little thrill of satisfaction go through me. Not that I'd really describe either encounter as being *satisfying*. But you know—crawl before you walk and all that.

"Alright, try these." Ben suddenly turned around with his frying pan and started transferring some amazing-looking fried items onto a plate.

"Is that bacon?" I leaned forward eagerly and practically drooled on the table.

Within seconds, all three of us were biting into dates stuffed with manchego cheese and wrapped in crispy jamón. It was absolute heaven.

"These definitely need to be on the menu," Kalina said, her eyes closed as she savoured the taste.

"Definitely," I agreed.

# 21

My phone bleeped with an incoming text and I immediately shifted my attention away from the document I was trying to read over on my desk.

My instant thought was that Lucas had finally texted me (it'd been five days since we exchanged numbers, after all), but then my more cynical side decided that of course it wouldn't be him because he probably wasn't interested in me at all and I was being completely delusional. Even though he'd suggested that he was, in fact, interested.

Nevertheless, when I opened my phone my heart skipped a beat to see that Derek Windsor had replied to the text I'd sent him the night before. Opening the message chain, I re-read over what I'd sent before checking his response:

(Me) Sunday at 5.18 pm:
*Hey, Derek—it's Laura. Just wanted to say I had a really fun time on Fri night & sorry about leaving so quickly. Hope you don't have any lasting injuries (& hope the swing isn't too broken)!*

Derek Windsor Monday at 10.16 am:
*Hey, Laura thanks for the text. I also had fun on Friday & no lasting*

*injuries. Sorry about the swing—dodgy make, apparently. I've got plenty of things that don't break, if you're in the area again.*

Hmm. Was that an invitation for more sex? I'd thought it was just a one-night stand? Although, I supposed I'd already broken the rules of one-night stands by basically stalking him through a friend to get his phone number and texting him afterwards. But you know. Most people don't potentially break a penis during a one-night stand.

Or do they?

I was still staring at my phone, unsure if I should reply or not, when my desk phone started ringing, "Rose Spencer" coming up on the display.

"Hello!" I said enthusiastically as I picked up the receiver.

"I want all the sordid details and you are going to leave nothing out," Rose hissed down the line.

"Is it time for that meeting?" I tried to suppress a giggle while keeping my voice even. My eyes slid back to the document on my screen. It was nothing *super* urgent, and a quick coffee break wasn't going to make much of a difference. "Okay, I'll pop around now."

Rose managed not to say anything as she joined me at the lifts. Once we were inside one, squished up the back with a group of executives in front of us, I surveyed Rose out of the corner of my eye. She was dressed in one of her usual stunning outfits, although there was something a bit different about her today. I couldn't quite put my finger on what.

"Okay, spill," Rose said once we were safely out on the street and heading towards our coffee shop. "Tell me everything that happened on Friday night."

"Shh!" I tried not to laugh as I glanced around to see if anyone from the office was following us. Luckily, we were out on our own, the myriad other office workers from different buildings paying us no attention.

I looked back at Rose and took a deep breath, letting her hang in suspense before answering. She watched me intensely, her face carefully neutral.

"Well," I began, a grin creeping across my face. "I went home with Derek Windsor. To his *penthouse*."

"Oh my God!!" Rose gasped. "Are you serious? I wasn't sure if your message was a joke! And then when you asked for his number ... well, wow." Rose frowned, a distracted look coming across her face.

It was then that I realised what was different about her. Her hair was tied up in a messy bun, but it wasn't one of those stylish messy buns that were purposely dishevelled. It actually just looked *dishevelled*, as if she just hadn't been bothered that morning. And her eyes had dark circles under them, something Rose almost never had.

"So, tell me about it." Rose seemed to pull herself together, and looked at me again. "Was it amazing?"

Did her voice sound kind of hollow?

"It was pretty good." I gave Rose an abridged version of the evening, unsure what was bothering her. And then I suddenly realised—oh no, maybe she had a thing for Derek Windsor? I mean, obviously she had a long-term boyfriend, but did it bother her that I'd slept with Derek?

"Rose?" I asked hesitantly. "Are you okay? I mean, are you okay with me having gone home with him?"

Rose jolted. "What?" Her face transformed, and she gave me an incredulous look. "Of course! Why wouldn't I be okay with it?"

"Oh, I don't know," I said, feeling caught off guard.

"I'm happy for you," she said, smiling at me, although it wasn't her usual genuine smile. "Of course you should be sleeping with different people. I mean you're single now! You're allowed to."

I was still confused as we made our way into the coffee shop. Rose seemed to recover as we walked towards the counter; a few men's eyes were drawn to her as she crossed the room.

Once we'd ordered and were waiting at the collection area, I turned to Rose again, determined to get whatever was bothering her out in the open.

"Are you sure you're okay?" I prodded, then decided to take a guess. "Is everything alright with Christian?"

A momentary freeze came across her whole body, then she melted back into motion just as fast, a tight smile on her face as she surveyed the room. "Things are fine," she said quickly.

I stayed silent, waiting for her to look at me. When she finally did, I simply raised my eyebrows.

Rose sighed, caving. "I don't know. We had a huge fight on the weekend."

"What happened?" I asked gently.

Rose shrugged and looked away. "I don't really know. He was just sitting there, playing Xbox again like he does every weekend now. And I wanted to go out and do something, you know, actually get out of the house for a change. And he was like, 'Well, if you want to go out, then just go out.' Because he'd already been out so much for work, so he didn't want to do anything."

"That sucks."

"Yeah, so I did go out, on my own." Rose paused, her mouth still open as if she was about to keep talking. Then she closed it hastily, blanching again, and looked away from me.

"Where—"

"He's just become so *boring* lately," Rose cut me off, turning back towards me and speaking rapidly. "It's like he doesn't get that just because he goes out all the time, I don't get to. I mean, we used to go out heaps and now we just spend every weekend in."

"At least you have someone to spend the weekends in with," I offered kindly.

"Yeah," Rose said, but she sounded morose.

I was about to ask her more when our names were called for our coffee and we picked them up and headed back outside onto the street.

"So, tell me, what's the latest with your other boys?" Rose asked, although her voice sounded a bit odd. I glanced at her sideways again, but she was looking straight ahead.

"Which ones?" I asked, realising she probably didn't want to talk about Christian anymore.

"Tinder Boy. Pete from sales," Rose supplied.

"Oh no, well nothing with Tinder Boy! Not after the tarts, anyway. And nothing's really going on with Pete. We're just training buddies at the moment."

"Ah," Rose nodded, relaxing.

What was wrong with her? There was something definitely up, and it seemed like more than just a fight with Christian.

"What—" I started to say, but Rose cut me off again.

"Have you heard about the new deal that the sales guys are working on?" she said, changing the topic. "Apparently, there're some big investors involved. I'm trying to get in on the marketing side."

"No, I haven't heard," I said, frowning.

For the rest of the walk back to the office Rose talked about the deal, but I was barely listening. She was deliberately avoiding something, I could tell. She said she didn't have a problem with me sleeping with Derek, so what was going on?

It was still a mystery when we arrived back at the office and headed inside, and as we made our way up to level five I knew I'd lost my chance to ask Rose again.

❧

When my clock hit 4.25 pm, I grabbed my gym bag from under my desk and logged out of my computer. My plan was to slink out of the office without anyone from my team noticing that I'd left early, but Belinda caught me.

"Are you leaving *already*, Laura?" she said, eyeing my gym bag.

The emphasis she put on the word was *so* accusatory. Honestly, it wasn't that bad to leave work a little early every now and then, was it? I mean, my work would still be there in the morning. I could just come in early and make up for the lost time.

"Yep, I have a training session," I replied, squaring my shoulders and trying to push any guilt away. I mean, really, I certainly didn't need to justify my actions to Belinda, of all people. Though, I did glance around to make sure Cara wasn't within sight (luckily she wasn't). "Bye, then!"

I went down to the lobby and hovered around near the front doors waiting for Pete. Every minute or so the lifts opened and people stepped out, all heading home for the day. As I watched them hurrying past, I vaguely wondered what Rose was doing that afternoon. She hadn't been at her desk when I'd left, and a lack of handbag underneath it meant that she'd already gone. I hoped things were going to work themselves out between her and Christian. Maybe she just needed to have a good chat to him. Many things could be worked out by simply talking.

*And speaking of* ... I pulled my phone out of my bag and stared despondently at the lack of message notifications, feeling disappointed again. There'd still been no contact from Lucas. Why was that bothering me so much? It wasn't unexpected. I mean, if I thought about the situation rationally, then I wasn't actually expecting him to call. But then, I didn't want to be rational. And I *did* really want to have a drink with him. And possibly do some other things with him, too.

I glanced up at the people in the lobby again, but there was still no sign of Pete. Looking back at my phone, I opened a new text message to Lucas and felt my heartbeat irrationally fire up.

*Hi, Lucas, it's Laura, the meditating girl—*

Oh no. I quickly deleted it.

*Hi, Lucas, it's Laura. Was thinking of checking out some bars in Manly this week. Would be great to bump into each other again!*

Ick, no! I deleted that one, too.

*Hi, Lucas, it's Laura. Was thinking of checking out some bars in Manly this week and thought you could help me out with some food recommendations. What night are you free?*

I re-read the message a few times. Was it too forceful? But then, something told me I needed to be a bit forceful with this guy if I wanted anything to happen.

The lifts opened again and I caught sight of Pete's hulking figure out of the corner of my eye. My eyes darted back to the message and I felt my heartbeat increase again—*quick, decision time!*

I hit "send", before hurriedly burying my phone in my bag and then turning to smile at Pete, who was approaching.

"All ready for another sesh?" Pete asked as we left the building.

"Absolutely! Are *you* ready?"

"Definitely. I'm always ready. I could lift weights all day if I had more time."

"Erm, right. Yes, I'm sure I could do a lot more … *reps*. If it wasn't for the whole time thing, of course."

Pete raised his eyebrows at me speculatively.

"So how was your weekend?" I quickly asked, feeling my body returning to its regular non-giddy state as we stepped out onto the street.

"It was epic! A few of the boys and I went to the footy, then hit the pub afterwards. Didn't get home until about three. How 'bout you? Do anything good on the weekend?"

My mind flew immediately back to Friday night; going home with a wealthy Sydney playboy, sailing through the air on a sex swing. Had that really been only three days ago? And here I was texting and thinking about a different guy altogether, while heading to the gym with a *third* one.

"Nothing too adventurous," I said.

We arrived at the gym and our conversation ended as we went inside and then moved to our respective locker rooms to get changed. I pushed all thought of Lucas—and Derek—out of my mind, determined to not let them interfere with my workout session. I was only interested in those guys for *sex*, after all, I reminded myself. Thoughts of them shouldn't interfere with my self-improvement time. Or my time hanging out with Pete.

When I came back out onto the gym floor, I found Pete in the weights area.

"What should I do today?" I asked him, feeling positive and more confident in the gym.

"What areas do you want to work out?" he countered, already sitting on a bench with a pair of gigantic dumbbells.

"I don't know," I said, looking around dubiously at the equipment. "What areas should I be working out?"

Pete seemed to take this question as an invitation to do a full assessment of my body, and his eyes travelled the full length of me slowly. I was caught off guard. I mean, I thought we were just training buddies? Wasn't it established in our last session that Pete was definitely not interested in me in *that* way? He'd spent the whole time staring at Leopard-print Girl. But perhaps I was mistaken.

"Well, you've got fairly good arm tone, so I'd say you'd benefit the most from doing core work and also legs and glutes," he said eventually, his eyes returning to mine.

I raised an eyebrow. "I have good arm tone, do I?" I echoed.

"Yes, pretty good," he said, grinning.

"But what, my 'glutes', or rather my *butt*, needs more work?" I was trying hard to keep a straight face.

"Not a lot of work," Pete said, his eyes returning to stare at my backside. "But a few squats and then you'd take your already hot body to the next level."

My eyes widened, and I turned away, speechless, trying not to laugh. Hot body? Really?

"Uh-uh," I finally said, turning back. "I'm sure this is your professional opinion?"

"Nah, it's my personal one," Pete said. "You really should take the compliment. I'm not lying; you are hot." With that he lay down on his bench and started doing chest presses.

Okay ... what was *that*? You don't tell your friends they have a hot body and openly check out their butts! Was he ... I mean was this ...?

Who knew.

Pete was now studiously ignoring me, so I located a leg press and got myself set up on it. As I started doing a few experimental pushes, I caught sight of myself in one of the mirrors. And you know what? I wasn't looking too shabby. Leopard-print Girl wasn't at the gym today, so maybe Pete really did have some potential for Laura the Explorer.

I did a few more sets on the leg machine, then found a few other machines that promised to work my glutes. I was just trying to work out an awkward-looking one that was meant to do the sides of my stomach when Pete wandered over.

"How are you going?" he asked.

"Oh, great!" I said. "Just ... um ... well, actually I don't think I will use this machine, after all." I quickly disentangled myself.

"There're a couple of good machines over in the other corner that I think you'll like."

"Really? Where?"

"Come on, I'll show you."

We made our way across the gym together, and I saw the machines we were heading for.

"I don't know why people do dance classes at a gym," Pete said, as we passed the group fitness studio, and I looked over as well.

I could see the entire class through the glass wall, and it looked like they were doing a kind of street-funk routine. Once again, there were the lost-looking women at the back, struggling to work out foot–arm coordination, followed by some fairly good people in the middle and then a couple of dancers at the front who looked like they were performing a Mariah Carey warm-up act.

That guy at the front was really good. Really great energy and form. In fact, he looked familiar. The hair, and the way he moved, and the …

Oh my God.

I stopped walking. I was frozen, staring in disbelief into the class.

Pete had walked on, oblivious to the fact that I was no longer beside him.

I couldn't breathe. I felt like time had frozen. Because that person at the front—I knew his body so well. I'd loved him, and lived with him, and shared everything with him for over a decade.

I *thought* I'd known him so well. I thought I'd known everything about him. Until the day I realised that I didn't know him at all.

It was Jack.

And Jack was *dancing*.

My heart suddenly started thundering in my throat, like the gates at the Melbourne Cup had just opened and twenty-four horses were now stampeding around in my chest.

I was hyperventilating.

"Laura? Laura?"

Suddenly, Pete's voice penetrated through my thoughts, and I tore my eyes away from the sight of my ex-husband dancing, and dancing so *well*, to stare wide-eyed at Pete.

"Are you okay?" he asked, looking alarmed.

I couldn't speak, I just stared at him. Then I was moving, walking past him and away, away from the class, away from my startlingly good, jazz-dancing ex-husband.

"Hey, what's wrong?" Pete said, catching up to me.

"I just need to go," I managed to say, heading as fast as I could for the change rooms.

"Well, wait, okay, I'll leave as well."

I barely even heard him as I walked into the change rooms, grabbed my bag, and walked out again. I was trying to stay calm and to move normally, but I was feeling completely disconnected from my body.

So many thoughts were spinning around my head. What was Jack even doing there, at a city gym? He didn't work nearby, or at least he hadn't. And he hated gyms, he never used to go and do any exercise.

And dancing? I mean really—*dancing*?? I'd once suggested we go to a salsa class together and he'd hated the idea! Wouldn't even consider it! And yet there he was, doing street-style funk?

Pete caught up to me as I walked out the front doors.

"Laura—hey wait! Are you okay? What happened?" he asked.

"Sorry," I muttered, feeling a tiny bit of sanity returning once I was back out on the street. "I just ... saw someone in there."

"An ex?"

I nodded.

"Shit. You mean, what, dancing? What is he, gay?"

My heart, my eyes, literally *everything* froze ...

"I mean," Pete hastily backtracked. "Not that you'd have to be gay to do a dance class. Or even ... I mean, was it a girl? Was it a, uh, a bad breakup?"

"You could say that," I managed to say, not deigning to answer his other questions.

"Oh shit. Well that sucks. Do you want to get a drink? There's a bar just around the corner from here."

I hesitated, unsure. But then, maybe I did need a drink. "Yes. Sure."

My legs felt like they'd turned to jelly, and I was pretty sure that wasn't from the leg press.

"Okay. Come on, it's this way," Pete said as he led me away from the gym.

# 22

There were so many reasons for relationships to end. One person could cheat on the other, or you could simply grow apart. You might fight constantly or have other commitments pull you in different directions. But these were all quite normal reasons, and they were things that happened to lots of people, all the time.

God, how I wished my marriage to Jack had ended for one of those reasons. Then perhaps I could have accepted it more easily. I could've told myself I wasn't alone, or unusual, or a freak; many people had gone through the same thing I was going through, and there were probably lots of movies and songs I could relate to. At least then I would have known that in the beginning, in fact for most of the eleven years we were together, that it was real. That we were happy. That he did genuinely love me.

But when your husband tells you he's gay, you don't really have this same level of rational thinking. Oh yes, of course I could accept that he loved me like a friend. That we were best friends for all that time. But how could it be that I saw him as so much more—as a life partner, and a soul mate, as someone I accepted exactly as he was, flaws and all. Yet the whole time he'd been trying to push down the fact that he didn't accept all of me. That there were fundamental things wrong with his choice of partner, and ultimately it was his own dishonesty that was causing his unhappiness.

While he'd taken his time working himself out, trying to play along in the role everyone saw him in, he'd let me be his shield against reality. And when he finally gained the courage to be himself, to throw the shield aside, I was the one who had been destroyed. A necessary sacrifice. Collateral damage.

And everyone felt so sorry for *Jack*. How tragic that he'd felt the need to hide his sexual orientation. How awful for him, being forced by lingering societal pressure, by the set opinions of older generations to conform to "normal" boy–girl relationships.

Of course I understood. There was a part of me that knew, and felt for, the internal struggle he'd gone through. But what about *me*? What about the person who was lied to and tricked for all those years? The one who'd spent every waking moment with that man, and yet didn't work out anything was wrong? Yes, my friends and family had all sympathised with me. But none of them really got it. None of them really understood the deep, deep humiliation of it all.

Because how could I not have seen it? That's exactly what everyone wondered about me: how had I not *known*? Weren't there hints? I mean, I'd *slept* with him, for years. Surely, if he was truly gay that whole time, I should have known?

The worst part was the pity I got from people who knew the truth. It wasn't even an angry pity, where they put an arm around your shoulders and say, "Fuck that arsehole!", like they would if he'd left you for another woman. No, it was the purse-lipped, pat-on-the-arm type of pity, the kind where no one really knew what to say. Because you couldn't blame Jack, could you? He was the true victim here.

I was just the poor, blind fool who'd wasted ten years with him.

∽❍

All night I tossed and turned, unable to sleep. My one drink with Pete had been a lesson in speed drinking. I'd downed it so fast, but then felt so sick that I almost threw it up.

I think I mumbled something vague about not wanting to talk about my ex, so we'd just sat in the bar together for a while, Pete valiantly trying to lift my spirits by talking about a crazy girl he used to date, but I'd barely even listened, just nodded vaguely. Eventually, I'd said I had to leave and Pete had walked me outside and even offered to walk me down to the ferry, but I'd shaken my head and thanked him and went on my way, the cool evening air and the walk through the city alone all that I'd wanted.

I checked the time on my phone and saw that it was 5.26 am. For a minute I pressed my arm over my face, trying to block out the black thoughts creeping through my brain. I'd been doing so well up until that point, really getting past things and getting on with my life. But I could feel that despair beginning to snake its way through my chest again.

I knew the sun would be rising soon, and it wasn't like I was sleeping anyway, so I got up. I quietly padded my way into the kitchen in my pyjamas, my stomach feeling empty and hollow. I hadn't eaten dinner the previous night, and even though I still wasn't hungry, I knew I should force something down.

As I went about making myself some toast and a cup of tea, the sky outside began to lighten. The kettle had just finished boiling when I heard another bedroom door open down the hall, and a moment later Ben appeared looking sleepy, his pyjama pants as crinkled and fuzzy as his hair.

"Morning," he said, yawning.

"Morning," I replied. "You're up early,"

"I was going to say the same thing about you."

"Yeah, couldn't sleep. You want a cup of tea?"

"Nah, I'll grab a coffee," Ben moved around me and started getting the coffee out while I spread strawberry jam onto my toast.

"You working today?" I asked.

"Yep, got a job out at Alexandria. Need to be there by half-past seven."

I moved around the bench and slid into one of the bar stools with my breakfast. "What sort of job is it?"

"Studio job for a fashion company."

"Really?" I perked up, my interest genuinely sparked. "What company?"

"Can't remember," Ben said, yawning and scratching his head.

"You're such a boy." I rolled my eyes.

"They're all the same." Ben shrugged. "My mate Reggie is in charge of the job. He does the camera work and directs."

"I'd love to go on a film set." I sighed wistfully. "I'd have no idea how to get involved with anything like that, though."

"It's pretty easy once you're in. It all just comes down to knowing people really." Ben put some more bread in the toaster. "Most of my work all comes through friends and connections now."

"Did you have to do much training to be an audio engineer? And was it hard getting started, or getting 'in' as you say?"

"I did a certificate at a private college. To be honest, though, you can learn it all on the job. As I said, it all comes down to word of mouth and knowing people."

"Too bad I don't know any directors," I said, taking a big bite of toast.

"Hey, you know me, and I know lots of people. What sort of stuff would you want to do on a set?"

I scrunched up my nose, thinking and chewing, before swallowing the mouthful. "Honestly? I have no idea. I love looking at cinematography and sets and landscapes and things. Or maybe I just like the idea of travelling around to different places."

Ben looked thoughtful for a minute, but before he could answer his phone started ringing from down the hall and he disappeared back to his room to answer it. Left alone in the kitchen, I stared down into my tea and let my imagination wander.

How cool would it be to work on film sets? Being surrounded by actors and directors, or just watching the cameraman work. Even getting involved, being an assistant and just helping out everywhere. I'd always imagined that sort of thing as one of those fantasy dream jobs. Something that only made-up people did, or hugely creative people. And yet Ben seemed so normal. He was just a regular guy who got to do that sort of cool stuff for work.

While I sat in a financial office in the city looking at spreadsheets all day. At what point had I even *made* the decision that was what I wanted to do with my life? If I was being honest, I used to think that I *was* a creative person. I used to dabble a bit with painting and sketching, making artworks that Mum valiantly hung in the hallway for a few years before they were relegated to being stored and forgotten under the bed. There were those few years when Mum and Dad bought a family video camera for Christmas and then I'd spent heaps of time forcing Elle to star in my movie shoots, making our own music videos or coming up with play ideas that we'd turn into movies. One of our favourite things to do was film our own versions of TV commercials, selling random household products in comedic ways. It might have even been the lingering memory of making those fake commercials that had led me to study marketing and advertising at uni. Well, that, and the fact that Jack had thought it was a good option. A good career move, he'd said, back when we were choosing our university preferences and I had no idea what to do.

I felt that weight of sadness press down on me again. Thinking about my past inevitably led me to thinking about Jack. He'd been such a big part of my life, had been the main actor for so many years that now all my memories were tainted.

I glanced outside and saw that the sun had risen, early-morning sunlight bathing the balcony. I picked up my tea and the rest of my toast and went to sit outside, not needing to get ready for work for another hour.

The image of Jack dancing in that studio appeared in my mind again, as vivid as if he was right in front of me. Then it wasn't him dancing that I was seeing, it was his face, looking at me, smiling and laughing and sitting beside me.

Somebody that I used to know.

As if on cue, the lyrics to Gotye's famous song swam through my mind. *How accurate those words were*, I thought. And yet I was the one that had cut Jack off, wasn't I? I was the one who'd told him I didn't want to stay friends, didn't want to attempt to keep in touch. Sorting out the house and the finances was one thing, but my parents had been able to step in and do most of that for me. Jack had probably felt too guilty to fight me for anything, and on the flip side I hadn't really *wanted* anything that would remind me of our relationship.

So, why was it bothering me now that I didn't know him? Because that was what was getting under my skin—the fact that Jack had looked like a completely different person in that dance studio. He'd looked carefree and confident and just so comfortable with himself. So different to how I'd last seen him.

It struck me that I simply didn't know who he was anymore. That boy that I'd started dating when I was fifteen, the guy I'd grown up with who used to tell me everything, I suddenly didn't know. Since when did he dance? Since when was he in the city on weekdays? What had happened with his life in the past six months?

Jack used to be the one person who knew me best. I used to be the person that knew *him* best. I'd cut myself off from him, thinking it was the right decision for myself. But was it?

Was I moving forward with my life? Or was I just hiding?

ᏻᏝ

I was in a terrible mood all day at work. My confusion—sadness, or whatever it was that'd kept me awake all night—had morphed into a shitty, angry cloud. I was annoyed that I'd seen Jack. I was annoyed that Jack had looked so happy. I was annoyed that seeing Jack looking happy was making me annoyed. And then I was super annoyed at myself for letting it all get to me.

I know—total drama queen, right? But whatever. No matter how much I tried to block it out, it wasn't working. And my work keyboard was taking a total beating in response.

*Input formula. Smash, smash, SMASH on the keyboard. No, that's wrong. It's WRONG! Delete everything! DELETE!!!*

I sighed and leaned back in my chair. I really shouldn't be taking things out on the keyboard. It wasn't a subtle way to vent my frustration. Belinda had even peered over the partition a few hours earlier to ask if everything was alright. Well no, Belinda, no, everything was certainly not alright! But I didn't say that. I'd just glared at her and smiled tightly and snapped back that yes, everything was perfectly peachy, I just had a headache.

I probably shouldn't have yelled at Olive, the marketing junior, in the tea room, either. But really, I just needed to get some hot water for my afternoon tea, and there she was in there, talking to Bonnie from design, and they were gushing all over Olive's new engagement ring and her wedding plans. I mean really, she'd only known her boyfriend for eight months and they were engaged already! Plus, she was only twenty-one! That was just ridiculous— she barely knew the guy. And she was going on and on about how perfect he was, and what a lovely proposal it was, and how she couldn't wait to marry him, and should she get a strapless wedding dress or something with lace sleeves like Princess Kate wore? Let's be honest, *anyone* would have told her that she needed to stop and have a good think about whether or not she was making the right decision. Although, perhaps my advice came out sounding a little condescending. Because Olive and Bonnie's expressions did look a bit fiery when I left.

But as I said, whatever. It hadn't even made me feel better, being able to impart my wisdom on someone so young and stupid.

Five-thirty rolled around, and then so did 6 pm and then 6.30. I was still in the office, trying to get some work finished. I think I was also just feeling kind of listless and annoyed still. I didn't want to go home. I couldn't be bothered walking down to the ferry. I just wanted to sit in my office chair and make the stupid spreadsheet work properly. Because at least that was something I could fix. This spreadsheet *would* obey me.

"You're here late," said a voice behind me, making me jump.

I turned around and saw Pete standing there, dwarfing everything around him, looking curiously at my desk.

"So, this is where you work," he said, nodding as he took in all the random crap I had stuck up in my work station.

"What are you doing up here? Shouldn't you be at the gym by now?" I asked.

"I wish." Pete rolled his eyes. "Got stuck in a meeting with some of the sales managers. And then they sent me up here to give this folder to Cara, but I have no idea where her office is."

"Yeah, she's gone already."

"So how are things?" Pete asked, leaning an arm on my partition. I hoped it wouldn't break.

"What do you mean?" I asked innocently.

"You know. You seemed pretty upset yesterday."

"Oh right, that. Yes, sorry about that. I just was a bit surprised."

"Feeling better today?"

*No.* "Yes." I forced myself to smile. "Much better."

"Cool. So, can you show me where Cara's office is?"

I had to suppress a sigh. None of this was Pete's fault, after all. Plus, he'd been incredibly nice to me with all the training. The least I could do was help him out.

I led Pete over to Cara's office and hovered by the door while he put the folder in her in-tray. He was goofing around a bit, obviously trying to make me laugh, and it was rather infectious. I felt my lips twitching, my bad mood starting to dissipate.

"Are you going to give me a tour of the marketing floor now?" Pete teased. "I am still new, after all."

"You're hardly new anymore!" I countered, rolling my eyes. "But sure, I can give you a tour. Though, it's nowhere near as exciting as the sales floor."

"I hear there's leftover giveaway stuff and free shit all over the place up here?"

I laughed. "Yeah, if Tiger Finance–branded post-its and pens are your idea of cool freebies, then there are plenty of those."

I showed him around the floor, even though it was deserted, and gave vague indications of where various teams sat.

"And here is our awesome tea room," I said, heading into the pokey little kitchen.

"Ours is way bigger downstairs," Pete said, taking up about eighty percent of the available space in the kitchen.

"I told you level four was way cooler."

There was a pause in the conversation and I noted that I was stuck in the kitchen since Pete blocked the whole doorway. God, he really was big, wasn't he?

"You'll have to move if you want the tour to continue," I said, putting a hand on my hip and huffing dramatically.

"Aww, surely you're strong enough to barge past me now." Pete challenged. "What have you been doing all those weights for?"

"I'm totally strong enough!" I said and made to shove him out of the way.

He raised his eyebrows at me.

Okay, it was totally game on. Good thing I was in a fighting mood.

Narrowing my eyes, I leaned my whole body weight on him, trying to make him budge, but he barely even moved.

"Come on, you can do better than that!" he said.

"You're super heavy!" I tried pushing harder.

"You need to tense your stomach muscles," Pete said, and poked at my sides.

That just made me squirm and laugh, though, so I poked his sides, and to my delight this did actually make him jerk away and squirm.

"So, tickling makes you move, then?" I went in with two hands, trying to poke and tickle his sides, possibly a bit more aggressively than intended.

"Hey—hey!" Pete was laughing as he blocked me, and then he was tickling me again. And honestly, that aggression, that weird, tickle fighting, it was exactly what I needed.

For a second, we were both squealing and laughing and trying to poke at each other's sides, and then Pete managed to catch both my hands in his large, meaty, iron-fisted ones.

And then we were kissing.

*Okay—whoa!* How did that happen? My eyes were squeezed shut and I was standing a little stiffly, but that was possibly also because I was having to do an almighty backward head bend. And it was a bit weird, because there wasn't any of that electric-feeling stuff that had happened when Tinder-boy Darren or Derek Windsor kissed me. But then, was that just because we were in the work kitchen?

Because Pete was attractive, right? He was hot, wasn't he?

If we went by Rose's opinion, *she* certainly thought he was hot. And Rose had good taste. Therefore, he must be hot.

So, why did us making out in the kitchen feel really surreal and kind of non-personal? I felt like I was having one of those out-of-body experiences. Like I was floating up high somewhere, on the roof of the tea room, looking down at a weird puppet-version of myself who was kissing Pete and doing all the right things—the things you'd expect someone to do in that situation—but I wasn't really connected to it.

Maybe because I was still thinking about Jack? But then no, look at that—the thought of Jack was making puppet me more passionate. Or aggressive. Either way, I was pressing forcefully against Pete and raking my nails down his back. It was almost like angry kissing. Like the more aggressively I could kiss Pete, the more I could drive stupid Jack and his weird happy dancing out of my mind.

Because Pete was *straight*. And look at this, Jack—a straight, hot guy was making out with your wife. And he was actually attracted to her. To me. See—*someone* found me attractive.

Oh Lord, I was going nuts.

I snapped back into myself and suddenly Pete's face was right THERE smooshed into mine. I quickly broke away, gasping for air.

Pete smiled lazily down at me, his eyes smouldering.

"Well, that was, um, probably not appropriate for the workplace!" I laughed skittishly, taking a step back.

"Yeah," Pete agreed. "Lucky we're the last ones up here."

"So, I've got to …"

"Yes, I should get back, too."

Okay, good. At least we were both feeling slightly awkward.

I straightened my top as we left the tea room, Pete tucking his shirt back in and grinning at me slyly sideways. I smiled back, but it felt fake. My stomach felt hollow, empty.

"See you later." Pete gave me a knowing kind of look as we parted directions, like he was saying, "We'll definitely be doing that again."

Once Pete had gone, I sagged. What was wrong with me? Shouldn't I be feeling elated and happy? I mean, I just made out with the cute guy at work, the "hot guy from sales" as he was known around the office. He'd made out with *me*, he'd wanted to hook up with *me*. But if anything, I was just feeling a bit ill.

At least all the fight had gone out of me. I no longer felt like murdering my keyboard. Instead, I shut it down nicely, giving the keyboard an apologetic little pat. Then I picked up my bag and made my way out of the office, heading for home.

# 23

It was dark when I got on the ferry. At least being late, the ferry was less crowded than usual. I took a seat in a back corner where I could stare out at the dark night and the lights along the headlands sailing past. I wondered what the lives of the people in the houses and apartments I passed were like? Were they all easy and happy? Or did they feel shitty and lost, like I did?

My mind was still reeling from what had just happened with Pete in the work kitchen. Part of me couldn't believe I'd just made out with him. I didn't feel triumphant and excited like I did after going home with Derek Windsor. Even with Darren—well, aside from the weird tart thing—I at least felt *good* after that encounter.

What was wrong with me?

My thoughts turned again to Jack. To how happy he'd looked. How joyous and comfortable and free. Just the *confidence* of him.

I felt tears prick at my eyes, and I hastily blinked them away. How was any of this fair? He was the one who was meant to be lost, meant to not know who he was. *He* should be the one crying on a ferry, not me. But he wasn't crying at all, was he? That guy I'd seen dancing—he hadn't looked lost at all. He'd looked happy.

Which was so different to when I'd last seen him. How he'd been that day—how he'd acted—when he'd shattered the illusion of our marriage and revealed a truth that I wasn't expecting and struggled to accept. I felt as if I was back in that place, all over again. That sad wreck of a person who had existed in the few months after that conversation.

I hadn't even left straightaway. For the rest of that weekend, I'd wandered around our house in a daze. Jack had been there, too, sort of following me, sort of giving me space. Ready to jump in, to keep talking, to discuss the logistics of how we needed to leave each other.

It was Louise who finally broke my stupor. After two days of wondering around feeling numb, Louise had suddenly turned up. Jack must have called her. We sat on the patio and I cried. A lot. Louise made me tea. She wrapped a blanket around my shoulders and rubbed my back. And then she spoke calmly about the things I needed to do. How things would need to proceed from here.

Remembering Louise—how nice she'd been and what a good friend she was that day—brought a whole new wave of guilt over me. How had I let things fall out between us? We'd been friends since high school. Why had I shut her out? All that silliness about the "incident". What did it even matter? In the long run, what did any of that matter?

I called Louise later that night.

"Laura? Hello!" came her bubbly voice over the phone. I wasn't sure how I'd been expecting her to sound—sad, or suspicious maybe? But she sounded genuinely happy to hear from me.

"Lou, hi, how are you?" I said, feeling a huge rush of relief.

"I'm fantastic! Really, really good. How about you?"

"I'm great as well!" I said positively. "Everything is really good here."

It was like nothing had even happened between us, wasn't it? Like we were just talking the way things used to be, all notion of the "incident" forgotten. Our conversation turned to polite chitchat about how things were going for a few minutes, but soon there was an awkward pause and I knew I needed to raise the topic.

"Look, Lou, I just wanted to say I'm really sorry about what happened, you know, last time I saw you," I said.

"Oh, Laura, don't even mention it!" Louise replied. "*I'm* sorry. I shouldn't have dragged you off to go baby shopping with me after ... well, after what you were going through."

"I had no right to speak to you that way," I said, still feeling awful. "I should have been able to put everything behind me and just be happy for you."

"No, Laura, I should have been more caring about what *you* were going through. It wasn't fair of me."

We both chuckled skittishly, probably in relief, and I knew that our fight was over.

"So, how is the pregnancy going?' I asked after a moment.

"It's so strange!" Louise said. "I've got this giant stomach now, and I've still got a few weeks to go! I'm terrified to think how much bigger I'm going to get! Honestly, pregnancy is really quite awful. I miss wine terribly, and brie, and there are so many things I can't do now ..." Louise trailed off and I found myself smiling. I knew she was talking it down to make me feel better.

"Listen, Laura," Louise said, suddenly sounding uncertain. "I ... um ... well, I hadn't asked you because we hadn't spoken, and I wasn't sure if you'd want to come or to see me. But it's my baby shower this weekend, and I'd really love for you to come. Only if you want to, of course—no pressure or anything!"

My stomach clenched involuntarily. Louise was having a baby shower and she hadn't invited me? I really had been a terrible friend.

"I'd love to come," I said.

"Good," Louise sounded relieved. "I mean, I wasn't sure …".

"Oh, don't worry about me, I'm totally fine now!" I said, my voice sounding a little too high even to my own ears. "But anyway, how is Simon?"

Our conversation veered off for a little while into stories about Louise's husband and our families. Eventually, we hung up after Louise said Simon was waiting for her to watch the next episode of their latest Netflix show.

Only after we'd ended the call, and I was sitting in my room alone, did I really think about what it would mean to go to Louise's baby shower. It wasn't that I didn't want to see Louise. I could even deal with seeing her happy, perfect life, her loving, doting husband with her. I could deal with the fact that I'd basically be looking in through a window on a life that I thought I'd be having.

But no, it wasn't that which suddenly bothered me. It was the fact that I'd be seeing all those other people—old friends of Jack's and mine, who'd no doubt be there. People I hadn't seen since before our separation. People who'd attended my wedding and who'd watched as Jack and I said vows to each other.

People who quite possibly knew more about Jack's current life than I did. What would they say to me? Would they ask me about Jack? Or worse, just start talking about his life as if I was fully across it?

# 24

I'd made a decision. I wasn't sure if it was the *right* decision. But it was likely to happen sooner or later, wasn't it? So I might as well just dive right in and get it over with.

I was going to meet Jack for lunch.

As the lift doors closed in the Tiger Finance building and I started descending to the ground floor, I tried to control my breathing. It was Friday, only four days since I'd seen Jack dancing at the gym, and now I was meeting him for lunch.

Oh my God, *why* was lunch even happening?

The thought had been chasing itself around and around my mind ever since I'd sent him that initial text the previous day. Did I seriously want to see him? *Surely*, I thought, *I should just turn around, go back to my desk and cancel the whole thing.*

But then, a small part of me *did* want to see him. I wanted to see his face up close, to see if it looked the same. I wanted to know what he'd been up to since we parted. At the very least, I felt it was information I needed to know before I saw Louise and all my old acquaintances at her baby shower. Plus, as I kept telling myself, I'd probably have to see him again in another few months when we were finally able to apply for a legal divorce.

The lift arrived in the lobby and I trailed behind everyone else as we exited the building, my hand gripping tightly around the straps of my handbag. I forced myself to take steady, calming breaths as I walked down the street towards the chosen restaurant. My steps were slow, and I felt other people hurrying around me, but I couldn't seem to walk any faster. The restaurant was close to my work anyway, so there was only so long I could delay getting there.

Le Café was located on a street corner, a beautiful French-style restaurant with little Parisian tables and chairs spilling out onto the street, perfectly manicured pot plants along the pavement and a bright-red awning over the door.

Despite my reluctance, I was a couple of minutes early when I arrived. The restaurant looked deceptively cheerful and happy from the outside. It was the kind of place people met for business lunches or stylish morning teas. It certainly didn't look like the kind of place where you met up with your ex.

Pushing back my shoulders, I made my way inside and straightaway my stomach jolted in shock—Jack was there already. He was wearing a business suit, one of the same ones he used to wear, sitting at a table by the window. For a second it felt like nothing had changed, that we were still together and I was simply meeting him for a casual lunch. His dark hair was slicked back off his face the way he'd always styled it for work, and for a moment I was transported to our old little house, seeing him as he used to walk in the door in the evenings.

Then he looked up and spotted me, and a strange mix of emotions flashed across his face—surprise first, then a cautious, closed-off look immediately afterwards. And that made me remember that we weren't together anymore. He was not in love with me, or even attracted to me.

*Okay, Laura, focus.* I was the one who'd set up this lunch. I was the one who'd wanted to catch up. So I needed to act like an adult.

I pulled myself up to my full height and walked over to him, plastering my best professional smile on my face. I figured that if I just pretended he was a business contact and that we were meeting for a business lunch, like most other people in the restaurant, then it wouldn't be so awkward.

"Jack, hi!" I said, overly perky, and gave him a brief kiss on the cheek as he stood to meet me. I could see he was stunned as I pulled away, but I couldn't do anything about my overt cheeriness—it was masking the fact that I was shaking.

I took my seat and he followed suit, sitting again.

"Have you been here long?" I asked.

"No, not long, I was a bit early," Jack said quickly.

"It's a nice place this, isn't it?" I indicated the restaurant in general. "I haven't been here before."

Honestly, I was acting like we really were just business contacts rather than a recently separated couple in their first post-split meeting.

"Yes, it's great," Jack said, and I saw him relax more. At least things were civil, if a little formal.

"And how are you? Is … is everything good?" I asked, belatedly hoping he wouldn't jump into anything heavy.

"Yes, I'm good, all good," Jack said, babbling a bit himself. "How about you? How are you doing?"

"Oh, I'm great! Really, really great …" I trailed off and silence stretched between us.

Shit, things were getting awkward already. Why had I wanted to do this again? It certainly wasn't so we could make weird, polite conversation for the next hour.

I took a deep breath and looked up. "So, do you—" I started to say.

"I'm so glad—" Jack said at the same time.

We both stopped and smiled sheepishly at each other.

"You go," I said.

"I was just going to say that I'm so glad you wanted to meet up again,"

Jack said. "I still feel so bad about what happened with us. I really never meant to hurt you, Laura."

I felt my stomach twist uncomfortably and I was forced to look down. "Yes, well," I mumbled, not sure what to say. Should I get angry? Or sad?

"You were my best friend for so long," Jack continued quietly. "And I loved you—I really did love you, you know that don't you? That wasn't … I mean, I wasn't pretending with that or anything."

Oh God, this was really not what I wanted to hear him say. I mean, it'd been nearly seven months since we'd split. I didn't need to hear all this again. I gathered my strength and looked up.

"I know," I said. "It just was what it was."

Jack nodded, looking earnest.

"Anyway," I changed the subject, "we don't need to talk about what happened. That was all … well, I've dealt with that. That's not why I wanted to meet up."

"Okay." Jack nodded in agreement and I felt my stomach begin to unknot.

A waitress suddenly appeared beside us. "Are you ready to order?"

I quickly scanned the menu and ordered the French onion soup, not sure I'd be able to handle anything else, and a glass of water. Jack ordered a steak and then the waitress walked away.

"So," Jack said shyly.

"So," I said, attempting a smile. "I saw you in that UNLEASH gym the other day. In a dance class?"

To my surprise, Jack turned red. "Yes … ah, I've been going there quite a bit," he said. "I didn't think I knew anyone who went to that gym."

I grinned, taking a huge amount of pleasure from Jack's embarrassment. "I've been training there a bit lately. With a guy from work," I added.

"Oh really?" Jack looked curious. "Is he … ah, your boyfriend?"

"Oh no, no!" I shook my head vehemently, horrified that Jack would think that. "He's definitely not my boyfriend. He's, well, just a friend. How about you? Do you have a ... um ... a boyfriend?"

Oh shit, why did I ask that? Of course I didn't want to know that. I braced myself as Jack opened his mouth to answer.

"Sort of. I mean, it's very new," Jack said softly.

I felt my smile freeze to my face. Shit. SHIT! Jack had a *boyfriend*? I had no idea how to process this information. I wanted him to stop talking now.

"No one you know, don't worry, just a guy I met ... but well, yeah I've been seeing someone."

Oh. My. God.

"But we shouldn't talk about that. I mean, it's a strange conversation," Jack continued hurriedly, obviously spotting my expression.

"Right, no, I mean yes," I said, unfreezing. "Let's talk about something else. I mean, so long as you're happy, that's the main thing."

"I am happy," Jack said, leaning forward and looking at me intensely. "Really, Laura, it's hard to explain it. I was happy when we were together, don't get me wrong. But now it's different. It's like I'm one hundred percent happy, whereas before there was a tiny percent of me that knew something was wrong."

I nodded my head mutely, unable to find words to reply. So, it was confirmed, then. Jack truly had found happiness.

Our lunch arrived at that moment, and I gratefully took the opportunity to lean back in my chair, as if I could physically distance myself. Once the waitress had left I stared down into my soup, hoping the smell of my lunch would ground me.

"So, anyway," Jack said, drawing my attention back to him. "I just wanted you to know that. That I ... well that I feel like I'm in the right place now."

I nodded again and lifted a tentative spoonful of soup to my mouth. Even though I knew rationally it was probably delicious, I struggled to swallow.

"But enough about me. Tell me about you," Jack said. "Are you ha—I mean, how are you?"

Jack was about to ask if I was happy but then backed out of the question, didn't he? Did he think I was an unhappy mess? Could he *see* that? I was sure my facial expressions weren't helping right then.

I forced myself to sit up straighter, drawing my professional mask on again. Just because I may have been in a place of uncertainty with my life, Jack didn't need to know that.

"I'm good, Jack, don't worry about me," I said, making sure I didn't overdo it on the fake this time so I sounded believable. "And I am happy. At least, I'm a lot happier than I was a few months ago."

Jack nodded. "I'm glad. You deserve to be happy."

That constricting feeling gripped my stomach again. "But anyway!" I said, desperately needing to change the subject. "Tell me, what are you doing in the city during the week? And why are you now going to a city gym?"

"Oh, yes, I transferred to the CBD office. It's a lot easier for me now as it's closer to where I live."

"Where are you living?"

"Just near here, actually. I have a studio place near Chinatown."

"Seriously? Wow, that's, um, that's great."

"Yeah, a friend helped me find it."

"Do you still keep in touch with anyone?"

The conversation turned to our old friends, whom we had seen, whom we hadn't seen and any gossip we'd heard about them. It was a good change. I think both of us untensed as we veered away from personal topics. There was even a moment when we both started genuinely laughing as Jack told me about how one of our old friends had started dating a self-proclaimed cougar.

While we were talking I felt myself genuinely start to relax, lulled by familiar topics. Weirdly, I realised, this was what I missed the most about our relationship. The nights when we'd go out for dinner or sit at home with a glass of wine, just talking. I found myself appraising Jack over the table; examining his forearm beneath his rolled-up sleeve, the curve of his neck and Adam's apple. Strangely, even though I used to lie next to him every night, our bodies pressed against each other and my head resting in that curve between his shoulder and neck, he didn't seem familiar anymore. Nor did I find myself *drawn* to him like I used to.

It hit me as he was recounting a story about his sister. He was talking animatedly, the way I used to love watching him talk, but there was something different about how I was seeing him. I was no longer attracted to him.

Yes! That was *it*. I was no longer *attracted* to him.

And, for the first time, it was like I was seeing something fundamentally *gay* about him. Like when you do one of those magic eye puzzles, and the picture that was there all along suddenly snaps into focus.

God, how had I not seen it before?

A strange calmness settled over me after my revelation. I suddenly didn't feel scared, or nervous, or worried about what Jack thought of me. And after days of my stomach being twisted in knots, I felt it relax properly.

Our conversation turned to our new apartments and what the neighbourhoods were like, followed by how our families were doing. And I found myself laughing and smiling—actually properly smiling—and enjoying myself. Before I knew it, our lunch was finished and Jack was looking at his watch, saying he'd best get back to the office.

I checked my watch, too—shit! I'd been gone for well over an hour.

We split the bill then walked outside together, pausing on the pavement before leaving. The sun was warm on my face and I looked up momentarily to savour it.

"It was so good seeing you," Jack said, smiling at me again.

"Yes, it was good to see you, too," I said, genuinely meaning it.

"Let me know if you want to do this again. I can't believe how much I've missed talking to you," Jack said, looking hopeful.

"Yes, maybe. I'll let you know."

"Okay. Well, bye."

"Bye."

We hovered awkwardly for a second, as if not sure if we should hug or kiss. Then, chuckling, I leaned in and kissed Jack on the cheek again.

"Bye," I repeated, then we both turned and walked in opposite directions, heading back to our respective offices.

** TINDER ALERT **
Congratulations! You have a new match!

** TINDER ALERT **
**New Message: Guy, 26**
*Hey, want to come over and sit on my face? :P*

[User Unmatched]

** FACEBOOK ALERT **
**Elle Baker uploaded 10 new photos to the Album Bolivia:**
*Shenanigans at the salt flats* ♡
– with Marrika Bentley and 3 others.

** NEW MESSAGE **
**From: Mum at 1.36 pm**
*Hi, darling! Dad and I are going to the RSL for dinner tonight if you want to come too. We haven't seen you in weeks! I'm sure Eric will be there working and he'd love to see you. I could put in a word for you if you can't make it?* 😉 😍

# 25

I still had the strange, light feeling coursing through me as I walked back into the office.

I didn't find Jack attractive anymore.

The realisation was probably one of the most amazing things I'd ever felt. My whole life, my whole adult life anyway, had always been connected to Jack. Even in the last few months when he hadn't been there, it was as if there was still a link that attached us. There was an emptiness in my heart where something was missing.

But it was no longer there.

I didn't know what I was expecting to feel when I saw Jack again. I'd probably been terrified that I was going to be dragged back to that same horrible place I'd been lost in when he had first told me he was leaving. But it hadn't been like that at all. It was like I could suddenly look at Jack and realise that we hadn't been the perfect couple, and that actually I didn't need him beside me.

"Laura?"

Cara's voice right behind me made me jump, and I realised, belatedly, that I'd been sitting in a daze, my computer still on standby mode since I'd left for lunch almost two hours previously.

"Hi, Cara." I turned around and smiled blandly at her.

Her eyes flicked to my screen and I saw annoyance trace over her face. "Do you have a moment?" Cara said, and indicated that I should follow her.

*Shit.* I knew I was going to get told off, and rightly so. I'd been gone for two hours for lunch—again. As I followed Cara to her office, I was running through excuses in my head. I couldn't say I'd had another "appointment", I'd already used that excuse too many times. Or could I? Should I pretend I had some terrible health problem and I needed specialist treatments? But no, that would be too dramatic. Plus, she might ask for a doctor's certificate or something.

"Please shut the door," Cara said as we entered her office, moving around to take the seat behind her desk.

My heart started beating skittishly, but I did as requested and then slid into the visitor seat on the other side of her desk.

"Firstly, how are you going with the third quarter reports?" Cara asked, her voice neutral.

Oh no, the *reports*. They'd been on my to-do list for weeks, but I'd been putting them off. I mean, monthly reports were bad enough, but *quarterly* reports ... they were probably the least favourite part of my job.

"I've made a good start on them," I lied, forcing a cheerful smile. "I thought they weren't due for another week?"

"They aren't, but I was hoping you'd have them ready a lot sooner than that," Cara said. "To be honest, Laura, I'm a bit worried about you."

"What do you mean?" I could feel my face flushing, my smile faltering.

"You used to be right on top of the ball, always having things finished ahead of schedule and impeccably checked. You were one of my star performers. But I've noticed you slipping lately. Many of the reports you've sent me have errors, they're either late or coming in right at the eleventh hour, and I'm not sure if I'm imagining things, but you seem to be hardly ever at your desk anymore. Is something going on with you that I need to know about?"

Oh God, I hadn't realised things had become so bad! Or rather, I knew that my work had become pretty poor, but I didn't realise it'd become *noticeably* bad. Should I pull out the sickness thing, after all?

"I'm so sorry, Cara," I said, forcing myself to meet her eyes. "It's just that I'm ... well, I'm still trying to sort things out with my ex. And you know ... the divorce."

I hated myself as soon as I'd said it. *Look at you*, the little voice in my head admonished, *still blaming your separation almost seven months later*. Cara at least did know most details about my marriage breakdown and my subsequent personal meltdown. But that had all been months ago; things should've been back to normal. In fact, I'd had a special meeting with HR after all my time off so that everyone could make sure I was fit to return to work. And yet here I was, throwing the divorce thing around like it was new again. The funniest part about it was that for the first time since I'd separated from Jack, I felt like I was actually starting to move on.

Cara nodded, her expression carefully blank. "I know what you're going through must be very difficult, Laura, but when these things start interfering with your work—and your attitude to your co-workers—then we have a problem."

My mind flashed back to earlier that week—snapping at Belinda, yelling at Olive in the tea room. Who'd dobbed me in about that? Weren't we women allowed to have one moody, emotional day every now and then? I mean as far as they all knew, I could have been going through the worst PMS of my life! Surely they could've given me a little leeway?

I dropped my gaze in embarrassment, feeling my face heat up again. "I'm not sure what you're talking about," I mumbled.

"Do you really not?" Cara looked at me sternly.

I took a deep breath. "I might have been having a ... a really tough day earlier this week. I may have acted a little ... unprofessionally."

Cara watched me for a moment then nodded. "We all have bad days now and then. When things start creeping into our professional lives, sometimes we just need to take a step back," Cara said kindly. "Now, is there anything else going on that I should know about? Anything besides what you're going through in your personal life?" Cara asked.

I shook my head. "No, everything else is fine," I said. "I'll have that quarterly report done by the end of the week."

Cara nodded again, and I knew I'd said the right thing. "Good. I'll expect to see an improvement with your work."

I forced myself to smile before standing up to leave.

"And, Laura?" Cara called.

I paused with my hand on the door.

"If anything does come up, or you are having any personal issues, you know my door is always open. Make sure you let me know if anything is interfering with your work life."

I nodded before vanishing from her office.

*Damn. Damn, bugger and damn.*

I mentally kicked myself as I returned to my desk. There I was thinking that I was finally working through things, and work had given me a big kick up the bum.

I opened up a blank spreadsheet template to start the third quarter report but found myself just staring blankly at the page. For a while, I felt like I was having another one of those weird, dissociative moments. I felt like I was sitting up on the ceiling, looking down at a puppet version of myself at my desk. And the real me was up there somewhere thinking, *What are you doing, Laura? What are you really doing?*

# 26

"Which fragrance are you?" Kalina asked in a fake presenter-type voice.

"Oh gosh, my life won't be complete until I find out!" I replied dramatically.

"Quizzes used to be far more entertaining than this." Kalina sighed, dropping the magazine next to her on the sand and draping her arm across her face.

We were lying on the beach at Fairlight, soaking up the gloriously warm sunshine on what was an unusually hot spring Saturday.

Kalina sighed again and rolled over onto her stomach, clearly restless. "Do you think you'll meet his boyfriend?" she asked me.

The previous evening, I'd told Kalina all about my lunch with Jack. We'd got stuck into a bottle of wine after dinner and I guess since I'd seen him that day and he was still on my mind, it had all just come tumbling out, details about Jack's boyfriend and all.

I scrunched up my nose thoughtfully. "No," I finally said, reaching my hand up to block out the sun. "I don't think we're even really friends now. It was just the one lunch."

"Didn't he say he wanted to do it again, though?"

"Yeah ... but that might have been him just being polite. As much as I didn't mind seeing him, I don't think I want us to become buddies."

"Fair enough."

We were silent for a while, the sounds of the beach around us. I was being lulled into a deliciously apathetic mood, and it'd been highly cathartic sharing all my Jack history stuff with Kalina.

"Do you think it's a serious relationship?" I asked after a moment, thinking about Jack and his boyfriend again.

"Who knows," Kalina replied. "Guys are weird. One minute they say they're not ready for a relationship, the next minute they're impregnating some poor girl and having a shotgun wedding."

"I don't think Jack will be impregnating some poor girl anytime soon."

"Nah, he'll just be enjoying another man's arsehole."

"Eww, Kalina!" I gave her a little slap on the arm. "I don't want to think about him having sex."

"What do you reckon, though?" Kalina grinned at me. "Do you think he's the dominant one or the submissive one?"

"Oh my God, I don't even know what you're talking about!"

"Like, does he do the giving or the receiving?"

I frowned in confusion. "I don't know. I assumed gay guys just sort of took it in turns. Don't they?"

Kalina laughed, and I put my arm over my face. "Stop it! I don't want to imagine Jack doing anything with anyone!"

"Is it weird or different, though? I mean, if Jack had just dumped you and had a new girlfriend, then obviously you wouldn't want to imagine that. Like him with another girl. But is it different 'cause it's a man?"

I took a moment to think about that. *Was* it different?

"I still have no idea," I replied eventually. "I just don't want to think about it. It's like being told you have to imagine your parents having sex. I don't want to go there!"

"Really?"

"What—you imagine your parents having sex?"

"Argh, no! Not that! But like, you know, the other thing. An ex."

"You don't have a gay ex," I said, looking at Kalina quizzically. "Do you?"

"No."

"But ..." I prompted.

"I have an ex that cheated on me," she said quietly. Then she plonked her face down onto her towel and covered her eyes with an arm.

For a moment I just looked at her. Kalina had never opened up about her past relationships. Well, aside from being very vocal about *not* having relationships. Even the night before, we'd spent so long talking about Jack and me, and no time talking about Kalina and her men.

"What happened?" I asked gently.

After a moment, Kalina propped herself up on her elbows again. "Usual story. Was living with my boyfriend. Thought we were totally in love, that he was totally the one and all that. Then found out he was cheating on me."

"Shit. Were you together long?"

"Four years."

My eyes widened. How had I not known Kalina had been in such a long-term relationship before?

"That sucks," I said, trying to think of something better to offer.

Kalina sighed again and rolled over onto her back. "It was my best friend," she murmured.

"I know how you feel. Jack was my best friend, too. It's like losing everything in one fell swoop."

"No, I mean it was my best friend sleeping with him," Kalina said, laughing at my misinterpretation. "Apparently, they'd been sleeping together pretty much the whole time. Always behind my back."

"Oh my God!" I said, shocked and indignant now. "What, for four years?"

"Something like that." Kalina shrugged.

"What arseholes! Not only your boyfriend, but your friend, too!"

"I know, right? Just goes to show. Don't trust anyone. You'll just end up getting stabbed in the back. Or the heart. Or both."

I stared up at my hand blocking out the sun again, a dark outline haloed in blinding light. A sense of sadness washed over me—not only for what had happened to Kalina, but for how it had affected her. But she was right in a way, wasn't she? The same thing had happened to me. You trust someone, give them your whole heart, your soul. And they just shatter it.

"Anyway," Kalina continued. "That's why it's so much better not having any strings attached. You can't hurt anyone and they can't hurt you. Everyone wins."

"I totally agree." I said. "I'm only doing no-strings-attached things at the moment."

"Oh yes, and how are your 'things' going?" Kalina cocked an eyebrow at me.

"They're good."

"So, let's see. There's been the strawberry-tart-fetish guy, and Sydney playboy Derek Windsor who owned the sex swing. Have you had any *non-kinky* sex yet?"

"It wasn't ... I mean, I didn't know about Tinder Boy's tart fetish until afterwards," I protested. "And Derek Windsor has actually invited me around again. Well, sort of vaguely anyway."

"Uh-uh." Kalina looked at me sceptically.

"Oh, and I made out with a guy at work!" I said, suddenly remembering.

"Really?" Kalina sounded excited now. "You didn't tell me about that!"

"Yeah ..." I trailed off. "I think he's cute. At least my friend Rose thinks he's hot."

"Oh Lord, this isn't sounding promising."

I laughed. "No, I mean, he is hot. He is. He kinda looks like a footballer."

"Go on ..."

I shrugged.

"But?" Kalina prompted.

"I dunno. I'm not sure I'm really that *into* him, you know?"

Kalina laughed again. "This is classic."

"What would you do?" I asked her.

"Me? I'd totally sleep with him. I mean, if he's into me and I don't really care, well then great. He can do all the work."

I rolled my eyes at her. "You're terrible."

"Terribly good at having fun," she countered.

"So, how are *your* boys going? I haven't seen 'Maverick and the Lyricists' around much. And don't you have another one?"

"Who, Ethan?" Kalina rubbed her nose. "Yeah, I haven't seen him in a while. I should give him a call."

"Uh-uh," I repeated Kalina's earlier sceptical sound.

"The trouble is, there are just too many cute boys around," Kalina said, pressing her hand to her forehead dramatically.

"Like Ben's brother?" I grinned at her. "You never told me the story about him."

"Ah ... Ben's brother!" Kalina smiled up at the sun, using her hand to block it from her eyes like I was doing. "You'll have to meet him soon. He's such a hottie."

"How did the sleeping-with-him thing happen?"

"Oh, you know, the usual way. He was coming round a bit to see Ben, I got chatting to him." She winked at me. "That's all it takes."

"So, how come you didn't keep seeing him? Or sleeping with him, at least?"

Kalina shrugged. "Things just didn't really line up back then. He was going overseas. I'd only recently arrived in Australia. And I was still in my full-on man-hating phase."

"What, you're not in that phase now?"

"Ha-ha. Nah, I was all over the place. He was all over the place. What else can I say—one night of passion and then it was all over." She sighed dramatically.

"You're such a goose."

Kalina laughed softly. "Yeah," she agreed after a moment. "It's funny, but I always kind of think of him as the one that got away. You know, like if the timing had been different, then maybe we would actually have really hit it off."

We lapsed into silence for a while, and I turned her words over in my mind. I wondered what the real story was with Kalina and Ben's brother. It wasn't like he was a stranger that she'd never see again. In fact, she probably had seen him many times since their one-night fling. So, what had really happened? Had they just lapsed naturally into friendship instead? And if so, why did she talk about him with such a wistful tone in her voice?

Then again, if Ben's brother was about to open a bar and Kalina was going to go work there, then perhaps their romance would be rekindled?

"How long until the bar opens now?" I asked casually.

"The what?"

"The bar? You know, Ben's brother's bar. The one you're going to work at?"

"Oh, that! A few weeks still. Maybe three, I think?"

"That's pretty soon!"

Kalina shrugged. "It could be four?"

Huh. Well, whatever wistful note I'd imagined in her voice before had definitely disappeared. Maybe I was just imagining things, after all, and they were just friends now. Which was good. I mean, don't get me wrong, of course I wanted Kalina to be happy. But a horribly selfish part of me wanted her to stay single with me as well.

# 27

As I packed up my beach things, I realised that I'd completely forgotten to tell Kalina about Lucas. Not that there was anything to tell on that front—I'd messaged him five days ago, and he'd written back three days ago to say he was really flat out and couldn't meet up anytime soon. I couldn't even rouse any energy to feel disappointed by it at the time—I was still quietly obsessing over seeing Jack.

Kalina had already left to get ready for work, but it was still early afternoon and I didn't feel like going back to the empty flat by myself. Instead, I decided, I'd head down to the 4Pines, one of the local Manly pubs, and get myself a pint while I read my book.

I walked around the headland between Fairlight and Manly, a gorgeous walkway filled with people out dog-walking or wandering along between beaches. There were signs on the pavement indicating that we should all "watch out, penguins about", but despite my best efforts I didn't spot any penguins.

I dodged through the crowds of people near the ferry terminal and crossed the road, heading up the small staircase to the 4Pines main upstairs pub. It wasn't too busy inside, and after buying myself a pint of cider, I managed to nab a nice corner table outside on the balcony. Perfect.

For a minute I sat, enjoying the view and sipping my cider, while surreptitiously checking out all the other groups of people nearby. It was mostly hipster-types with neatly trimmed beards and board shorts, drinking beer and relaxing. The girls looked similar to me, with sandy feet and summer dresses, most looking like they'd just rolled in from the beach.

Smiling to myself, I took my book out of my bag and started to read. But barely ten minutes later, my mind was pulled back to the present abruptly when somebody slid onto the couch next to me. I looked up, startled, and was completely taken aback by who it was.

"Here you are, drinking on your own again," Lucas said, his disconcerting blue eyes sparkling at me.

Oh my—he was even hotter than I remembered him being. He had rough stubble across the lower half of his face, and his skin was tanned a deep golden colour, making his eyes appear more vibrant than they already were. There were barely a few centimetres between us, and as I inhaled sharply, the most delicious cologne hit my senses—a sort of earthy, smoky scent. I think my heart immediately went into overdrive.

"And here you are, stalking me again," I countered, telling myself that I must keep breathing. "Even though apparently, you have no time for casual drinks."

Lucas grinned. "Hey, I wasn't lying. I'm only here because it's a friend's birthday." He nodded towards the side of the pub, and I spotted his tattooed friend, Tom, amongst a small group of people.

"Are you here with anyone?" he asked.

"Nope. Just hanging by myself. Which I realise I seem to be always doing when I run into you."

"Aww, don't worry, I'm sure you have friends."

"Hey!" I gave him a playful push on the arm. Although, my hand *may* have lingered a bit too long on his bicep afterwards. "If someone wasn't so busy all the time, then maybe I wouldn't have to be here alone on a Saturday afternoon."

"I like that you're hanging alone at the pub on a Saturday." Lucas smiled again. "And as I said, friend's birthday. Prior commitments I just can't break. But since we are both here, why don't we have that drink right now? What can I get you?"

"Oh! Cider would be great, thanks. Here." I started fishing around in my bag for my purse, but Lucas shook his head.

"Don't worry about it," he said, getting up from the table and heading inside towards the bar.

As soon as he'd gone I felt a bit stunned, and I also became, just like last time, hyper-aware suddenly of everything around me. I glanced over to the group of friends he was with again. There was a pretty blonde girl in a lovely sundress and an attractive Japanese girl wearing the shortest shorts I'd ever seen also in the group now. They were talking and laughing with the guys there, and for a second I felt a stab of envy—was one of them here with Lucas? Were they friends with him? Was one of them angling to go home with him tonight?

"Here you go." Lucas suddenly appeared again, making me start. He put two drinks down on the table and slid the cider over towards me, then sat on the couch next to me once more.

"Thanks," I said, trying to squash the silly jealousy I'd started to feel. "So, aren't your friends going to wonder where you've disappeared off to?" I asked, taking a sip of my drink.

"Nope," Lucas said, glancing over at his group. "They can do without me for a while. Besides, I think we're all heading off to another pub soon."

"And you're going with them?"

"I will be," Lucas said, his eyes on mine.

"That's a shame. It might have been nice being able to hang out with you tonight."

He shifted, and then our legs were pressing together, causing my breath to catch.

"That might have been nice," he said, and his eyes were looking at me intensely.

I raised an eyebrow. "You know, you *do* have my number in your phone. It would only take one call and we could actually be hanging out together. You know, intentionally."

A small smile crept across his mouth. "Maybe I'm better at being sensible when I'm not around you."

"What am I, toxic or something?" I asked, feeling incredulous. "You really need to stop sending mixed signals."

He laughed softly. "Okay, let me ask you a question, then. What is it that you're after? From me?"

I felt my mouth open and close again. Felt my heart stretch slightly ... and then recoil. "I'm ... well, I'm not looking for anything serious, if that's what you're wondering," I said. "I mean, why should people settle down with just one person?" My earlier conversation with Kalina swept into my mind and I felt that same anger spark in me at the memory of what her ex-boyfriend did to her, what Jack did to me. We all had enough scars on our hearts—no-strings-attached dating was the way everyone should go. "See, people are always let down by other people," I went on, warming to my topic. "You know, you let someone in and then it ultimately ends, usually with someone being stabbed in the back. Or the front. So, it's much better for everyone to just not get involved emotionally and stick to casual things."

Lucas raised an eyebrow at me. "See, I think that sort of thinking is exactly what's *wrong* with people nowadays," he said. "People treat each other badly, they use each other, and no one is really happy. The whole 'casual' thing is just an excuse to sleep around and not commit to anyone."

"That's not true!" I replied defensively. "Keeping things casual is a way to just have fun and explore things *without* people treating each other badly. When you let yourself get attached or involved emotionally, *that's* when things go wrong. Because really, things always end nowadays, don't they?

It's almost inevitable. Just look at the divorce rate." To which I would be adding soon.

"You think people should just sleep with whoever they want, whenever they want, and that's all okay?" Lucas was looking at me hard, as if this question was a challenge.

But all I could think of was how dare he ask this question? He didn't know that I'd spent a whole eleven years in a monogamous, loyal relationship only to have it all blow up in my face. Monogamy hadn't worked well then, had it? And take Kalina and her ex-boyfriend! He'd been sleeping with her best friend the entire time behind her back.

Plus, I felt like there was a deeper meaning to this conversation. Like, we were now talking about the fundamental differences between men and women. Hadn't men been able to sleep around for centuries without any consequences? Wasn't it even today, still, expected for guys to do that? And now, when the girls were finally catching up and coming to the party, suddenly it was not okay?

"Absolutely," I replied, staring him down. "If people are single, then yes they should definitely be able to sleep with whoever they want. And as many people as they want."

Lucas looked away from me, shaking his head. "See, I just don't agree. It's like those people you see in the social pages, like that Derek Windsor moron."

As Lucas said his name, I felt my stomach twist in annoyance and surprise. There was so much scorn and disdain in his voice.

"The amount of women he goes through is disgusting," Lucas continued. "Every week he's photographed with someone new, like they're disposable. He treats them like shit."

"How would you know?" I said, my voice rising. "I'm sure the women who sleep with him have a great time and definitely want to be there! It's their choice, after all. And just presuming that they're *victims* or some crap like that is really insulting. You know, to women in general," I quickly added.

He looked at me, eyebrows raised again, but I just glared at him. God, there was really something about him—his words, or his annoyingly good looks maybe—but he was making me really angry. How had we even started on this conversation anyway?

"I can see I'm not going to convince you," he replied, and I realised his eyes had softened and he had a half-smile on his face.

I also realised that I'd become super tense. Kind of poised like an angry, spitting cat.

"Well, you know," I muttered, embarrassed by my outburst. "Girls should be able to do all the same things that guys have been doing for centuries."

Lucas gazed at me for a long moment, and he looked almost … what, sad? Disappointed? Or just curious?

"You're right," he conceded, nodding once. Then he looked away, over to his group of friends again. I looked too, and saw that they were all getting up from their table.

"Looks like the party's moving on," Lucas said, turning back to me with a look of regret.

I felt like I was sinking into my chair, my body deflating. "You should probably go, then. Sorry about the … um … discussion." I looked down into my drink, too mortified to look at him now.

"It was … enlightening," Lucas said lightly, and I looked up to see him smiling at me again. Not in an ironic way, but in a genuine way.

I shook my head. "You are one of the most confusing guys," I blurted out.

Lucas chuckled and shook his head. "Probably best you don't get to know me."

"Okay, okay, hint taken!" I held up my hands dramatically. "You don't want to get to know me, I get it. Don't worry, I won't try again."

"That's not it," he said, then he hesitated, as if not sure what to say next.

I just rolled my eyes. "Look, it's fine. Go. Your friends are leaving."

Lucas made to get up from the table, but then he stopped, and instead slid right up next to me, nudging my arm with his shoulder.

"Hey," he said, and I looked up into his face, only inches from mine. "If things were different, you're someone I'd definitely like to get to know more."

I could barely breathe. We were so close together—our bodies were actually touching—and I was so hyper aware of the pressure of his arm on my arm, his leg on my leg. We were looking into each other's eyes and I shifted towards him. His eyes were searching mine, and then—

"Lucas!" a male voice suddenly called. "You coming?"

We both jumped, and a second later, he was looking at his friend, his body shifting away from me. I felt like all the air had suddenly been sucked out of my lungs.

Lucas stood up from the table and grinned at me again. "Later, Laura." And then he walked away, merging with his group of friends heading out the door. The blonde girl was looking at me with interest, and I felt my cheeks flush.

What had he meant by that last thing he'd said—that if things were different, he'd like to get to know me? And had he been about to kiss me, or had I just imagined that?

God, the whole point of casual dating was to not get involved in anything confusing. Shaking my head at myself, I finished my drink, shoved my book in my bag and started to head home.

# 28

I was just walking in the door of the flat when my phone started ringing, its distinct "Mum" ringtone (Michael Bublé's "Come Dance With Me", at her insistence) letting me know who it was. I managed to juggle my bag and towel around, grabbing my phone and answering it just before it stopped ringing.

"Hi, Mum!" I said, only just getting myself in the door properly.

"Hi, darling!" Mum replied warmly. "How are you?"

"I'm good, you?"

There were a few minutes of chitchat as I made my way into my bedroom, before Mum started fishing around again.

"So, how are things on the social front?" she asked, her voice sounding hopeful.

"It's pretty much the same as usual, Mum. I'm getting out and being nice and social," I replied, knowing my vague answers would annoy her.

"Oh good. And how are things with Ben? Have you met any of his nice friends?"

I rolled my eyes. "Actually, no, I haven't met *any* of his friends."

"That's a shame." Mum sounded disappointed.

"It's hardly a shame," I scolded. "But don't worry, I've been spending lots of time with my *friends*."

"No *boy*friends, then? Have you met any boys? You know, your father and I went to the pub for dinner and Eric was there! We had a lovely chat with him—you know he's still single."

"Muuum," I whined.

"I really wish you'd consider going on a date with him, Laura. He's such a *lovely* boy."

"I've already *been* on a date with someone else, you know," I replied hotly, but regretted it as soon as I'd said it.

"Reeeaally?!" Oh God, Mum sounded like she'd just won the lottery.

"It's nothing, though," I replied hastily. "It was just dinner, and um, well … nothing else." I certainly was *not* telling my mother about the strawberry tarts. Or the sex swing. "Anyway," I quickly pushed on. "How's Elle doing? Has she called lately?"

"Oh yes, she's having the time of her life! Although, your father is rather worried about her. I gather she's hooked up with a couple of French backpackers, a pair of lovely girls she tells me, so at least she's got a larger group now to travel with."

"Where is she now? Last time I spoke to her she was making her way up towards Mexico."

"Honduras!" Mum replied enthusiastically. "She posted a whole album of pictures from some amazing Copan ruins just this morning. It all looks amazing of course!"

"Erm, right." I'd have to remember to google where exactly Honduras was later.

"I saw on Facebook that your friend Louise is having a baby shower tomorrow," Mum said a bit too casually.

Aha! So, *that* was the real reason for the call.

"Yes, I'm going to that," I replied equally casually. I'd given up long ago wondering why my mother thought it was okay to "friend" all my friends on Facebook.

"You are? Good! You've spoken to Louise, then?"

"Yes, we've spoken."

"And how is her pregnancy going?" Mum asked eagerly. "Is she glowing?"

"I don't know, Mum, I haven't actually seen her."

"Gosh it will be so lovely for her." Mum sighed. "Her first baby."

"Uh-uh."

"She'll be feeling so scared and nervous probably. It can't be long now until she's due!"

"Yep."

"Laura, why are you sounding annoyed? Don't you want to know about all this?"

"Not really!"

"But why not? It could be you someday soon. You do still want children, don't you?"

My stomach twisted and I could feel myself getting annoyed at my mother again. "Mum, it's *really* not at the top of my priority list right now."

"Well, it shouldn't be too far down! You were all ready to have kids just a few months ago!"

"Yes, and I had a husband back then, didn't I? One who wasn't gay."

"Laura, you'll meet someone again soon. You just need to be open to the possibility. I really wish you'd let me set up a date with Eric."

"So, what?" I laughed. "I can go on a date with him and say, 'Hi, Eric, my mum *really* wants me to have babies right now, so what do you think?'"

"You're not taking this seriously." Now Mum sounded annoyed.

"No, Mum, *you're* not being serious. Or realistic. Or whatever."

"Your biological clock isn't going to sit around and wait for you to make up your mind, you know."

Stomach twist. My mother really knew how to dig in the knife.

"It will just have to wait, won't it?" I said angrily. "Look, Mum, I've got to go."

"Don't get angry with me! I'm just being realistic."

"I don't need realistic at the moment, okay?"

"Okay, darling, okay. I'm just trying to help you."

Argh, why were all mothers so good at guilt-tripping their children?

"Yes. Whatever. Look, I really have to go, though."

"Bye, darling," Mum said, her voice all warm and kind again.

"Bye, Mum." I sighed, feeling defeated.

As soon as I'd hit the "end-call" button, I threw my phone on my bed and flopped down after it.

Why was everything so hard? Was my mother right, and I should be desperately out there trying to meet someone again just so I could have children? But honestly, the idea of having kids right now seemed absurd. Sure, it seemed like a good idea back when I was with Jack, when we were living together in our cottage with the big backyard. I could see it then, really *envision* it.

But now. Now I was living in a shared flat in Manly, with two equally single, party-loving people. For the first time in over ten years, I was simply doing whatever I wanted, whenever I wanted, without having to worry about what anyone else wanted to do.

Was that such a bad thing?

❦

"*The Bachelor*!" I suggested, gesturing at the TV with my beer bottle. "Ooh! Or *The Block*?"

"I'm *not* watching *The Bachelor*," Ben said with disgust. "Let's see what's on the Food Network!"

"The Food Network?" I rolled my eyes. "God, how much sadder can we get? Sitting at home on a Saturday night watching the Food Network."

"Hey, I like the Food Network!" Ben said.

"Oh whatever." I shrugged. "We really need to get a Netflix subscription in here." Though, to be honest, I did actually like the Food Network, too.

"How's work going?" I asked Ben after a few minutes of watching a food fight involving strawberry mousse.

"It's pretty cruisy," Ben replied, taking a swig of beer. "I haven't taken any new contracts because the bar's opening in just over a week."

"Is it that soon?" I asked, surprised. "Kalina told me it was still three or four weeks away."

"Yeah, it's been brought forward. Everything's gone to plan, and my brother wants to get in with all the work Christmas-party functions which will start up soon."

"Cool. So, you're going to be working there full-time once it opens?"

"Yeah. It's worked out really well, actually. The bar will run until February, and then I've got a great gig booked in to start in April."

"What kind of gig?"

"Movie contract. Some new Aussie film being done in Sydney, so it's a four-month project."

"Oh wow!" I exclaimed, clearly far more excited about this than Ben was. "What's the movie?"

"No idea. Sorry," Ben added, grinning at me.

I rolled my eyes and shook my head at him dramatically.

"What?" he asked defensively. "It's just a job."

"Just a job?" I repeated incredulously. "I'd love to be part of a movie production! I can't believe you're not enthused by it." I shook my head again. "Well, you'll have to give me blow-by-blow details of everything that happens on the set. And then I can live vicariously through you while I'm slogging away at my stupid job."

"Not enjoying your work?" Ben asked.

I sighed, thinking. "I dunno," I said eventually. "I mean, it's a job, right? No one really likes their job."

"I like mine," Ben offered.

"Yes, but you have a dream job."

Ben laughed. "Why do you stay if you don't like yours?"

"It pays the bills," I replied automatically.

"Yeah, but lots of jobs pay the bills," Ben challenged. "Why not just get a different job?"

I went to reply with all the reasons that were already in my mind, but I stopped myself. Because the truth was, I suddenly realised, that all the reasons no longer mattered. There was the financial-security factor of having a stable, well-paid job that would always pay the mortgage. But it wasn't like I had a mortgage anymore, was it? Jack and I sold the house months ago.

There was also the maternity-leave factor, as Tiger Finance had a great maternity-leave scheme. But that wasn't going to happen anytime soon. (Although, I was sure my mum would kill me for throwing that away).

Plus, how had I even entered marketing analysis in the first place? My job as an incentives coordinator was never meant to be quite so heavy on statistics. I'd actually enjoyed myself far more when I was working at the PR agency, even though the pay was way lower. At least there I'd had more interactions with people and had helped organise some cool events. Now I didn't know what I even wanted to do.

"Maybe I should just chuck my job in and get you to get me a job on the film set," I said, half joking.

"Well, why don't you?" he challenged.

"Oh yes, because it's that easy!" I laughed. "Just switching careers. Besides, I wouldn't dream of really asking you to help me get a job!"

Ben shrugged. "I don't mind. Like I said, it's all who you know. If you were really keen, I could reach out and see what positions are still available on the film production."

"Really?" I looked at him quizzically.

"Yeah. Really."

"That's something that you could *actually* do?" I clarified.

"Yes." Ben grinned at me. "In fact, I think Celeste is in town at the moment. She's one of the producers and does most of the hiring."

"Interesting ..." I trailed off, still looking at Ben and waiting for the catch.

He just raised his eyebrows at me. "You don't look very sure about it," he said, urging me to say something.

"Well, it's just ... I mean, it would be a bit crazy, wouldn't it? And what would I *do* exactly? I don't have any movie-production skills at all."

"There're always runner jobs going. Although they're pretty junior. But who knows. There's set design, costume design. You do marketing stuff, don't you? There's probably some crossover with skills there."

I tried not to laugh, but a smile split across my face. "You have no idea what marketing is, do you?"

"Hey, I'm not that bad! But really, if you're thinking about changing jobs then why not just give it a go? What have you got to lose?"

I turned to stare at the TV for a bit, mulling over Ben's words. I couldn't chuck my job in to go chase some dream of working on a movie set, could I? People didn't really *do* that sort of thing.

But then ... I'd wasted so many years of my life in a relationship with Jack because I'd thought that was the right thing, hadn't I? And now here I was, twenty-seven and single for the first time. Had Jack not happened, I could have done all my single dating and exploring when I was in my early twenties or late teens, and then I might have actually met the right guy by now. I'd wasted all that time in a relationship I'd been too blind or naive to see wasn't quite right. Was I doing the same thing with my current career? Was I staying there just because it was safe and easy and because it felt like what I should do, what people expected of me?

I'd studied marketing and communications not because it was something

I had always wanted to do, but because it had felt safe and interesting. Then I went and got jobs in PR and marketing, using my degree, and now I was up to a fairly good salary in the marketing team at a prestigious bank. Shouldn't that have made me happy? I was doing the whole ladder climb, wasn't I? Moving forward and upwards. Wasn't that what everyone aspired to do?

So why had I started dreading work every morning?

"She's thinking about it," Ben said, jolting me out of my trance. I turned to look at him and saw him grinning at me over the top of his beer again.

I rolled my eyes. "Let's just say I was *thinking* about it, as you say. How would it work?"

As soon as I'd asked this I felt my heart start to race, like I'd just made a huge decision. But I hadn't—yet. I was just considering things. Weighing the options.

"I'd send Celeste a message and ask what jobs are going. Say I've got a great friend looking for work. They love getting referrals anyway, makes it way easier for them when hiring."

"You have an unskilled friend," I clarified.

"She doesn't need to know that. Besides, you need to back yourself. Fake it till you make it."

"Ha. Yeah, I suppose so." I turned back to the TV. "Let me have a think about it."

"Alright. But I think Celeste's going to be in Melbourne next week, so if you want me to contact her it should probably be soon."

"Got it. And Ben, thanks." I smiled at him.

"No problem at all."

A few minutes later, Ben's phone started ringing from his bedroom and he left the room to answer it. I could vaguely hear him talking to someone about heading out, and with a stab I realised I'd be left home alone. Home alone on a Saturday night.

"That was Hobbs," Ben said, walking back into the lounge room. "There's a bunch down in Manly I'm gonna meet up with. You want to come?"

"No, thanks," I said. As much as sitting home alone on a Saturday night wasn't a great prospect, hanging out with Ben's fellow twenty-three-year-old mates wasn't a much more appealing one. "Have fun."

"Cool. See ya later, then," Ben said, grabbing up his keys and wallet and heading out.

I turned my attention back to the TV and swigged at my beer moodily. I couldn't concentrate on what was going on in the show, though. Now that I was alone, it felt like all the events of the past forty-eight hours were suddenly cramming for attention in my mind.

It had only been a few hours ago that I was sitting at the 4Pines, Lucas sitting beside me. I could practically still feel his shoulder brushing against mine, still smell the scent of him. Before the conversation had deteriorated into an argument about monogamy, we'd been having fun together, hadn't we? We'd been joking around—laughing. And then he'd leaned in close and said, *You're someone I'd definitely like to get to know.* Although he'd preceded that statement with, *If things were different.*

*Different?* Different how?

I automatically reached for my phone, opening the message app, but then I froze. Not only because I didn't want to be the one chasing him, but because right near the top of my message history was Jack's name, the messages where we were confirming our lunch meeting.

Had it really only been the day before that I'd had lunch with Jack? Only one day since we'd sat opposite each other in a restaurant, talking and laughing like old friends. Something he'd said swam through my mind, clear as if he was sitting next to me repeating it right then:

*I am happy, Laura. Really, it's like I'm one hundred percent happy, whereas before there was a tiny percent of me that knew something was wrong.*

Jack had found his place in the world. It was funny, I thought I'd begrudge him that. Thought I'd be horribly mad and hurt and betrayed still by what he'd done. I mean I still was, don't get me wrong. But there was a part of me (a tiny, TINY part) that did understand.

How many times had I heard Jack's dad make a disparaging comment about homosexuals? How often had I heard him call someone a "bloody poofta"? Even my own parents—I know they try not to judge, but it was kind of like that's just how their generation was raised, wasn't it? When our parents' generation was growing up, sodomy was literally illegal. And even though my parents say they're all open-minded, and of course they see being gay as totally okay, I still remember a few years ago when one of my mum's friend's sons came out as gay. Mum had *cried* about it. She kept saying, "Oh poor Maggie, now she'll never have any grandchildren. What a tragedy!" The way she'd spoken, you'd think the son had died.

But anyway. My point was, that I kind of got why Jack refused to admit, even to himself, what his sexuality was. Logically I could see that. I'd just always resent him, society and his parents, for pressuring him into that. And taking me along for the ride.

But still. Although it took him twenty-seven years to work out he was gay, now he was happy. He'd found his place in the world. He knew where he was heading.

So why didn't I? My mum's voice in my mind reminded me of the whole biological-clock thing. Which just made me angry. I mean, how was that fair? Why do women have to deal with that crap? Men didn't have to give a damn, did they? They could swan about for years and didn't have any time pressure on them about kids. In fact, they could swan about, *period*. Or sleep around. They were allowed to sleep with whoever they wanted, whenever they wanted, no consequences whatsoever.

Suddenly I was jumping to my feet, downing my beer in one last chug. *Fuck all of this*, I thought. What was it Lucas had said that afternoon?

That sleeping with people casually was what was wrong with society nowadays? Well stuff that—I could and *should* be sleeping with whoever the damn hell I pleased. In fact, Lucas was probably still out drinking with his birthday crew, that bloody Japanese-short-shorts and blondie there with him. I wouldn't be surprised if after his spiel about not liking casual dating, he took one of them home, anyway.

And Jack—God, Jack was probably at home now with his *boyfriend*, wasn't he? Doing ... I don't even know what. Some sort of sixty-nine blow-job scenario, no doubt.

It was just me who was the Saturday-night loser, then, wasn't it? Well I could change that.

I stormed through the apartment looking for my phone, before remembering it was still sitting on the couch. I grabbed it up and started scrolling through my contact list. There were little warning bells going off in my mind, reminding me that I had to go to Louise's baby shower the next day, and that perhaps going out tonight wasn't the best idea. But I decided to ignore them. The prospect of having to sit around with all those girls talking about their happy, married lives was another reason why I needed to distract myself.

Tinder-boy Darren? Argh, no, he might have ideas involving a cheesecake. Or baklava. *Imagine* the stickiness if he wanted to play with baklava?!

Derek Windsor? Hmm ... No. No, I wasn't in the right mood to visit someone's penthouse. Plus, I highly doubted he'd be alone on a Saturday night.

Pete?

Huh. Pete. I wondered what he was currently doing?

With a giddy smile starting on my face, I dialled Pete's number.

# 29

Pete's apartment was in Darlinghurst, not far from the office, and as my car sped along towards his place, I tried to breathe normally. This was going to be great! I felt just like an old Hollywood movie star, zipping along to a late-night rendezvous with my secret lover. Not that Pete and I were lovers, yet. Making out in the kitchen at work didn't really count.

I sat up straighter and watched the city lights speed past outside the window. My hand closed around the bottle of wine on the seat next to me, which I'd pilfered from Ben's stash. I also may have helped myself to a few shots from the resident vodka bottle in our apartment before stepping out.

Was the back seat spinning slightly? Oh no, no, it wasn't.

The Uber pulled up outside a modern building and I felt my stomach give a weird kind of flip-flop. Oh God. I had arrived. Was I ready to go in? Couldn't I just stay in the car for a bit longer?

"So ... this is it," the Uber driver said, turning around to look at me. He totally knew I was drunk.

"Yes, thank you!" I said a bit too enthusiastically.

I made it out onto the street, winning the battle against the tangly seatbelt, and quickly adjusted my trench coat. Because, yes, I was wearing a trench coat and nothing underneath except sexy lingerie, my feet in the sky-high heels that made me feel like a stripper. And okay, I'll admit the underwear-and-trench-coat combination had *seemed* like a fantastic idea an hour earlier, but that I *may* have been having second thoughts about it right about then. I think I'd had some delusional vision of me doing a sexy striptease in Pete's bedroom, it all just sort of naturally coming together. But I couldn't do a striptease! How on earth does one even *start* a striptease? What, would I put some Spotify music on my phone and raise an eyebrow at him? Whip the belt off my coat and pull it back and forth between my legs like I was riding a horse? Then what? I only knew about three dance moves and I was sure they would all result in excessive, and immensely unflattering, jiggling.

I stepped up to the front door and rang Pete's buzzer.

"Laura?" Pete's voice came over the intercom.

"Hi!" My voice came out all squeaky and high-pitched.

"Come on up." I heard the lock click open on the door.

*Okay, here we go. No turning back. Try not to embarrass yourself with unflattering dance moves.*

I stepped inside and moved into the lift, pressing the button for Pete's floor. I could feel my heart beating rapidly in my chest, as well as up near my ears and throat, and I forced myself to take a few deep breaths as the lift ascended. When the doors opened on level nine's hallway, I was reminded of a luxury hotel, right down to the nice jasmine smell emanating from a nearby floral arrangement. As I moved down the corridor, glancing at the door numbers, I could feel my coat rubbing my mostly bare skin underneath.

I passed a mirror halfway down the corridor and paused in front of it. Shit, I'd gone a bit overboard on the eyeliner, hadn't I? At least the trench coat, even with nothing underneath, made it seem like I was fully clothed. So, if I chickened out on the whole striptease thing, we could just sit around drinking wine and chatting, right? But no, no. I'd come here to have sex and I could do it. I stood up a little straighter, lifting my chin in the mirror. There was a vase sitting on the side table, and for a moment I considered pouring water over my hair à la Jamie Lee Curtis in *True Lies*.

Except that would be a bit weird. He might think I'd been out swimming.

Just then a door opened at the end of the corridor and Pete peered out into the hallway, looking for me. He smiled when he spotted me and held the door open, waiting for me.

"Hi," I squeaked again as I tottered forward. My smile felt a bit fixed and my legs a bit shaky as I walked inside, taking in the simple, if a little sparse, furnishings of the unit.

"You look nice," Pete said, closing the door and moving inside.

"Oh thanks! I just thought it felt like a trench-coat kind of night!" What did *that* mean?

"Erm, right. Isn't it a bit warm outside for a coat?"

"Yes. I mean no! Um, I mean, coats are a fashion thing." Why were we talking about my trench coat so much? I put my bottle of wine and purse down a little unsteadily on the kitchen counter.

"Right. Well, can I take your coat for you, then?" Pete asked, sounding flummoxed.

Oh no, was this the moment already? I wasn't really going to sit around in my coat all night, was I? I needed to do this while I was still feeling the effects of my earlier shots and before I totally lost my nerve.

Right. Go time.

I turned slowly to face him, smiling as seductively as I could. He was looking at me with his eyebrows raised, one hand outstretched as if ready to take my coat. I watched his face transform with surprise as I deliberately unbuttoned my trench coat, letting it slide off my shoulders and fall to the ground, so that I was standing in just my heels and lacy underwear.

His expression was priceless.

But then the weirdest thought crossed my mind. As I was standing there, wearing nothing but lingerie and heels, the cool air making my skin chill, my eyes tracked upwards and I thought, *I wonder if Pete's hairline is receding?* The thought—and moment of the thought—was so strange that I almost laughed. But then, weirdly, I *did* hear a laugh. A sort of chuckle.

And the laugh hadn't come from Pete. Nor had it come from me. It had come from *behind* me.

SHIT!

There was someone else in the room getting a great eyeful of my bare bum in a G-string. I sort of half froze, my eyes widening. My first thought was, *Stay very still and they won't see you.* But that was ridiculous. I wasn't going to become invisible simply by not moving.

Pete's eyes shifted over my shoulder and they widened even further in surprise, confirming, if I had any doubts, that someone else was now behind me.

Taking a little yelping gasp of air, I swivelled quickly around, my throat making a further choking noise. I grabbed my coat back up off the floor and pressed it to my chest, simultaneously searching for the stranger in the room.

And oh no.

Oh no, no, no.

My eyes landed on the other person and I felt a sprawling swell of doom and horror expand out from my stomach to encase me.

It was Charlie. Friendly, outspoken, loud-mouth *Charlie* from sales.

"Hi, Laura." He said. He didn't even look uncomfortable.

"Oh … um … hi, Charlie," I said, feeling heat flaming into my cheeks as I tried to shimmy back into my coat without exposing myself further. "I didn't realise anyone else was here."

"I do live here," Charlie said, grinning and leaning casually against a wall.

"You do?" I looked at him now, surprised. Were there two of him standing there?

"Yeah of course. How else do you think I knew Pete and managed to get him the job at Tiger?"

Oh, *of course*. How else did I think Pete got the job? Honestly, I hadn't really been thinking much about bloody Pete's logistics. God, why hadn't I asked him more about his personal life? How could I have been so unaware that he and Charlie were friends outside work, nay that they *lived* together?

"Right," I heard myself say. "Pete didn't mention that."

Actually, Pete hadn't mentioned flatmates at all.

"Shall we have a glass of wine?" Pete asked after a moment of uncomfortable silence. To be fair, he at least had the good grace to look embarrassed.

"Yes," I said, a bit too quickly. "Yes, wine would be great."

"I'll leave you guys to it." Charlie winked at Pete and gave him a look that clearly said "way-to-go!" before disappearing down the hallway. The look made me feel a little bit ill.

"Don't worry about him," Pete said, pouring two glasses of wine.

"If he tells anyone at work about this ..." I started furiously.

"He won't," Pete said quickly, though I was pretty sure there was a look of doubt on his face.

I closed my eyes briefly and forced myself to take a deep breath, holding onto the kitchen bench to steady myself.

"Alright?" Pete asked.

"Let's go to your room," I said, picking up my glass and the bottle, too.

"Okay," he agreed swiftly and led the way.

Once safely ensconced with the door closed, I felt relieved, despite my mortification. I gulped my wine hastily, looking around at Pete's room rather than at him. The room was surprisingly spacious, even with the large king-sized bed in the centre (I wasn't sure Pete would fit in anything smaller). It had drawers and a small couch on one side, even what appeared to be an enormous walk-in wardrobe. Why would a guy need a walk-in wardrobe? That wasn't fair. Couldn't I just transplant it over into my apartment building?

The balls of my feet were starting to ache in my stupidly high shoes, plus I was finding it difficult to stand still without swaying, so I took a seat on the bed. Pete sat down next to me.

"So," he said, eyeing me sideways. "I was wondering why you suddenly wanted to come over. But I guess that mystery is solved."

"Yep, mystery is definitely not my middle name, is it?" I replied, taking larger gulps of wine. I was struggling to look at Pete. I was super embarrassed, and drunk, and his presence next to me just felt a bit, I don't know—*friend-zone*. Could he tell that I was drunk?

Pete chuckled. "Sorry about Charlie. I wasn't really expecting you to be wearing nothing under your coat."

"Yep. It seemed like a great idea before I got here. Now I'm not so sure."

"I'd say it's still a great idea." Pete smiled at me and shifted closer. His leg brushed against mine and I found myself looking down at what could only be described as rather powerful thighs.

"How's everything going at the office?" I asked the first thing that sprang to mind.

"It's good," Pete replied. "There's a huge meeting happening on Monday with a really big new client, so it's been all hands on deck for the past few weeks."

I leaned closer to him, so our shoulders brushed together, rather than responding.

"How are things up in marketing?" Pete asked, shifting towards me more.

"They're okay." I crossed my legs so that my trench coat fell open across my thigh. "You know, pretty average. Pretty market-ey."

"Market-ey? Is that the new way of saying—"

"Sshh." I pressed a finger to his mouth to stop him talking. His eyes went wide. "Less talking," I said as I leaned in close. Then I dropped my hand and suddenly our mouths were together, Pete tasting like salt and white wine.

And woo ... the room was spinning a bit. But I discovered that if I held on to Pete tightly and crushed my body against his, then it was alright. He was like an anchor. A big, heavy anchor.

And if there was one thing to be said about drunken sex, it was that the mind tended to shut down and become rather sluggish, the body and the feel of things taking a much more centrestage role. And once my coat was gone and his clothes were off, then it was all skin on skin, mouths and hands and hips and soft things and hard things and pressure here and there, and urgency and pleasure ...

# 30

I fell asleep at Pete's house.

Fuck.

I could tell it was morning because Pete's apartment had those shitty old venetian blinds that didn't close properly, and the dawn sun was blinding me. I could also tell that I had a massive hangover. God, had I drunk *any* water the night before?

I had vague memories of rather wild sexcapades—there was some standing action, and kneeling action, and various other acrobatic action. One thing I did at least remember clearly was the condom being deployed. Thank goodness for that.

I slowly sat up, my head feeling like an anvil being hammered on in a *thud-thud-thud* kind of way. Pete was still asleep next to me, snoring.

Well, there at least was another thing to tick off my list. Drunken sex with a co-worker. Laura the Explorer was certainly getting herself out and about.

I eased myself out of the bed, and as my eyes landed on the trench coat and heels splayed out around the floor, I had the horrible sinking realisation that I'd have to wear them home.

I tried to sneak around the room looking for my underwear, and managed to whack my shin into the bed frame. Luckily Pete didn't wake from that, or from the subsequent expletive that erupted from my mouth. When my clothes were once again adorning my body, I eased the door open and backed out of the room without waking Pete, heels in one hand, purse tucked under the other.

Thankfully, there was no sign of Charlie in the apartment's common area, and I was able to make a clean break out the front door and towards the lift. An elderly man with a small cavoodle emerged from another apartment, and he did a double-take as he spotted me, before smiling politely even as his face turned red.

I took out my phone and booked an Uber, noting that it was 6.15 am. With a jolt, I realised I needed to be at Louise's baby shower in just under eight hours. But I couldn't think about that right then. All I wanted to focus on was getting home, taking a shower, and going back to sleep.

The Uber arrived and I climbed in. I wound the window down and leaned back in my seat with my eyes closed, letting the cool breeze blow on my face.

What a night. What a bizarre, crazy, random night.

A small smile cracked over my face and I opened my eyes again to watch the city streets sailing past. It was actually funny, really, to think that in a few hours I'd be sitting among a host of married mothers. And there I was, being taken home early in the morning after a night of hot sex. Well, exuberant sex, at least.

I suddenly had a flashback to when Pete was putting on the condom. I think it was the first time I really stopped and had a proper look at him naked, and okay, this will sound awful, but his penis looked so small compared to the rest of him that I started laughing! And then I remembered him looking at me in surprise, so I had to cover and say I was laughing because the condom was green, and that it looked like a dragon, and since Pete's name was Pete it was now Pete's Dragon, just like in the movie!

Oh dear. I was surprised he hadn't kicked me out of the house right then.

I took a deep breath and squeezed my eyes shut. Well, things could always be worse. Right?

~⁂~

Turning my key in the lock of my apartment's front door, I was super aware of how dry my throat was and how much I desperately needed a glass of water. I pushed my way inside and spotted Kalina straightaway, getting her own glass of water in the kitchen. She was already fully dressed and looking far too chirpy for so early on a Sunday morning.

"Here she is!" Kalina practically shouted as I walked in, still carrying my heels and my purse. "Looks like someone had a big night!"

"Water," I croaked, dumping my things and walking straight to the sink.

Kalina handed me her glass and I drank from it greedily.

"So?" Kalina was watching me with a gleeful look on her face, one hand on her hip. "Where've you been? Did you see Derek Windsor again? Or Tinder Boy?"

I finished the water and shook my head, gasping for air. "Pete. The guy from work."

"Really!" Kalina squealed. "I love it! Tell me all about it!"

"Does my trench coat not tell you all you need to know?"

As Kalina laughed delightedly, Ben walked out from the hallway, also fully dressed and looking like he'd been up for hours.

"Doing the morning runner, eh Laur?" Ben teased, grinning at me as he walked over to the dining table where a few laptops were set up.

"Well, as a wise man once said, if you wake up next to them they expect pancakes or some—"

I stopped talking abruptly as someone else walked out from the hallway, following Ben.

And oh no.

Oh no, no, no.

He looked at me, eyebrows raised as his own surprise was quickly masked by a guarded, curious look. His eyes—those brilliant, sky-blue eyes—slowly took in my messy coat, my bare feet, my stripper heels lying next to the door, before returning to my face and my no-doubt dishevelled morning-after look. His mouth quirked up in a half-smile, his eyes narrowing ever so slightly. His amazing blue eyes.

No. No. No. He couldn't be here.

What the fuck was *Lucas* doing in my apartment?

Kalina turned, trying to work out what I was staring at. "Oh, don't worry about him," she said, waving a hand dismissively. "That's just Ben's brother. He doesn't care about any of this stuff."

Ben's ... brother ...

"Oh yeah, you guys haven't met, have you?" Ben chimed in, now looking between us as well. "Laura, this is my brother Lucas. Lucas, Laura."

Lucas. Ben's Brother.

Oh. My. God.

I couldn't move. My eyes had gone a bit too wide, the glass I was holding felt in danger of breaking, and a weird kind of choking sound came out of my throat.

"Nice to meet you, Laura," Lucas said smoothly, as if I really was just a friend of his brother's. But his eyes were twinkling with way too much enjoyment. "Sounds like you've had a good night."

Had he heard that? All of it? My mind raced over everything we'd just said—the mention of Derek Windsor. The clear morning runner from a casual hook-up I'd just had. What must he think of me? But then ... then the other truth hit me.

Lucas was Ben's *brother*. Which meant Lucas had slept with Kalina.

Lucas was Kalina's "one that got away".

And there I'd been, coveting, flirting with, trying to chase him down. Sending him text messages. Bumping into him in bars and cafes. Last time I'd seen him we almost kissed. I'd wanted him to kiss me. I'd been fantasising about it for weeks.

But that could never happen now, could it? Because he was the guy Kalina had a history with and an ongoing thing for. Kalina, my friend, the girl whose best friend had been secretly sleeping with her boyfriend for years.

The situation was awful. It was a big, fucking, shit-heap pile of awful. And everyone was still staring at me.

"Yes," I managed to choke out, forcing myself to unfreeze and blink a few times. "Nice to meet you."

"So, come on, tell me!" Kalina said excitedly, clearly missing my mortified horror. "Did you have an *amazing* night?"

"Yes, tell us, Laura," Lucas chimed in, his eyes burning into mine even as a half-grin still adorned his face. "How *was* your night. With ... a guy from work, right?"

I swallowed, my gaze darting about between them all. "It was fine," I managed to say.

"Just *fine*?" Kalina sounded disappointed. "Oh, come on, we need more than that!"

"Well actually, I *really* need to go to the bathroom," I said, and made a sudden dash past Kalina down the hallway, not making eye contact with anyone.

"Fine, but I want to hear all about it later!" Kalina called after me as I locked the bathroom door behind me.

Fuck. Fuuuucckkkk!!!

I stood there leaning against the door, my heartbeat pounding in my ears. Outside in the lounge room, I could hear Ben, Kalina and Lucas all talking, discussing things about the bar. Because it was opening this week,

I realised. That was obviously what Lucas was doing at the flat. Finalising things with Ben and Kalina. No wonder there'd been three laptops on the table.

I slid down against the door until I was sitting on the floor tiles, feeling a bit shaky. I could hear their muffled voices chatting away in the other room, and I pressed my hands to the sides of my head, trying to squeeze my skull and stop the headache from pounding into my brain.

Oh God, how had this happened? How had I never actually mentioned Lucas to Kalina? Or Ben? And how had neither of them ever named Ben's brother?

How the fuck had I never realised that he was all the same person?

All this could have been avoided. And yet, all this could have been far more disastrous, couldn't it? What if Kalina *knew*? What if I had started talking about Lucas and how he had almost kissed me and how I desperately wanted to sleep with him. Kalina probably would have lost the plot. Or worse, just become all quiet and hurt and then she wouldn't want to be friends with me anymore. Because what kind of friend sleeps with a friend's ex?

I suddenly felt dirty, like I might throw up. I managed to strip off my coat and underwear while sitting on the floor, then dragged myself up and into the shower. I wasn't sure how long I stood under the water, but I desperately hoped they would all leave the flat while I was in there. I didn't think I could face Lucas again. Or Kalina.

** NEW MESSAGE **
**From: Rose Spencer at 9.17 am**

*Hey, I need to talk to you urgently. Call me when you can xx*

** NEW MESSAGE **
**From: Pete at 10.35 am**

*Hey, Laura. Had a great night last night—you should have stuck around this morning 😜 You want to train later this week? Either at the gym or my house.*

** NEW MESSAGE **
**From: Mum at 12.02 pm**

*Hi, darling! I've just sent you an email with some information from a company called Genea that specialises in egg freezing. It's been highly recommended by a lovely girl from my work, and I think it's something you should consider! Also was talking to Jenny from across the road and she said she met Brad on a website called Tinder—have you heard of it? Might be worth getting on there, I hear there's lots of single men all looking for relationships! xxx*

# 31

I pulled up outside Louise's suburban house and turned off my car engine. There were pink balloons tied to the letterbox, bobbing around in the breeze. I saw a girl I used to know, Marie Chu, walking up the footpath towards the house with a brightly coloured gift in her arms.

I closed my eyes for a moment and swallowed my nausea. It wasn't just the headache and the hangover, which were still there despite the Nurofen and Berocca I'd taken. No, the gut-wrenching, sick feeling in my stomach had nothing to do with how much I'd drunk last night.

It was dread. Pure, cold, dread.

It had been six hours since Lucas, Ben, Kalina and I had all stood in the same room. Six hours since the pieces had fallen into place—for Lucas and me, at least. But would Lucas have told Ben and Kalina by now that, actually, we'd already met? Would he have mentioned that we'd swapped numbers, that we'd shared a drink in a bar? I don't think men really discussed such things in detail, but Kalina might put the pieces together and then she would be horrified and feel really betrayed …

Oh God.

I was still having trouble processing who Lucas really was. And yet … Kalina's the one who'd been encouraging me to get out there and sleep with as many guys as possible. Plus, it wasn't like I'd known Lucas's identity.

So did that make it okay? Or if I just completely abandoned any further thoughts of Lucas and me together, then would *that* make it okay? … But did I want to do that?

At least I hadn't had to see any of them again this morning. They'd all gone out of the apartment when I (finally) emerged from the bathroom, and neither had they been there when I'd woken from my nap hours later. But I was just delaying the inevitable, wasn't I? It would all come out. Sooner or later, the truth would come out.

And I knew I had to go to work the next day and Pete would be there, and Charlie … I shuddered and reached for my bottle of water.

Thinking about work reminded me of Rose. I needed to call her. I didn't know what that message she sent meant. I grabbed my phone and fired off a quick message back to her:

*Ahh I need to talk to you too! I spent the night at Pete's place last night!!! Then had massive drama this morning!!! Running late for party now, talk tomorrow xx*

Chucking my phone back in my bag, I turned my gaze towards Louise's house again. *Well*, I thought, *there was no point delaying the inevitable.*

✧

"So, the plumber didn't show up on Thursday night, nor did he show up on Friday or Saturday, so now Harry is back at home and we're stuck with a toilet that doesn't work! He threatened to dig a hole in the backyard, but I've absolutely forbidden him from doing that. Instead, we're driving down the road to the shops every time one of us needs to use the loo."

A general tittering of laughter followed this scintillating story, while I tried to stifle a yawn. There I was, at the baby shower. Louise's backyard had been decorated so nicely with pink balloons, pink streamers, pink blow-up flamingos and just an all-around sea of pinkness. There were pink tablecloths, pink flowers; even the food was pink. There were also about fifteen women there, all dressed up as if they were heading out to the races. I felt like I was standing out like a sore thumb—what with my giant sunglasses, casual clothing and shitty mood.

*Why* had I drunk so much last night?

Every time my mind strayed back to my night with Pete, the fun night I remembered morphed into a gut-twisting vision of the look on Lucas's face when he had walked in this morning. Me in my stripper coat, with rumpled sex hair and smeared panda eyes. And Kalina standing there, all bubbly and excited, chatting away so loudly about my diverse sex life.

*Kalina and Lucas would make a nice couple, wouldn't they? And let's face it, they'd already slept together…*

My stomach twisted again, and I took another sip of my watermelon mocktail. I needed to get it together and focus on the conversation I was meant to be partaking in.

"She's been such an angel," Rachelle was cooing at her infant daughter. An old uni friend of Louise's who'd recently had her first baby, I'd never much cared for Rachelle's superior attitude. Four-month-old Annabelle didn't look impressed with her mother's conversation either, nor with the sparkly pink headband adorning her tiny head.

"Have you been getting much sleep?" asked Gabby, the other participant in our conversation, as she pushed one of her fingers into Annabelle's little hand. I'd known Gabby since high school, in a distant-friends kind of way. We'd always moved in the same social circles, although never been that close personally. Even though we were the same age, she already had three kids of her own.

"Oh absolutely, Annabelle is such a good sleeper," Rachelle gushed, looking down adoringly at her child in the baby carrier. "She goes to sleep right on nine o'clock every night and doesn't wake up until we go and get her at six-thirty."

"Really?" Gabby said. "You must have one of those lucky babies I've heard about."

"I'm not sure *luck* has anything to do with it."

I tried not to sigh as I looked around the patio, searching for any conversation better than this one. In addition to the mocktails, there was sparkling grape juice being served, an alternative to champagne, and even though I was driving and hungover, I started to desperately wish there was alcohol on offer.

"Don't worry, Laura," Rachelle said, a patronising hint in her voice. "When you have kids, you'll find out what we're talking about."

"I'm sure," I replied disinterestedly, ignoring the fact that Gabby was now shooting Rachelle a pointedly shut-up look.

"So tell me, how *are* things with you?" Rachelle asked, directing her full attention at me. She made the comment sound casual, but loud enough that I could sense about five heads in the near vicinity suddenly perking up and homing in on us.

"They're great," I replied stiffly.

"You've moved over to the northern beaches I hear?" Rachelle pushed, that fake, caring smile still plastered to her face.

"Yeah, I'm living in Manly. It's great, I go to the beach all the time."

"Oh goodness, I haven't had time to go to the beach in months!" Rachelle replied with a proud little laugh. "I've barely even set foot out of the house since Annabelle came along!"

"You should be enjoying it now while she's still little," Gabby warned. "Once she's walking, good luck trying to get her to cooperate anywhere!"

"I'm sure things will be fine. James dotes on us both as it is—if my feet aren't up in the evenings he's right there, making me take it easy!"

I didn't even bother with an excuse as I stood up abruptly and walked away from them.

At least things were back to normal—or at least mostly normal—with

Louise and me. She was sitting in a throne-like armchair that had been specially brought out to the patio and was deep in conversation with three women. Her pretty sundress showed off the large bump of her tummy—and rather enlarged boobs—which I'll admit I hadn't been quite prepared for when I arrived.

Lunch was served and I managed to survive some more inane conversations, then there was a round of absurd games in which I was forced to maintain a cheerful expression while quietly wishing I was back home in bed. We had to make tiny baby figurines out of Play-Doh (mine had a head like Stewie from *Family Guy*), followed by a round of "baby-shower bingo". Then we were all handed a stack of nappies and some permanent markers and told to write funny messages on them.

"Did you hear that Eloise is now engaged?" asked a girl called Claire to the table in general.

"Is she really? Oh how lovely!" gushed Louise.

"So, Lou, when are you starting your maternity leave?" asked Rachelle.

"I'm stopping work two weeks before the baby is due. I think that will really give me time to settle in and hopefully relax a bit in the last couple of weeks."

"Oh, maternity leave it the *best*," Gabby enthused loudly from across the table. "You're going to *love it*, Lou."

"I know! I've been dying to leave my job for ages and now I can! Well, technically it's not leaving, but you know."

"Oh, I know! Who wants to go back, right?"

"Hey, did everyone hear that Tina and George bought a house?"

"No! Did they? I thought they were having all sorts of trouble getting their loan approved."

"No, it all got sorted out in the end. It's a lovely three-bedroom place, a bit old, but they're going to renovate."

"Aren't they still trying to get pregnant?"

"Yes, still trying poor things. It's been almost a year now. I think Tina is keen to try the IVF route, but I have no idea how they'd afford that now with the mortgage."

"Well, the two of them are still drinking like fishes, aren't they? Maybe they should start by giving up the booze for a while."

"Gabby!"

"What?"

"I heard that Matty lost his job—did anyone else hear that?"

"He didn't lose it, he's on workers' comp. Had a hammer drop on his knee or something."

"God, is he okay?"

"Oh, he's fine. He's just milking it now. I went around to their place a couple of weeks ago and he was up a ladder cleaning out the roof gutters!"

As the talk droned on, I couldn't have felt more like an outsider. My thoughts kept returning to the previous night, and then also bouncing back to being in Derek Windsor's penthouse, straddling the man on a sex swing. It was all such a contrast to how my life used to be when I was with Jack, which was exactly the kind of situation these women were describing.

The weird thing was, had Jack and I stayed together, I would have been exactly like them. I probably would've been eagerly participating in the idle gossip, sharing stories about my life, right down to Jack and me trying to get pregnant and how much I was also looking forward to taking maternity leave.

Now, the idea of being like them felt like a rash. They were all just so ... *typical*. Grow up, get a job, get married, leave job, have babies. They'd all followed the same formula. Sure, I may not have any idea where my life was going at this point. But somehow, that fact didn't bother me the way I was once terrified it would.

I looked down at the nappy still in front of me. I'd written "Special Midnight Delivery" on it. Was this what life was meant to come to?

Standing quietly from the table, I made an escape into the kitchen, needing somewhere to just hang out and get away from all the suburban talk. I was sneaking down the hallway towards the lounge room, looking for somewhere to hide for a few minutes, when I heard low voices talking.

"... surprised she came at all," someone was saying.

"Well, she is still friends with Louise," I heard Marie's voice replying. "Although, after that *incident* in David Jones. Did you hear about it?"

"I heard something, but not the full story! What happened?"

"It was *such* a scene. Security was called and everything. Apparently, she just lost it for no reason, started yelling and swearing and ripping baby onesies off the racks and throwing them across the department."

"No!"

"Yes! And there was another mother there with her child, and she was going to press charges and stuff."

"Really? God, how embarrassing!"

"*Of course* Louise has forgiven her, though. I mean, her husband was *gay*. Can you imagine that? Talk about humiliating."

"There must be something seriously wrong with him. And her. I mean, how do you go out with someone for eleven years and *not know*?"

"He was fooling her the whole time. And everyone. He kept the whole thing completely under wraps, really pretended to be straight."

"He must be cracked in the head. To be able to lie, and keep up the lie for so long—"

I couldn't listen anymore. I imagined not just what those girls were saying, but what everyone, at any time, must have been saying about Jack and me. The ridicule, the criticism, the *judgement* of us. I was so angry—not necessarily at Jack for this, but on his behalf. Because whatever happened between us, no one else had the right to gossip bitchily about it.

I stepped around the corner and cleared my throat loudly, startling the girls into silence. It was Marie and another girl called Amanda, who had recently married. I'd never really liked either of them much.

"Having fun in here?" I asked sweetly, narrowing my eyes.

"Oh, Laura ... hi," Marie stammered, looking embarrassed. "We were just ..."

"Just talking about me? Yes, I know."

They looked at each other warily.

"And let me tell you both something. My life—and Jack's life—are none of your business. And for the record, Jack had a really tough time working out who he was. But at least he made a decision on what he wants and he's no longer just blindly following what society expects of him, unlike the two of you and everyone else here!"

And with that I turned on my heel and stormed back towards the party, leaving them staring at each other in disbelief.

I was fuming when I stepped out onto the patio, and the sight of everyone still writing encouraging messages on nappies while discussing the lives of all their distant friends didn't help calm me. I needed to get out of there. Also, I was pretty sure I'd just insulted everyone at the party to Amanda and Marie. I thought it might be prudent to leave before they decided to share my delightful sentiments.

"Louise, I've got to get going," I said to her quietly, trying to look remorseful. "Good luck with everything. It was really great seeing you again."

I gave her a quick hug and then I was free of the party. As I left, I passed Marie and Amanda making their way back towards the patio, but I deliberately ignored them.

Climbing into my car, I felt a rush of relief and a sense of freedom. It wasn't just escaping the party, it was escaping that life. The suburban, husbandy, baby-having life. I'd thought that was the life I wanted. But now that I was an outsider, now that I'd seen a whole different side to living, that suburban existence I'd just witnessed was a world I was glad to no longer be a part of.

# 32

Okay, so how bad were things really? It's not like anything had *actually* happened between Lucas and me. Sadly.

No, no stop that. I couldn't think about him wistfully. He was now off limits. In fact, he probably was always off limits, or at least beyond my limits. I didn't need him. Didn't need to see him or talk to him or just be around him. But then, he *was* my flatmate's brother. And Lucas, Ben and Kalina were all going to imminently be working together. So … could I even avoid him?

My head was all over the place as I arrived at work early on Monday morning. I felt a bit like I'd had a horse run into the side of me.

By sheer luck I hadn't seen Ben or Kalina for the rest of Sunday, and there'd been no sign of Lucas again. And I'd left the flat deliberately early this morning so there was no chance of bumping into them. But I was just delaying the inevitable, wasn't I? It was all just a big time bomb, waiting to erupt. Soon, Kalina would work out how Lucas and I knew each other, and she'd be devastated. Worse, she'd feel betrayed. Oh God, I'd have to move out of the flat. And we wouldn't be able to be friends anymore.

Walking across the marketing department, which was empty this early, my eyes fell over Rose's desk, and with a pang I realised I'd forgotten to call her again. Hopefully, whatever she'd wanted to talk to me about wasn't that urgent. I mean, surely she would have tried calling or messaging me again if it was?

I sat down at my desk and stared blankly at my computer for a while as it booted up, then started idly clicking through emails. I was still doing this when Cara suddenly appeared beside me, making me jump.

"Oh good, Laura, you're here early!" she said, her voice far too enthusiastic for my liking.

"Ah, yes," I replied cautiously, wondering where this was going.

"We need some extra people down in Conference Room Three. There's a big presentation happening today, and they need someone from marketing down there right now."

Conference Room Three was in the sales department. As I stuffed my phone into my pocket, I felt a sweeping sense of doom flopping around in the pit of my stomach. Because Pete had mentioned something about helping out on a big presentation, hadn't he? So I'd likely see him down there. And probably Charlie, too. They'd better not make any lewd gestures or comments to me. I swear, if I so much as got one raised eyebrow, one bloody impression of a trench coat coming off …

When the lift doors opened, the sales floor was a hive of activity. I crossed over to the conference room and found two of the sales managers inside.

"Hi!" I said cheerfully, moving inside. "Cara said you might need a hand?"

"Who are you?" barked Evan Gough, the vice-president of sales.

Well honestly, I'd only worked there for four years.

"Laura Baker," I replied, smiling tightly. "I'm from marketing?"

"Where's Rose Spencer? She was meant to be here half an hour ago."

Shit, it wasn't like Rose to be late. I hadn't realised she was so involved in this. "I'm sure she's just, um …" I trailed off lamely, no idea what excuse to make for Rose.

"Look, we need the gift bags *now*," Evan snapped at me. "You're from PR, sort it out."

I bit down on my annoyance and refrained from mentioning that I wasn't actually in the PR team.

"How many—"

"Six."

I nodded and fled from the room.

Back in the marketing area, I had no idea what gift bags he was talking about. I had a little snoop around Rose's desk, but there was no sign of gift bags there. I also tried calling her, but her mobile rang out.

Sighing, I walked into the PR cupboard and decided to just make my own version of gift bags. It wasn't like Tiger Finance had anything really exciting to offer anyway. A few branded post-its and notepads? How about some Tiger Finance–themed pens? And a Tiger Finance–monogrammed stapler! Ooh, aren't these people in for a *treat*.

Once the bags were done, I went back down to the conference room, noting that there was still no sign of Rose.

"Here are the gift bags, Evan," I said, holding them up.

"Great," he replied brusquely, sparing only the most cursory glance at my carefully curated bags.

I hovered for a moment in the conference room, which was now full of people bustling around (including Charlie, whose gaze I was studiously avoiding), unsure if I was needed for anything else. Someone was putting little name tags in front of seats around the table, and I saw that "Rose Spencer" was one of them. I pulled out my phone and checked it, but there were still no messages from Rose. I quickly fired off a text asking where she was.

I'd just started edging my way out of the room to try to escape back to my floor when the phone in the conference room rang. Evan strode over to it and grabbed the receiver.

"They on their way? Good." He hung up just as fast, then turned and clapped his hands together to get everyone's attention. "Okay, listen up, team! They're en route, ETA twenty minutes. Kate, get the food brought up now."

I swallowed, edging further towards the door, but Evan spotted me.

"You! Marketing," he barked. "Where is Rose?"

"I'm not sure," I said, aware everyone's eyes were on me, including Charlie's.

"Should we take her name tag away?" asked Kate, Evan's EA.

"No, we need someone from marketing. You ..." he hesitated, frowning.

"Laura?" I supplied.

"Yes, Laura, if she's not here in time, you'll have to take her place, at least until the morning break."

"I'm sure she's not far ..." I tried, but Evan had already turned away.

Crap. Where on earth was Rose? I had no idea what this meeting was about. I checked my phone again, but there was still no response. I sent her another quick message as I raced back up to marketing, desperately hoping she might've magically appeared at her desk.

I failed to find Rose, but Belinda called out to me cheerily as I swung past my own desk.

"Morning, Belinda. You haven't seen Rose, have you? Or Cara?"

"I think Cara is in meetings all morning," Belinda replied calmly, taking out little containers of cheese cubes and mixed nuts and assembling them in a neat row on her desk.

"Damn. If I'm not back here in twenty minutes, can you tell Cara I've had to go to the sales presentation? I think I'll be there all morning."

"You're not coming to Xena's farewell morning tea?"

"Oh bugger!" I made a face. "I think I'll be stuck downstairs. Could you grab me a cake or something?"

"Sure," Belinda replied blandly, adding a chocolate bar to her snack line.

Sighing, I wrote a quick note to leave on Rose's desk, explaining the situation, then went back down to level four.

As my lift pinged open in the sales department, the lift next to mine simultaneously opened and out stepped a group of six men wearing "visitor" lanyards, being escorted by Pete.

Shit! I'd completely misjudged the time, because that was the entourage for the meeting, and I should've already been in the meeting room. I fell in behind them, hoping I could just sneak in the back unnoticed, but then the guy at the back of the group turned and our eyes met.

I froze, recognising him instantly.

He did a double-take. "Laura?" asked Derek Windsor, recovering first.

"Hi!" I replied, my voice sounding choked.

"Long time." A slow smile spread across his face.

My own eyes slid over to Pete, who had stopped to wait for Derek, and was now watching us both curiously.

"Yes, it's been a while, hasn't it?" I replied, starting to feel flustered. "I didn't realise you'd be here."

"And I didn't realise you worked here," Derek countered. "But I suppose we didn't really spend long talking, did we?" He gave me a conspiratorial wink and I felt like the bottom of my stomach had dropped out. My eyes skittered over to Pete again, and I could see he was still watching and listening to us, a frown on his face. If only the floor could open up and swallow me.

"We're through this way, Mr Windsor," Pete said stiffly, indicating the conference room.

"Sure, sure," Derek replied dismissively, his attention still on me. "Are you joining us, Laura?"

"She's not—" Pete started to say, but I cut him off.

"I am actually, at least for the morning," I replied, giving Pete an apologetic look.

We walked into the conference room and I saw that my name tag (or rather Rose's name tag) was positioned next to Pete and directly opposite Derek Windsor.

Perfect.

I slid into my seat and glanced around at the other five members of Derek's party, as if I was completely aware what this meeting was about. There was a lot of talking, a lot of handshaking, a lot of golf references going on. Then stacks of paperwork were handed around to everyone. Evan addressed the group, officially welcoming the party, and making a speech about how much Tiger Finance was looking forward to working with them. Then the lights were dimmed and the presentation began on the big screen.

I started watching, quietly trying to absorb the information for a minute or so, when Pete nudged me on the shoulder, and surreptitiously pushed a piece of paper in front of me.

*How do you know him?*

Well honestly. This wasn't high school. I tried to ignore him and turned my attention back to the presentation, but a moment later he nudged me again.

As I turned to give him an annoyed look, my eyes fell across the glass partition in the meeting-room wall and I saw Rose hovering outside, looking furious. She was staring in at the meeting, her eyes darting around the table. They rested for a second on Derek Windsor, then they skated over and met mine. I raised my eyebrows at her, trying to say, "What happened?" She pursed her lips, and I saw her clench her fists. Then she turned on her heel and disappeared.

Feeling slightly confused, and somehow weirdly guilty, I turned back to the presentation. Pete nudged me again, harder, causing me to jolt visibly. This drew the attention of Derek, who looked over at me, his eyes then sliding to Pete and back to me again. He raised his eyebrows, giving me a little smile as if this was highly entertaining.

Oh, honestly.

When we finally broke for morning tea, I couldn't escape fast enough. Thank goodness Rose had arrived—she could take over for the rest of the day. I checked my phone again as I raced to the lifts, but weirdly there was still no response from her.

Back upstairs, marketing seemed to be buzzing more than usual. I crossed straight to Rose's desk, but she wasn't there. Feeling frustrated, I walked past Cara's office, but that was also empty. As I made my way back over to my own desk, I finally spotted Rose striding towards me, a scowl on her face. We met exactly in front of my cubicle.

"Rose, what happened? I had to—" I started to say, but Rose cut me off.

"Did you enjoy that?" she asked, her voice icy.

"What do you mean?" I noticed that Rose had huge bags under her eyes again, her complexion pale.

"Sitting in my place in the meeting? Did you enjoy it?" Rose repeated, her voice still cold.

"Oh. Well, not really. I was only filling in because they needed someone from marketing—"

"You know, I've been working on that project for *ages*," Rose cut me off again, giving me a furious look that made me flinch.

"I know! I wasn't meant to—"

"And *you* of all people take my spot."

For a beat, there was a charged silence between us.

"What does *that* mean?" I finally said, feeling my own anger igniting. I was vaguely aware that a few people nearby had started watching us.

"It means haven't you done enough? You just get whatever you want now, don't you?"

"*Excuse* me? How can you *say* that?"

"Oh, please." Rose gestured at my desk as if exhibiting evidence. I looked over and saw a little strawberry tart sitting on my desk, courtesy of Xena's farewell morning tea.

"A gift, is it? Or a souvenir from one of your many men?" Rose crossed her arms, glaring at me.

"What are you *talking* about?" I hissed, glancing around warily at the crowd we were drawing.

"You seriously don't know what I'm talking about? You know, I was *fine* with you sleeping with Derek Windsor. I even encouraged you to get out there and do that. But Pete—really? You couldn't just leave him well enough alone, could you."

My mouth dropped open. I was absolutely mortified that Rose had just said all of that so loudly! Through my peripheral vision, I could see our audience was growing.

"You know what, Laura? Just stay away from my projects, okay? You might take whatever you want outside the office, but don't steal my shit in here."

And with that she turned and stormed away, leaving me standing open-mouthed and humiliated. I realised everyone in the near vicinity was staring at me, including Pete, who was on the marketing floor for God knows what reason. His eyes were darting between the retreating Rose and me, looking startled. I opened my mouth to say something, but nothing came out. Then suddenly Cara was there, grabbing me by the elbow.

"Laura, my office, now," she said quietly, and basically frogmarched me across the department towards her office.

"Cara, that … I wasn't …" I tried to explain, but I was still in shock after Rose's outburst.

Cara held up a hand. "Not here," she said firmly, and I shut my mouth, allowing myself to be led into her office. Once inside, Cara shut the door and turned to me.

"What was *that*?" she demanded.

"That … I-I," I stammered, still trying to work it out myself.

Cara sighed. She walked around her desk and sat down, gesturing for me to do the same. Feeling a bit weak, I sank into the chair offered.

"I don't know what is going on with the two of you, but making a scene like that in the middle of the office is not acceptable," Cara said calmly. "Especially when there are such important potential clients in the building."

"But I didn't! I mean, it was Rose," I protested, but Cara held up a hand again.

"I will be speaking to Rose's manager about this as well. But *you're* the one I'm concerned about. You're the one in my team."

I slumped in my chair.

Cara looked at me levelly for a moment, then sighed again. She tapped her fingernails on the table thoughtfully for a moment before continuing. "Why don't you start by telling me what's going on."

"I don't think there's really anything going on," I mumbled.

"Are you sure about that?" Cara raised her eyebrows at me.

I swallowed, meeting her eyes. "Yes."

Cara breathed out heavily, looking disappointed. "Laura, do you remember what we spoke about last week?"

My mind darted back to that previous meeting. Cara telling me my work had been slipping. That I was never at my desk. That I'd become unreliable. That I needed to improve. My throat felt so tight that I didn't think I could respond. Instead, I just nodded my head.

"Laura, I've been watching you carefully for a while now, and I must say I've been disappointed. Aside from today, you've been late most mornings. Your work is continuing to slip and you're missing deadlines. And to be honest, after today and seeing that argument with one of your colleagues, I'm starting to think that you're just not a team player anymore."

I could feel tears pricking at my eyes. It wasn't that I didn't agree with everything Cara was saying—even I knew she was right. But hearing it from your boss, hearing the disappointment in her voice—it was awful.

Cara looked down at something on her desk, as if reading notes. "Laura, I want you to consider this as a verbal warning," she continued, and my stomach clenched unpleasantly. "I know this is hard, but at the end of the day this is a business, and we want people who *want* to work here. I'm just not seeing that in you anymore."

I couldn't hold the tears back any longer. My eyes overflowed, and I looked down at my lap, wiping furiously at them.

Cara handed me a tissue. "Look, why don't you to take the rest of the day off," she said after a moment. "Go home, get some rest, take a long walk or a hot bath. I want you to really think about what you want. If you do still want to be here, then I'll need to see an improvement. Otherwise, maybe you need to start looking for something else that will make you happy."

I nodded my head, still staring at my lap, which was swimming foggily.

"Are you okay?" Cara asked kindly, and I wiped the tears away, looking up at her.

"Yes. Sorry. I just … Well, it's just been a bad day. I think you're right—I need to have a good think about what I'm doing."

Cara smiled and nodded. "I'll put you down for sick leave for the rest of the day. Now go get your things and get some rest."

I nodded again and stood up. I tried to pretend I was invisible as I slunk back through the marketing floor and collected my bag. There was no sign of Rose, but she was probably already down in the conference room.

As I passed a cubicle, I overheard two of the graphic designers inside, who were huddled together talking, their backs to me.

"… thought she was married?" one was saying.

"No, she's getting a divorce. Didn't you *know*? That's why she had all that time off …"

I couldn't believe how humiliated I felt. I couldn't believe I'd just cried in front of my boss. And I couldn't believe what Rose had just done in front of the whole department.

# 33

I sat on the ferry trying to process what had just happened. What the hell had that been with Rose? It was like she was *angry* at me for sleeping with Derek and Pete and Tinder Boy—but why? I mean, she had a boyfriend, for God's sake, so she surely couldn't be *jealous*? And regardless of what her problem was, how dare she do that to me in the middle of the office! I clenched my jaw, anger boiling inside of me.

But I knew I couldn't completely blame her for what had happened with Cara. I'd been given a verbal warning—the culmination of weeks' worth of poor performance. Closing my eyes, I took a deep breath and tried to calm down.

When the ferry pulled into the wharf at Manly, I knew I didn't want to go back to the flat. Kalina might be there and I wasn't prepared to talk to her, not yet. Instead, I started wandering along the beach walkway, feeling the sun on my face. There were lots of people about, going on walks, some running. Just the sight of it and the fresh air helped my frayed nerves unwind a bit.

I briefly wondered about the lives of the people I was passing, ones who clearly didn't have jobs to be at on a Monday. Were they happy? Were their lives all neatly in order? Or did they feel lost, just like me?

Work had already started to feel horrible, even before today. Just the thought of going back there made me feel physically sick. I'd have to deal with Rose. And I'd have to see Pete. I wondered if he heard Rose say that I'd slept with Derek Windsor? Not that it particularly mattered … but I'd also have to see everyone on the marketing floor again. I could already imagine the tendrils of gossip, snaking their way around the building.

But if I was hating my job so much, why *was* I still there? Could the answer simply be that I was too scared to leave? So much else in my life had changed this year. I'd split from Jack, the only guy I'd ever been in a relationship with. I'd moved to the other side of Sydney, made new friends— who, hopefully, would remain friends. My job felt like the last part of my old self still hanging around.

But maybe it was time for that to go as well? Maybe I just needed to take the plunge, quit, and then work out what I wanted to do after that? After all, it wasn't like it was that *hard* to get a job in Sydney. Something would surely come up. In fact, maybe Ben could really get me a job on that film set he'd mentioned? Maybe I should do something that fascinated me, something completely different, if only for a few months? Hadn't he said that one of the producers was currently in Sydney? I could try to get in touch with them, at least find out if they had any jobs available that I could do.

Thinking about Ben made my thoughts bounce back to Lucas. His blue, teasing eyes swimming into my mind again. How on earth had I not realised they were brothers? All it would have taken was one comment, surely? One question, asked the right way, and everything would have been revealed long ago? I could have stopped obsessing over him, could have ended all this before it even had started.

I hated to think what Lucas's opinion of me was. The last conversation we'd had, only a couple of days ago at the 4Pines, was all about his disapproval of people having casual sex. And then he saw me walking into the flat, clearly having stayed the night at Pete's house. And then hearing Kalina make it really clear that I was obviously sleeping with multiple people. He probably saw me as the embodiment of everything he hated.

But so what? I didn't want to date someone judgy about that stuff. And even if I did want to date him, I now *couldn't*. Because Kalina was my friend, and she was there first.

I took a shaky breath. It was time to get myself together. And I supposed the best way to do that was just to face things, wasn't it?

I glanced across towards the Manly Corso, which wasn't far away. Ben would probably be at the bar with Lucas now, getting things finalised. And Kalina might be there, too, if she wasn't back at the flat.

I pulled out my phone and dialled Ben's number.

⁊つ

Ten minutes later, Ben appeared right as I was heading out of the Coffee Corner, two takeaway cups in my hands.

"Ben! Thanks for coming!" I said, smiling and handing him a coffee.

"That's okay, I needed a break anyway," he replied, taking the cup from me. "So, what's up? How come you're not at work?"

"That's sort of what I wanted to talk to you about, actually," I said as we started walking towards the beachfront.

Ben raised his eyebrows at me.

"You know how you mentioned that if I wanted a job in the film industry, you'd try to put me in touch with that producer?"

"Yeah," Ben said, a smile creeping over his lips.

"Well, is that still possible? I mean, to ask, at least?"

"Totally! As a matter of fact, I sent her a message yesterday to check if she's still on the lookout for people, and she said there're still a few jobs going. I'll give her a call now."

"Really?" I felt relief—and excitement—flooding through me. "That would be awesome!"

We walked over to a sunny bench looking out across the beach and took a seat while Ben pulled out his phone. I sat beside him, trying not to fidget, feeling my heartbeat start to jump around nervously.

"Celeste? Ben Hartcoat here. How are you?"

There was a slight pause and then he started laughing. I jiggled one of my legs nervously while Ben went through some general chitchat, and I could hear a faint voice on the other end of the phone laughing as well.

"So, look, that friend of mine who was interested in a job is asking to meet you. You're still in Sydney, right?"

I looked at him hopefully, holding my breath.

"Tomorrow?" Ben said. "Can you do the morning?" He looked at me with his eyebrows raised. "I'm sure she can do tomorrow morning."

I inhaled sharply and nodded, an eager smile on my face.

"Cool. Thanks, Celeste—you're the best."

There was another pause and then Ben laughed again. "Don't let my mum hear you say that!" he joked.

I waited, barely daring to breathe.

"Alrighty, great. I'll let her know. Thanks, Celeste." Ben ended the call.

"Well?" I squealed, feeling extremely jumpy.

"Coffee, ten o'clock tomorrow." Ben grinned at me. "Three Birds cafe in Double Bay."

"Oh my God, really?" I couldn't keep the radiant smile from splitting across my face.

"Yep. I know, I'm totally the best flatmate."

"You are!" I gave him a big hug, making him laugh.

"Just don't stuff up the interview," he said, although his voice was teasing.

"I'll try my best not to humiliate you."

Ben rolled his eyes. "So, what's the go with you and Lucas?" he asked casually, and I felt my stomach flop over like a fish.

"What do you mean?" I asked innocently, hiding behind my coffee cup.

"How did you guys meet? He said he's seen you a few times in Manly."

"Did he? Oh … well that's it really. We've just bumped into each other a few times."

I could feel Ben's eyes on my face, but I stared resolutely out towards the sea, pretending not to notice.

"Uh-uh," he said, clearly not believing me.

"What's the deal with him anyway?" I asked, trying to shift the conversation. "I mean, why is he not … involved … with, um, anyone?"

Ben raised his eyebrows again. "I have no idea. Why?"

"Oh, no reason. I mean it's just something he said …"

"Which was?"

"Well, he seems to have a problem with people, I don't know, *not* being in a relationship or something."

"Does he?" Ben seemed genuinely surprised by this.

"Yeah. Like he thinks it's really disgusting that people should be sleeping around casually. Which you know, considering how he saw me on Sunday morning, probably explains why he pretended not to know me!"

Ben thought for a moment, then started laughing again. "Oh yeah! That's even funnier now."

"Don't laugh about it!" I whacked him on the leg. "Your brother was *judging* me."

Ben kept laughing anyway. "So what if he was? Do you care?"

"No!" I said too quickly. "I mean, well, he's your brother. I don't want him to think I'm … you know. That I do that all the time."

"I'm sure he doesn't think that," Ben said, scratching his chin.

"Not that I think there's anything wrong with that," I said firmly. "It's just that we had a whole conversation about how he thinks that's what's wrong with people nowadays. Which, you know, is ridiculous."

"Ah." Ben nodded as if something had just dawned on him. "Yeah, I think I know what that was about."

"You *do*? Well what? Share please."

Ben looked at me sideways, as if not sure how much to say. "The thing is …" he began, then paused and took a sip of coffee. "See, last year Lucas was burnt pretty badly."

I raised my eyebrows, waiting for him to go on.

"He was with this girl for ages," Ben continued. "I think he even proposed to her—or so Mum says. But she broke up with him because, apparently, she thought she hadn't dated enough guys or something, basically wanted to go and sleep with heaps of other people. He was really cut up about it. Got really angry and started hating on girls for a while. Now, he just throws himself totally into his work, which is why he's got all these projects always on the go. Hasn't had a girlfriend since."

"Right," I said, taking a deep breath. "So, he thinks all girls are like that now?" No wonder things never "lined up" for him and Kalina.

Ben shrugged. "It was a while ago. I think he's mostly … over it." He didn't sound so sure, though.

"Huh," I said, looking out at the sea again.

"Anyway." Ben finished his coffee. "Speaking of my brother, I've got to get back to the bar. It's opening on Thursday, you know. You'll have to come by and have a look."

"Yes," I said, even as my insides recoiled. "Yes, I'll have to do that."

Ben stood up, shaking his head at me. "I'll never understand you girls," he said as he started to walk away.

"Hey! There's nothing … I mean …"

But he was already walking away, grinning and waving his hand over his head in farewell.

Shit. Did he realise I had a thing for his brother? Oh God. Now, I guess it was only Kalina who didn't know.

# 34

I took a sick day from work on Tuesday. Obviously I had to, because I had the interview with Celeste, but also because I didn't know what to say to Cara yet. But hopefully, my talk with Celeste at the very least would help me work out what I wanted to do with my life. Because really, it wasn't likely that I'd actually get offered a job on a movie set, was it? I didn't have any movie-related skills on my CV.

Yet, I hadn't felt this keen about something prospective in ages. I mean, just imagine—me, working on a movie set! Elle and I used to play around with a video camera when we were younger, filming mini-movies and things. Who'd have thought that maybe I'd get to work on a movie in *real life*?

But okay, I was getting ahead of myself. I should really look at things in perspective. It was probably—like ninety-nine percent likely—not going to happen. But regardless of the likelihood, I had butterflies in my stomach as I made my way to the interview. Celeste was flying out to Melbourne this afternoon, so it was really lucky that Ben had called her yesterday and she'd had time to meet me before heading to the airport.

Ben had showed me some pictures of Celeste last night, so I had an idea of what she looked like. And sure enough, as soon as I entered the cafe, I spotted an older lady with spikey blonde hair and bright-red lipstick, who was wearing a fabulous Camilla kaftan, sitting at the bench already drinking an espresso.

"Celeste?" I asked, coming up beside her.

"Aha! Laura, I presume?" she said, looking at me with deep-brown eyes over tortoiseshell glasses.

"Yes! Lovely to meet you." I shook her hand, warming to her immediately.

"Take a seat, darling, let's get another coffee. I've scoffed this one too quickly." She indicated the empty seat beside her and I slid into it.

"Waiter!" She clicked her fingers, which I found amusing. "Get this girl a coffee. Do you want a muffin or something, too, darling? Gosh, you're as skinny as my granddaughters are. All you girls nowadays have that half-starved look!"

"No thanks." I laughed.

"Well, while he's over there doing his thing with the coffee, we can admire his physique from over here." She winked at me. "You got a man around?"

"No. I'm getting a divorce, actually. My husband is now gay."

Wow—that just came right out. But there was something different about Celeste. I felt like I wanted to shock her.

"Is he really?" Celeste turned to me, looking fascinated. "My, my, now that's a story! I bet you've had a proper run-around in life's journey already, haven't you?"

"Erm ... I guess so?"

"What are you—twenty-five? Twenty-six?"

"Twenty-seven." I smiled.

"Let me tell you a secret, darling. You shouldn't settle for only one man, anyway. All women should have at least three great loves in their lifetime— I've certainly had my share!" She laughed, an almost musical sound, and I found myself feeling delighted. Her boisterousness was contagious.

"Besides, a young girl like you should be out seeing the world, not settling down with a husband!"

"I couldn't agree more."

"Now tell me, what brings you here, to meet with me? What makes you want to get into the movie business, besides the glamour of it all?"

"Aside from the all-around fabulousness of it, it's exactly as you said. I want to see the world. I want to do something exciting and different and something that I actually really care about."

"Did Ben tell you what the movie is about?"

"Um, no. He didn't."

"He's forgotten already, hasn't he?" Celeste grinned at me conspiratorially.

I couldn't help but smile back. "Well, I didn't want to say anything. But yes, he has no idea."

Celeste let out another delightful, musical laugh. "That Benny! I tell you what, there's something about that boy. I gave him his first job in the movies, did he tell you that? It was those good looks of his, I couldn't resist his boyish charm."

I laughed, trying to imagine Ben having any kind of conversation with Celeste.

"Let me tell you, Laura. There's action. There's adventure. There's romance of course. It's going to be a stellar film. And we're getting the best crew to go along with it. It'll be lots of hard work. Lots of long hours. But being part of creating something magical is a feeling you won't get from anything else. Now, let's talk your skill-set. What have you got."

The conversation turned to my work history, and I was surprised to find that I had good answers to all of Celeste's questions. I'd just finished telling her about an event I'd helped organise years ago when I was working at the PR agency—a snowfall-themed cocktail reception to launch a vodka brand from Russia. Celeste had been listening attentively, her eyes hardly moving from my face the whole time. Now, she took a sip of coffee and looked thoughtful.

"So, you're quite hands on and like working with people, then? How are you managing vendors and contractors and the like?"

"Great! My current job has me working with a lot of suppliers. I'd take a phone call with one of them over running a report any day!"

"Okay. Now, Laura, what roles in the movie production can you see yourself in?"

Crap. This was the question I was dreading.

"I guess that depends on what you have available," I said, but I saw her frown. Shit, wrong answer. What had Ben said? "I mean … I guess there might be some overlap in … costume, or set design?"

"Oh Lord, no!" Celeste laughed, and I felt my face flush. Shit.

"All those design positions are hugely coveted—lots of career people in those, and if it's not someone experienced then there're hundreds of fashion or interior-design students after those jobs every year. No, no, that wouldn't be right for you at all."

Oh God. That was all I had. What else could I suggest?

"Normally, someone with no experience on sets would start out as a runner. But honestly, Laura, they're really junior roles, almost intern-level. I don't think you'd be happy with that."

"No … I mean, I could be," I said tentatively. For some reason, I really, really wanted her to offer me a job on the movie.

Celeste laughed, a softer laugh this time. "Don't fool yourself, darling. You wouldn't be happy with that, and I wouldn't want to put you in that position. However."

My breath caught. However?

I looked up at her hopefully. She was tapping a finger on her chin and looking thoughtful.

"Hmm, yes. It could work …" she said vaguely, still doing that chin-tapping, thinking thing.

"What could?" I asked, unable to wait any longer.

"Well, my location manager has been asking for fewer hours. Has his own projects he's working on. He's the best there is, I won't use anyone else. But this new project was going to be already stretching him pretty thin, and that's before he'd asked for reduced hours. So, I've been considering hiring a junior, or an assistant for him to help with things. Now, as an assistant location manager, you need to understand the hours are long. And I mean really, really long. You'll be the first on set and often the last to leave. Plus, work will start before filming begins in April—early March we'd need you to begin. But it could be a good career start for you. You'll surely get out there and 'see the world' as you say, if you succeed in this role. And you'll be learning from one of the best in the business."

I barely even heard the last few things Celeste said. Assistant location manager. The title swam through my mind—all the glamour, all the fantasy, all the dreams suddenly becoming real.

"Now, I'm not saying I'm offering you the job yet. I've still got a few things to sort out, and there are other people after jobs like this, you understand."

My dream vision came to an abrupt halt.

"I like you, though, Laura, I will say that. I've always gone on gut feel with people and have never hired the wrong person. Well, almost never, but that's a story for another day."

"Thank you! And, well, can I just say that that job sounds amazing and I would definitely love to do it if possible!"

Celeste chuckled. "Yes, I thought you'd like that. Now, let me sort out some things and I'll let you know about it by the end of the week."

Celeste signalled for the bill and paid, shushing away my offer of money. Then we got to our feet and left the cafe.

"It was lovely meeting you, Laura! Ta-ta," Celeste leaned in and gave me air kisses on both cheeks. "I'll be in touch soon!"

And then she put a pair of fabulous Gucci sunglasses over the top of her tortoiseshell ones and strode off down the road, her kaftan billowing out behind her and sparkling in the sunlight.

⚬⌇⚬

It's a funny word isn't it: *career*. Like, there should be only one, and you should always be moving upwards and doing better on that one path. When my marriage ended, I remembered Mum saying to me, "Well, at least you have your career", like it was some consolation prize. And yet, that made it sound like my "career" was something that I'd chosen, something I was destined to do for the rest of my life. When I think about career women, I think of these really driven, focused people who chose the right uni degree, landed an amazing graduate position and then made the smooth transition into a corporate job, their gaze constantly focused on the top of the ladder they were now solidly on. I, on the other hand, chose my uni degree because I didn't know what *else* to do. And then when I finished that I got a job at the PR agency, because that's what Claire from my course was doing and she made it sound really fun. And then I moved to work at Tiger Finance because I saw an ad online and realised the pay was good. But was that a career? Was that what my life was meant to be all about?

I don't think I'd ever really stopped to consider what I wanted out of life. I was just going along for the ride, doing the things that were expected, the things that were easy. Staying with Jack was easy, going to uni, getting a full-time job based on my degree—that was easy. But now, I found myself wondering how much of my life had come about because of choices I'd made? Or were they choices that others had made for me?

Whatever came from the meeting with Celeste, I knew that I had at least made one decision for myself: it was time to leave Tiger Finance. Because you only get one chance at life—that much was clear. And although I may not have known what I wanted to do with the rest of my life, I could now at least see the things I didn't want. And maybe that's what life was really about—the unknown. It was the things out there, waiting to be discovered, that pushed you onwards.

# 35

We met in Martin Place, Rose and I, an hour before work. I imagined us like two cowboys, approaching each other for a duel, as we cautiously walked towards each other. Rose was dressed impeccably, but she couldn't disguise the drawn look to her face, or the bags under her eyes I could see even through her heavy makeup.

We stopped walking a few steps away from each other. I folded my arms, waiting for her to speak. She also had her arms folded across her chest, and she raised her chin slightly in defiance.

"Seriously?" I blurted out, after a moment of silence. "You're not even going to apologise to me?"

Rose's jaw clenched. "I don't see why I should."

"Are you joking? You humiliated me at work! I got a verbal warning from Cara for your outburst!"

Rose's eyes skittered away, the first sign of uncertainty, of guilt. But then she met my gaze again firmly. "I got told off by my boss, too. And I still stand by what I said."

"You seriously think I'm trying to steal your jobs at work or something? Rose, I don't even care about work—I'm going to resign today!"

She looked surprised at that but covered it quickly. "Not that. I mean … okay, I probably overreacted about that. But the other thing. With Pete.

Why did you sleep with him?"

"What do you mean *why*? Does it even matter?"

Rose's eyes flashed angrily. "Does it *matter*? See, that's what I'm talking about. You don't even care!"

"What? *What?*" I spluttered. "Why *would* I care? I'm not trying to get involved with anyone! Why does it matter if I slept with the hot guy from sales?"

"So you think he's hot now, do you? I thought you weren't even into him."

"*You* thought he was hot!"

"Exactly! *I* thought he was hot!"

"So what is your problem, then?"

"My problem is that *I'm* the one who's sleeping with him!"

We fell into a shocked silence, staring at each other. Around us, business people rushed past on their way to their offices, earplugs in their ears. No one paid us any attention.

"You're ... sleeping with Pete?" I repeated.

Rose seemed to deflate, like the sails of a yacht that had suddenly lost their wind.

"But ... what about Christian?" I asked.

She looked away, her cheeks turning pink. "He's not part of this conversation," she said.

I couldn't help it—I laughed incredulously. "How can he not be? Are you still together with him? Or did you break up?"

"We're still together," she responded, not meeting my eyes.

"Well fuck, Rose! You've got more problems than I do!"

She turned a furious look on me.

"What?" I asked, my voice harsh now. "How is any of this my fault?"

"You should have realised I had a thing for Pete!"

"I knew you thought he was cute, but I also thought you had a boyfriend that you were happily living with and that you weren't planning to cheat on!"

"I wasn't planning on it!" Rose bit back. "But Pete and I ... Well, I thought we had a thing."

"You thought you had a thing? With *Pete*?"

"Yes." Rose glared at me.

"Then shouldn't you be angry at him?"

"I am angry at him! But I'm also angry at you! You're meant to be my friend!"

"And *you're* meant to be *my* friend! How was I supposed to know you had a thing with Pete if you didn't tell me!"

Rose looked away, letting out a slow exhale.

"Look," I said, feeling exasperated. "Whatever is going on with you and Christian—well, honestly, I can't even process that right now. So, if something is happening with you and Pete—I'm not an obstacle. I'm more than happy to never see him again."

Rose snorted. "I don't want him now. I mean ... I don't even know what I was doing. I thought ... but no. I was wrong about him."

There was silence for a moment and we couldn't quite meet each other's eyes.

"So, we've both slept with the same guy, then," I said after a pause.

"Yeah." Rose crinkled her nose as she looked at me. "Weird, right?"

"Did you think he was ..." I trailed off.

"Energetic?" Rose supplied, the tiniest trace of a smile on her mouth.

"I was going to go with ... overcompensating."

"You mean because of his, um ... size?" Rose's smile had definitely increased, a glint coming into her eye now.

"He certainly was interestingly proportioned."

"I suppose it may really have just been a problem of perspective. You know, because everything else about him is so big."

"Or that's why he spends so long in the gym. In order to make up for other … deficits."

Our eyes met properly, and our mouths twitched. Then we both burst out laughing. And it was probably because things were still a bit on edge, and we were still a bit unsure of each other, but we laughed harder and for much longer than our sad little jokes really called for.

As we both calmed down, I found I was wiping tears away from my eyes.

"Okay, so is this weird between us? I mean, are we friends again?" I asked, looking at Rose hopefully.

"I'm sorry about Monday," Rose said, looking actually remorseful and sheepish now. "I don't know why I got so angry. It was just … well, you were having such a fun, amazing time with everybody—"

"Hardly!"

"No, but it seemed like you were. And things with Christian were just … I don't know, they started feeling really stale. And then I was put on that project with Pete, and we started talking and flirting a lot and … well, things just got a bit out of hand and we slept together, and I would have told you, but then you messaged me saying that *you'd* slept with him and I just sort of lost it!" Rose finished in a rush, her eyes looking a bit wild.

"What are you going to do about Christian?" I asked carefully.

"I don't know." Rose pushed the heels of her hands into her eye sockets. "I don't know."

"Are you going to tell him?"

For a second Rose just stayed as she was, her face hidden. Then she shook her head, dropping her hands and looked at me. "No. Yes. I should. Shit—I don't know."

Our eyes met and I gave her what I hoped was an encouraging smile. "Well, I'm here for you, whatever you decide. And I'll try not to lose my shit and yell at you in front of your entire workplace," I added, mostly joking.

"I know I'd totally deserve that!" Rose threw her arms around me in a big hug. "I'm sorry. Did I say that already? I'm so sorry."

"Yes, you did. And since I'm going to resign today, it's just lucky for you that I don't care that much."

"Wait—so you were serious? Are you quitting?"

"Yes."

"Shit," Rose said, looking suddenly bewildered as she stepped away from me. "But why? When did this all come about?"

As I started explaining to Rose my decision to leave, I found myself relaxing. It was cathartic, talking through my rationale, and the more I said about it, the more I knew I'd made the right decision. Plus, it helped the lingering tension between us fizzle out a whole lot further.

"Do you think you'll get a job on the film set?" Rose asked when I'd finished speaking.

"I hope so. But even if that doesn't eventuate, I think I just need some time off, you know? I mean, I know I took a lot of time off work when Jack and I first split up, but I was in such a bad place then. This time, I'll be taking a break in order to just ... I don't know. Relax. Work out what I really want to do with my life."

"Aren't you worried about money?" Rose asked, frowning.

"Nope," I grinned. "I've got a lot saved up, and after the house was settled I actually ended up with a huge chunk back in my bank account. Obviously, I don't own a property any more, but after everything that happened with Jack, I'm just kind of glad to not be tied down to any commitments right now."

"Well good!" Rose said. "I'm glad. I mean, I'm glad that you know what you're doing."

I laughed. "I'm not sure I'd go quite that far yet! But I think that's the point. I'm on my way to finding out."

"God, I hope I can work out what I'm doing soon."

"You will," I reassured her. "We both will. And in the meantime, well, that's why we have friends, right?"

"Right. Come on, let me buy you breakfast before we go in to work. I'm going to need a massive chocolate brownie before I go and have a little chat with our dear friend Pete."

"You're going to talk to him?"

"*Talking* isn't quite how I'd describe it," Rose said, her eyes narrowing.

\*\* FACEBOOK ALERT \*\*

**Rachelle Lee tagged you in a post on Louise Hapshaw's Timeline:**

*Had such an amazing time at <u>Louise</u>'s baby shower! Can't wait till our bubs are playing together in a few months!! Now we just need **<u>Laura Baker</u>**, <u>Marie Chu</u> and <u>Tricia Simmons</u> to join the mummy crew* 👶👪🍼

\*\* NEW MESSAGE \*\*

**From: Ben Hartcoat at 2.43 pm**

*Laura! Celeste just called me wanting your number. Did she offer you the job??*

\*\* NEW MESSAGE \*\*

**From: Mum at 3.33 pm**

*Hi, darling! There's a free public seminar coming up at the RSL in a few weeks called "Making Healthy Babies". It's sponsored by the hospital and looks like a really good general information evening. Thought you might want to have a look! xxx*

# 36

I got the job!!

I could hardly believe it. I'd spoken to Celeste on the phone about an hour earlier and she offered me the job as Assistant location manager.

*I think I'm hyperventilating.*

The pay wasn't nearly as good as my job at Tiger Finance, but so what? The important thing was that I was trying something completely different and I don't think I had been this happy and excited about something in a long time. Plus, the job didn't start until March, so by the time I worked out my four-week notice period at Tiger, I would still have a solid three months off work over summer. Three blissful months.

I left work early that day and caught the 4 pm ferry home, no longer caring about appearances now that I'd resigned. Because yes, I had resigned earlier today. I'd gone to see Cara as soon as I'd arrived at work and handed in my notice. I would have liked to pretend she was surprised, but we both knew she wasn't. Plus, Rose took care of Pete for me—apparently, she had a massive go at him for sleeping with both of us and he tried to say that he didn't realise we were friends and then things ended with her accidentally saying in front of the whole sales floor that he was shit in bed. So, I wasn't sure he and Charlie would have much to gossip about for a while.

I made my way up to the upper deck on the ferry and got a seat at the back in the sun. The ferry was mostly empty, so I had the whole back section to myself. As soon as we pulled out of Circular Quay, I took out my phone and looked at it with a sigh. The buzz of my upcoming career change was dimmed to an extent by my mother's messages, and I was pretty sure I needed to have a word to her before she started picking out sperm donors for me. With a shake of my head, I dialled her number.

"Hi, darling!" she answered brightly after a few rings.

"Hi, Mum. Look, there's something I need to talk to you about."

"Did you read that information about that Genea company? And the seminar? Because Katrina from my work—"

"Mum, stop! This is exactly what I need to talk to you about."

"Is it? Good! I'm so glad—"

"No, Mum, not good!" I rolled my eyes, even though she couldn't see me. "Listen, I know you really want me to have kids and you're really worried that I won't be able to, but you need to just calm down and back off."

"What do you mean?" Mum sounded insulted.

"I'm saying," I continued calmly but firmly, "that I need to get my life in order right now, and thinking about kids is the last thing I need. I mean, if I *was* ever to have kids, then I'd want them to be with the right person. And I haven't even started thinking about moving on with someone new yet."

"Well, if you'd let me set you up with Eric—"

"Mum!" I said sharply, but I couldn't help laughing. "I'm not going out with Eric from the pub!"

"He's such a lovely boy."

"I'm sure he is, but that's not the point. I've been in a relationship my whole life! I need to just spend some time on my own. You know, get to know myself."

Mum was silent.

"Do you know what I'm talking about?"

I heard Mum sniffing on the other end of the phone. "Yes. I know. I'm just so worried—"

"Mum, you don't need to worry. Let me worry. It's my life—I'm the one who has to deal with this."

"Oh, but—"

"Maybe you should spend some more time worrying about Elle? She's the one flouncing around in South American backpacker hostels, after all."

"I *do* worry about her. Of course I do. But she's just so ... independent. Always has been."

"Exactly! Elle's independent, she knows how to live on her own, and she's a good six years younger than I am! I'm still figuring out how to be independent. And until I'm comfortable by myself, there is no way I'm going to even start thinking about another boyfriend or kids or anything like that."

"Okay, fine. So you don't want me to say anything, then? And what happens when you do decide you want kids and it's too late?"

I rubbed my forehead, feeling strained. "Can you at least give me a timeout? Like, stop asking me about it until I'm thirty-five or something?"

"Thirty-five!" Mum protested.

"Thirty, at least?"

Mum sighed. "You know I'm only doing it for your own good, don't you?"

"Yes, Mum, I know."

"Okay. Well, then. I suppose I'll try to stop *pestering* you about it as your father says."

"Even Dad thinks you're pestering me?" I grinned.

"Oh, he doesn't know what's what."

"Mum!" I was laughing again. "You're hopeless."

"I'm your mother. I worry about these things."

"Thanks, Mum. I'm ... glad that you do. But just not now, okay?"

"Okay, darling," Mum said, sounding defeated. "I'm sure you can decide what's best for you."

"Yes, I can. Oh, and guess what?" I said gleefully. "I quit my job today!"

"What?" Mum sounded horrified.

"Yep! I'm going to go work on a film set instead!"

Mum didn't say anything, but I heard the sound of a chair being pulled across the floor and an "oof" as she sat down.

When the ferry docked in Manly, I knew where I needed to go. It was the day before the bar opened, and I knew Kalina and Ben would both be there helping get things finished and ready. I'd managed to mostly avoid Kalina for the past few days—the couple of times I briefly saw her in the flat I pretended I had something pressing to do and either disappeared into my room or went out. But I couldn't keep avoiding her. After all, she was my friend and I didn't want to let a guy—any guy—come between us.

I walked past the glass window, peering inside. I could see Ben stacking some things behind the bar, and Kalina was sitting on a bar stool drinking a cocktail, clearly not helping with much other than taste testing. I hesitated for a second, waiting to see if Lucas appeared. There was no sign of him, though, and at that moment Kalina looked up and her face broke into a smile as she spotted me. I waved at her, then gestured for her to come outside. Following my prompt, she jumped off her chair and jogged over to the front door, unlocking it and stepping outside.

"Hey! Come on in!" she said, making to go back in.

"Wait!" I said, catching her. "Actually, I wanted to talk to you. Alone, for a minute."

"Oh God, what have I done? Is this why you're avoiding me?" Kalina looked worried, even as she stepped outside and closed the door behind her.

"No! I mean ... I haven't been avoiding you," I lied.

"Uh-uh." Kalina crossed her arms and raised an eyebrow at me, although she didn't look offended, just curious.

I glanced inside, but there was still no sign of Lucas. I turned back to Kalina. "Well ... okay, you're right. I have been avoiding you ... just a tiny bit." I cleared my throat. "Has Lucas mentioned that we sort of know each other?"

Kalina frowned. "I think he said something to Ben about it. Why?"

I felt my stomach hollow out. "See, we'd sort of bumped into each other a few times ... and I was messaging him. But that was before I found out he was Ben's brother!"

Kalina just cocked her head, her eyebrows creasing. "Okay," she said slowly.

"I wanted you to know that," I said in a rush, avoiding looking at her face, which had a confused look on it. "That, well, nothing has happened between us. And it won't—not at all."

There was silence for a moment, and I chanced a look at Kalina. She was looking at me like I was crazy.

"Laura, what are you talking about?" she finally said.

"Lucas. Ben's brother," I said, not quite believing she could be confused by this conversation. "You know. You and Ben's brother?"

She was still looking at me weirdly.

"Your 'one that got away'?" I added, exasperated.

I saw Kalina's eyes widen, then she burst out laughing.

"What? Why is this funny?" I demanded.

"Oh my God, Laura!" Kalina gasped out between laughs. "You think ... you think I've slept with *Lucas*?"

"Haven't you?" I demanded.

"No!" Kalina kept laughing.

"But ... but he's Ben's brother! You've slept with—"

"I've slept with Ben's *other* brother. Johnny," she clarified, no doubt due to the horrified and confused look on my face.

"How many bloody brothers does Ben have?"

Kalina laughed again. And it was rather infectious. I felt my own sides starting to clench hysterically.

"He's got four," Kalina gasped out.

"Seriously? How the fuck does Ben have *four* brothers and I had no idea?"

Kalina shrugged. "He doesn't talk about them much. He's the middle child. Lucas and Johnny are older, and then he's got two younger ones who are still in high school."

"Oh my God," I said.

"I know. I can't believe you thought I'd slept with *Lucas*!" Kalina started laughing again.

"Sshh!" I hissed, aware of how loudly we were speaking, as I glanced inside towards the bar again. "It's not that funny."

"Seriously? Lucas is *waaay* too serious for me. Although, I guess you haven't met Johnny, have you? He's *such* a babe."

"Hotter than Lucas? I can't imagine that."

Kalina's eyes sparkled, a sudden delighted expression on her face. "So, you've got a thing for Lucas, eh?"

"No!" I said quickly, realising I'd already put my foot in it.

Kalina laughed gleefully again. "Yeah, I'm sure."

"Speaking of Lucas—where is he? I thought he'd be here getting stuff ready."

"He is." Kalina looked inside as well. "He was out in the store room last time I checked. Want me to go get him for you?" she said suggestively.

"No!" I repeated. "I mean, I don't have a thing for him. Or at least I didn't ..."

Kalina raised an eyebrow again, a wicked grin on her face.

I rolled my eyes and gave her a playful shove. "Oh, stop it."

"Ben will love this!" Kalina laughed.

"No! There's nothing to love. I mean … okay, I *might* have had a thing for Lucas, but then … I don't know. I think I've moved past it."

"Moved past it?" Kalina repeated disbelievingly.

"Yeah," I said, taking a breath. Because, really, I couldn't quite explain what there was between Lucas and me. Right from the first time we spoke to each other, at the wine festival, it was like there'd been a barrier between us—an impenetrable blockage that couldn't be surmounted. And even now, with nothing tangible in the way, I still felt like there was a massive canyon between us, and for anything to actually happen, it wouldn't be a simple step but rather a giant leap. Plus, he might want nothing more to do with me after seeing the trench-coat-with-stripper-heels disaster.

"Anyway," I turned back to Kalina with a smile. "All I really need at the moment are my friends. Did I mention I quit my job today?"

"No! That's awesome!" Kalina said, and as we stepped inside the bar together I recounted my day's adventures for her.

# 37

I spoke with Kalina and Ben for a while, talking and laughing with them as they congratulated me on my new job. It was a great feeling, and made me happy and excited about the year to come. But while we were talking, I couldn't help but keep one eye on the back door, wondering where Lucas was and if he would suddenly appear.

Finally, I couldn't take the suspense anymore, and so when Ben and Kalina went back to their tasks I slipped out the back. The storeroom door was partially open, light spilling out through the gap. I could hear music playing inside and I hesitated only briefly before knocking a few times and pushing the door open.

There he was.

Lucas was stacking boxes on shelves, his t-shirt clinging to his back and shoulders in the most eye-bulging way. The radio was playing loudly, The Weeknd currently pumping away in the small space.

Lucas spotted me in the doorway, his surprised expression becoming a rueful smile as he leaned over and turned the music right down. Then he focused on me, leaning with one arm on a shelf and a half-grin on his face.

I hesitated momentarily, then stepped into the storeroom, looking around and nodding like I was on a scenic tour.

"Well, this is nice," I said, trying to sound casual.

"Exactly the kind of place you envisioned hanging out with me, am I right?" he replied, his eyes locked onto me.

I shrugged. "There are lots of canned tomatoes in here. Which you know, might come in handy if I found myself unable to afford groceries."

"Hmm. You do live with my brother."

I turned sharply to look at Lucas, but he seemed amused.

"Yes, apparently so. How long did you know?"

Lucas shrugged. "I didn't. Not until you turned up that morning."

"And yet you didn't seem that surprised to see me." I frowned at him.

"I was actually. But I heard you talking before I came into the room. I remember thinking, I know that voice. And sure enough, there you were."

"You ... heard us talking, did you?" Oh God, my worst fears confirmed. No doubt he'd heard it all.

"I did." Lucas nodded, still watching me with that same intensity.

"Right. So ... there's probably a lot you don't know about me."

"There is a lot I don't know about you." Lucas agreed. "But then, maybe I do know more than you think. See, I thought you were an interesting, if somewhat strange, girl who seemed to keep turning up everywhere I went."

I felt my stomach clench.

"But on the other hand," he continued, shifting away from the shelf so that he was standing ever-so-slightly closer to me. "Ben had told me a bit about his new flatmate. A fun, genuine girl, who had been hurt badly in a past relationship and was just starting to find her feet again."

I felt my breath catch and I looked up into his face. He was now looking at me with a mix of curiosity and warmth.

"Ben didn't say that," I said, my lips twitching.

"Those were his exact words," Lucas replied, deadpan. But I could see a matching twitching of his mouth.

"And here I was thinking you were the one with the emotional damage," I said lightly.

Lucas's expression became shuttered. "Yeah, well—"

"Ben told me," I cut in, and Lucas stilled. "I mean," I added quickly. "He told me his brother had been burned pretty badly by a girl."

Lucas's expression cleared and he nodded. "I guess that's the summary."

"Did he ... did he tell you that I was married?" I asked hesitantly. "Still am, technically. And my husband is gay."

Lucas looked at me carefully, as if to gauge if I'd continue talking. But I didn't.

"He mentioned something about that," he said eventually.

I nodded. Well, at least he knew.

We fell into silence, and I found myself looking around at the shelves of boxes around me, trying to find something to say.

"That really sucks," Lucas said suddenly, and I snapped my attention back to him. "What happened to you. You deserve better than that."

"Thanks," I said. "But you can see how I can get a bit confused when it comes to male signals," I added, keeping my voice light.

Lucas returned my smile, his eyes still resting on my face. "Well, we men are known to be rather confusing. Although, I can tell you that I am definitely straight."

"Yes, I'd believe that. I mean, you were totally going to kiss me at the 4Pines, weren't you?" I grinned at him, only half joking, and found myself holding my breath.

He raised one eyebrow at me. "I thought you were going to kiss me," he countered.

"And why would I want to kiss someone who pretends to not even know me?"

"Do you think we know each other?"

"I know we're both rather damaged," I said, my smile starting to fade.

Lucas nodded his agreement. "So it would seem."

"And two damaged things don't necessarily make a whole." Even as I said the words, I felt my own heart sinking, withdrawing.

Lucas stilled again, his attention on me. I let my eyes take him all in as he looked in that moment—hair messy, rough stubble across his lower face, blue eyes contrasted against tanned skin. The way his t-shirt clung to his chest, damp with sweat; even his smell, still deliciously intoxicating.

"I don't do things by halves," he said, his voice low and quiet. "Casual dating isn't something I'm interested in." His eyes burned into mine, and again I felt like I was standing on the edge of that cliff, a wide canyon between us. I could go to him—I could breach it—but it would take a huge leap and there would be no turning back.

My heart curled up, cowering. As much as I wanted to open myself up again, I knew, deep down, that I wasn't ready. And so that small gap—that tiny window that had tried to open again—I pushed it firmly shut. I closed my eyes and took a deep breath. When I looked at him again, he was still watching me intensely, as if holding his own breath.

"I know you don't," I said, stepping towards him so that there was barely a foot between us. "But I don't think either of us is ready for something more … whole."

Lucas smiled, and he lifted his hand, hesitated, and then tucked a piece of my hair behind my ear, his thumb brushing across my cheek. "I think that is a very sensible decision," he said quietly, but I could hear the regret in his voice as his hand dropped back down.

I released a breath and stepped away from him, feeling like we'd just made a huge decision using really cryptic phrases.

"So, I guess we'll still have to be friends, though, right?" I said, trying to stem the tide of disappointment I was suddenly feeling. "I mean, I do live with your brother, after all."

Lucas leaned back against the shelf again, tucking his hands into his pockets. "That probably can't be avoided."

"Good." I turned towards the door, knowing I should leave before I changed my mind. But as my heart plummeted, I felt the inexplicable urge to kiss him, now, before it was too late, before whatever this thing between us was truly over. So instead of walking out as I knew I should, I found myself turning back and closing the distance between us instead.

"But before I go ..." I said, looking up into his face.

He froze, his eyes finding mine.

I moved so I was right up against him, my mouth finding his and my hands drawing up and over his shoulders, feeling the shape of him that I hadn't been able to look away from since I'd first laid eyes on him. He tensed in surprise, but then his hands escaped from his pockets, snaking around my back and pulling me closer to him, and our bodies melted together.

I tasted his mouth, smelled his skin and lost all sense of thought as my body lit up, pressed against the hardness of him. For a moment—seconds, minutes—there was nothing but us, alone in that room, our mouths locked together, our bodies pressed together, in a completely earth-shattering kiss.

But then my thoughts returned, and I remembered that this wasn't supposed to be happening; not yet, not now. So I broke away. He took a deep breath as our bodies parted, his lips looking as swollen as mine felt, his eyes electrified.

"I just wanted to do that at least once," I said.

Before he could respond, I turned and walked out of the store room, my smile growing with each step.

"And you said I was the confusing one!" he called after me, but I heard him laughing as well.

⌀

As I left the bar the sun was beginning to set, casting Manly in a reddish glow. I strolled slowly along the beach walkway, heading for home. Summer was mere weeks away and the air was warm, though a cool breeze was blowing in across the ocean. Surfers sat out on their boards in the sea, bobbing up and down gently as they let the smaller waves pass, their figures smudges of darkness in the fading light.

I took a long, deep breath of the salty air, and looked up at the purpling sky. And I smiled.

Part of me thought it could be a giddy smile, stemming from a false or reckless happiness. I'd quit my career job, I was getting a divorce, and I'd just walked away from the hottest guy I'd ever seen. Yet I wondered as well about what happiness really was. Was it having the perfect job or the perfect guy? Did you ever reach a point in time when you could suddenly stop and claim to be happy?

Or was it an ever-changing thing that always had to be pursued? That could never be static.

I didn't know what the future would bring. But I knew I'd set myself up to discover it one day at a time, with no commitments, no firm plans, nothing holding me tethered.

I smiled again as I thought of the nickname Kalina gave me when I'd first moved into the flat—Laura the Explorer. Although it was intended as a bit of fun, a way to get me back out in the dating world, I couldn't help but think that there was a deeper meaning to it as well. Because the dating world was just the surface—there were so many more things I needed to explore, most of them to do purely with myself. Yes, I was still becoming Laura the Explorer. But the new map was me, and the journey was only just beginning.

# Acknowledgements

It is strange to think this is the first book of mine to be published.

It is not the book I spent over a decade working on through high school, university and later during full-time employment. It is the book I began when I decided to quit my job and focus only on writing, jumping straight in on the 1st November in 2015 with a first draft for NaNoWriMo. Huge thanks to that organisation for giving me the motivation to push through an almost-entire first draft of 50,000 words in 30 days! Since then, I've learnt a great deal about redrafting and just how many versions of a book can be created before it is ready (hint: it's well over ten!)

Thanks to Deb Doyle for your early notes on the story. A huge thank you to Ali, Lucy and James who believed in this story enough to give me such generous, wonderful feedback and notes, and for being amazing enough to read this story multiple times across various iterations! Thank you to Hazel for the amazing cover design, and being such a star to work with!

Thank you to my copy editor, Alex Nahlous - not only did you do an amazing job, but your love of the story and kind words rekindled my confidence when it had nearly burned out.

Thank you to the friends whose experiences inspired some of the scenes in this book. You shall remain nameless, but I hope you laughed when you read them. To my amazing support team & beta readers – Caroline,

Jeanette, Amelia & Louisa – thank you for reading the early drafts and for your positive feedback! To my sister, Hannah, for your feedback, belief, support and lunches – thank you! And to Mum, for wanting to read every version and loving them all. I know a proper author is not meant to trust their mother's reviews, but hearing how much you loved the story each time made all the difference.

Lastly, and most importantly, thank you to Linden. You brainstormed ideas with me, listened to me complain when things weren't working, and were there during the highs and lows of this whole publishing journey. You went from boyfriend to fiancé to husband while this book was in the works, and without you I don't think I would have made it. So thank you.

# Support an Author

# Leave a Review

Even a single sentence can make a huge difference!
If you enjoyed this book, please post a review online.

SARAH BEGG lives in Sydney with her husband and a dog named Ruby. She loves to travel and has been writing fiction for as long as she can remember. She decided she was going to become an author when she was seven and realised that was a real occupation. When she's not writing, she works in digital marketing.

*Laura the Explorer* is her first published novel.

Follow Sarah on Instagram, Twitter and Facebook
**@sarahkbegg**

Subscribe to Sarah's email newsletter at
**sarahbegg.com**

27619651R00184

Printed in Great Britain
by Amazon